PENGUIN BOOKS
THE ORDER OF LIGHT

Haroon Moghul graduated from New York University with a degree in Middle Eastern Studies and Philosophy. He is currently pursuing a PhD at Columbia University.

Haroon's first visit to Saudi Arabia is recorded in his novel *My First Police State* (2003). His essays, short stories and poetry have appeared in numerous publications.

haroon moghul

the order of light

PENGUIN BOOKS

PENGUIN BOOKS
Published by the Penguin Group
Penguin Books India Pvt. Ltd, 11 Community Centre, Panchsheel Park,
New Delhi 110 017, India
Penguin Group (USA) Inc., 375 Hudson Street, New York, New York 10014, USA
Penguin Group (Canada), 90 Eglinton Avenue East, Suite 700, Toronto,
Ontario, M4P 2Y3, Canada (a division of Pearson Penguin Canada Inc.)
Penguin Books Ltd, 80 Strand, London WC2R 0RL, England
Penguin Ireland, 25 St Stephen's Green, Dublin 2, Ireland
(a division of Penguin Books Ltd)
Penguin Group (Australia), 250 Camberwell Road, Camberwell,
Victoria 3124, Australia (a division of Pearson Australia Group Pty Ltd)
Penguin Group (NZ), cnr Airborne and Rosedale Roads, Albany,
Auckland 1310, New Zealand (a division of Pearson New Zealand Ltd)
Penguin Group (South Africa) (Pty) Ltd, 24 Sturdee Avenue, Rosebank,
Johannesburg 2196, South Africa

Penguin Books Ltd, Registered Offices: 80 Strand, London WC2R 0RL, England

First published by Penguin Books India 2005

Copyright © Haroon Moghul 2005

All rights reserved

10 9 8 7 6 5 4 3 2 1

ISBN-13: 978-0-14400-012-8   ISBN-10: 0-14400-012-1

Typeset in Perpetua by SÜRYA, New Delhi
Printed at Chaman Offset Printers, New Delhi

The Almighty Says in His Book

N. By the Pen and what is written
You are not, by the Grace of your Lord, mad.
Indeed, you have a reward, never to be cut off,
and you stand on a tremendous standard of character.
So soon you shall see,
and they too shall see: Which of you is
afflicted with madness.
Your Lord is best aware of he who strays from His
way,
and He is best aware of those who walk aright.

—The Qur'an,
The Pen (68), Signs 1-7

the end of islam

Could Kibr al-Akrad have known that he would perish by his own hand some years before his birth? Could he have grasped the chain of events that would bring him to such an impasse, to that strangest, rarest and most frightening of times, when the only way forward is backwards?

In the middle of the seventh century, the Byzantine city of Jerusalem had fallen into the hands of surging Saracens, bearers of an unexpected faith. Over the following decades, most of Jerusalem's native Christian and Jewish inhabitants—the indigenous peoples of Palestine—converted to Islam, gradually also exchanging their Semitic Hebrew and Aramaic for Semitic Arabic. Those Christians that remained in Palestine followed Eastern and Orthodox rites, meaning that they were, in the Pontiff's eyes, a heretic minority in territory ruled by Muslim heathens.

In 1095, the Roman Pontiff Urban II bound Catholic Europe to a supposed mission of recovery: the Christians would liberate Jerusalem. Shortly after the Pope's call, a swarm of Catholic warriors, nobles, daydreamers and criminals streamed into Anatolia, where they met stiff resistance from the noble Turkic nomads of the sunrise land. Yet even the formidable Turkic cavalry could not stem this sudden tide. In 1099, a divided Muslim world lost Jerusalem. Tens of thousands of Christians, Jews and Muslims—by some estimates, over eighty thousand—were slaughtered by the armies of the Roman cross. The Dome of the Rock, where Muhammad and the blessed Prophets of God gathered for prayer, became a Catholic citadel.

It seemed the victorious Crusaders would face no equals. North-east Africa was ruled by the House of Fatimah; from their capital of Fustat, these Ismailis audaciously allied themselves with the Crusaders against fellow Muslims. The Sunni Seljuk Turks had long since spent their vigour, leaving a feeble and worthless Caliph on the Abbasi throne in Baghdad. So God chose the Righteousness of the Faith, Joseph the son of Job, Salah al-Din Yusuf ibn Ayyub, to salvage lost honour and recover lost territory. Deposing the House of Fatimah, Salah al-Din made Egypt his stronghold, there gathering his forces while simultaneously bringing the population back to the mainstream of Islam.

On July 4, 1187, under the command of Salah al-Din, Islamic armies crushed the Crusaders at Hattin and followed this victory with another: the rescue of Jerusalem. The humiliations that had stretched nearly nine decades were ended; gradually, the remaining foreign outposts and fortresses fell back into the hands of a resurgent Muslim world. Yet Salah al-Din's ambition to raise a mighty host, and with it subjugate the ever unsatisfied Crusaders, was never realized. Rather, he passed to God some years after his earthly triumphs, remembered to this day as the great champion of an embattled faith.

For some time, his lessons were learned.

Under the House of Usman, known to the West as the Ottoman, Islam again galloped into Europe and across the

Mediterranean. For some centuries, Muslims had cause to feel not only secure but even exultant: the Ottoman Vicegerent of the Prophet, from the Sublime Porte of Constantinople, maintained their dignity. But, as before, what had risen began to fall. Learning new technologies and new strategies, the English, the Russians and many other peoples turned on to the Islamic world, driving it both from conquered lands and long-held ones. One by one, Muslim states fell to these humiliations.

1881 marked the Zionist Usurpation, with the immigration of foreign populations into the land of Palestine slowly but surely displacing her native inhabitants. In 1967, the pitiable Arab Muslim countries were cracked apart in a devastating six-day war that ended with Jerusalem in the hands of an expanding Jewish state. The Muslim masses had fallen into ignorance, deviance and despair, and while a few cried out for Salah al-Din, most suspected that no rival to the departed Kurd could be found. The faith weakened, and with it its followers, till the Islamic peoples began to be compartmentalized and assimilated into other ways of life, some of them new, some of them resurgences from the days before the Prophet.

But there was hope, albeit invisible. While the Muslim world knew much of Salah al-Din's actions in its defence, the Muslim world was ignorant of his last action. Salah al-Din sent his most trusted lieutenants and their families to Egypt, choosing the best, brightest and most pious of those who had struggled for and survived the liberation of Jerusalem. These men and women were selected to vanish from the world's eyes and tasked with living unnoticed in the corners of the newly founded Madinat al-Qahirah, the City Victorious. There they were to hold to their charge until the very meaning of victory had passed from Muslim tongues. Before leaving them to their responsibilities, Salah al-Din gathered them all together and delivered this message:

> Root yourselves and your families in the City Victorious. Through the long night of your expectation, let not the whims of other men distract you from your cause, for surely they shall obstruct and interrupt you.

> Recall in dark times that you are in the sleepless service of Jerusalem, the lot of you the promise of a coming and blinding light. For from among you shall one day rise a mighty warrior, perfecting your immortality.

> Verily, there is no honour and no power except with God. Place your hopes in Him. It is not for you to win by force of arms, for the defeat of Satan is in God's Unbreakable Hands. He asks rather, and only, for your allegiance, as His Will unfolds.

Almost eight hundred years later, Kibr al-Akrad was born, when many of the Kurds of the End of Days had begun to doubt even the fact of Salah al-Din's orders. But Kibr's father, Yusuf the son of Imad al-Din, nonetheless taught his son the ways of Islam, the sciences of its texts and the import of its history, binding Kibr to the fate his forefathers proudly shared. From a young age, Kibr was told of the magic in Abraham's blood, which had produced the great houses of Isaac and Ishmael. A similar if less potent spell was in Salah al-Din's blood, to whose line Kibr directly belonged. Kibr's family, however, witnessed the fading of Cairo's Kurdistan, as many Kurds abandoned their traditional ways in favour of Egypt's secularizing culture, marrying and mixing, diluting and eventually disappearing. Many wondered: Had Salah al-Din made a dreadful mistake, casting us to the awful fate of longing—and for nothing at all?

Until the great attacks. Words of war were spoken again, armies were gathered, and the Islamic world faced a defeat that would humiliate all previous humiliators. But then, a middle-aged preacher arrived in Cairo's Kurdistan, to fill the ears of a thankless city and a frightened Ummah. Those who had previously heard him, said that his voice was much bigger than his body, capable of puncturing the walls of Cairo's only Kurdish masjid. They said that it would deflate nations one day. So Kibr, with every other Kurd capable of the walk, went to listen. What he heard was a man calling himself, quite strangely, Rojet Dahati, a name which in Kurdish depicted the future. This Rojet declared that he too was of Cairene Kurdish extraction, though long ago his parents had set him on another path, a path he returned to only through the wisdom and the patience of an erudite scholar named Abd al-Bari.

But no matter what Rojet said, most of the Kurds remained in denial. Many of them refused to pay him any heed, and some of them even worked against him. Of his few supporters, among the most steadfast was Kibr's father. On his advice, Kibr followed Rojet and learned from him, till the Ustad took the young disciple into his confidence: Abd al-Bari had been the Qutb al-Aqtab, the Pole of Poles, and Rojet was appointed his Qutb. All they needed, then, were four Awtad, Pegs to form an Order of Light, disciples worthy of immortality. Those who thought themselves capable of a task too heavy for the stars were to meet with Rojet the following

Friday. An older man named Wanand was the first to answer; Kibr the second. The Order of Light resolved to gather its energies to liberate Jerusalem when the time for liberating came. Their sacred compensation would be the restoration of glory to Islam and dignity to her lands and people, a corrective justice in which the Order and its soldiers were to play a signal role.

But there was no new dawn. Attacks from a mysterious Base began another struggle, one which Rojet understood from the beginning was doomed to defeat. Again the Crusaders came, and again the Muslim world found itself divided and defenceless. Too early, Rojet was forced to launch his troops. Weapons the world had not imagined could be deployed were, and on multiple occasions, leaving the heart of the Muslim world a ruined, rotten and radioactive wreck. Tens of millions perished until, eventually, the Pole had lost his protector and had only his Pegs. So, alone in the Tower of Light, Rojet asked from the Almighty a most astounding request: to be allowed to go back, to try again.

Though he doubted the wisdom of this direction and its painful implications, Kibr forced himself to stifle his doubts. Years before, before the wars and the defeats and the massacres, he had pledged himself to Rojet and the path he preached. Whether Rojet's prayer would simply return the Muslim world to its ultimate defeat—albeit this time delayed—could not be known. All that the Pegs knew was this: They would have to take their own lives, and with them they would take all the memories and all the hurt born of a time when Islam was irresistibly forced from the earth.

embareh
yesterday

Let's die before dying, Bahu:
only then can the Lord be reached.

—Sultan Bahu

the apartment of
insufficient rainfall

Maybe I was the only one who felt like he wasn't making any
sense. Maybe I'd have to run alone. Again. We'd made it to
the masjid just as it was becoming crowded, Haris clapping
his sandals together and parking himself at the head of the
congregation, leaving me by the back wall. I faced a row of
bored, moustachioed men who faced the wrong way, their
backs to the holy city. I don't believe they much wanted to
be there, either, but something had made them come. Did
they have room-mates? Perhaps they came to sit on grass-
green carpets, relaxing under whirling fans, doing their best
to ape Elysium's cooling rivers, or to stave off the desert sun
hidden by a dome above us: a necessary nod to the (dead?)
civilization we (once?) belonged to.

And because I hadn't wanted to come to the masjid, I was
blessed to hear a sermon I'd never want to hear again. As if
yesterday's events weren't humiliation enough, the imam
rambled on about the importance of marriage and family in
this day and age. What was he blathering about? In our world,
inundated by individualism and the monopoly of machines,
how many people had the courage, drive or even the desire
to settle down, and in doing that, admit that we're an
impermanent species? The masjid became stuffier over the
course of the sermon, the humidity choking my reflections

before they had the chance to wander any further. I suffered prayer and met my room-mate on the burning marble steps.

The fastest way back was a long loop around a BMW dealership, itself tucked into the strangest place: a dilapidated apartment building facing away from every main street. From there, we travelled two blocks down a cluttered, interrupted street: the way home. Our apartment was on Shari al-Ghayth, on the fifth floor of a building in the middle of the block, equidistant from two rarely manned police posts, there to protect an important politician who lived across the street from us.

His apartment was nicer.

When we got past the showroom, my room-mate asked, 'What do you want to do for lunch?'

That question that has no answer. At least, not in Egypt. 'Why don't we figure that out once we're in the apartment?' I paused, looking both ways for a reckless vehicle. Martyrdom after Friday prayers: why not? 'Might as well think about it in air-conditioning.'

He didn't say a word. In other words, okay. I produced a cigarette and lit it, tossing the match behind me.

'Do you know how bad that is?' My room-mate. He fills in for the imam the six remaining days of the week.

'Oh no, I'd forgotten.' I grinned and blew smoke ahead of me. 'Thanks for the reminder.'

'Well, you never listen.'

My free hand gestured to the cars parked along the road. 'We breathe *their* crap in every day.'

'Why would you make it worse?'

I shrugged, taking another puff.

He concluded, 'It's a nasty habit.'

'So is telling other people what to do.'

Our apartment was like an Islamic Revolution: Considering everything we'd been promised, it was a big let-down. On entering, you faced a tiny foyer opening into a long and mostly pointless room the first half of which was a dining room complete with a gargantuan and worthless dining table. Who in the hell were we two foreign students going to entertain? The sitting room was devoid of anything but a cumbersome love seat and two lemonade chairs, so called because they were flimsy plaid-patterned lawn chairs that reminded me of happier summers with sprinklers and home-made lemonade. The space had not a table, nor even a respectable floor. We'd mop and mop, several times back and forth, but it remained dusty, as if the splotches were part of its design.

Behind the foyer was our kitchen, which lacked ventilation but made up for it with bright blue floor tiles and blamelessly white appliances, something out of a fifties' sitcom. Next to the kitchen was the first of our two bathrooms, this one totally useless, and not just because it was without a functioning light or toilet. Assuming the toilet worked, sitting on it would be impossible. One of my knees would scrape against a hideously rusted pedestal sink, while the other would get intimate with the wooden door. The second bathroom was the best part of the apartment: clean, spacious, well-lit, inviting. Of course, it was still just a bathroom. We had two bedrooms as well, both about the same size, though one had a bed and nothing else. The other bedroom anticipated this problem, coming equipped with two twin-size beds, a carpet, head tables and some other modern furniture.

It was our refuge.

While I waited in the dining room, my room-mate went into the kitchen, searching for some bottled water. Only after he was out did I venture in, to procure my own supply. We met each other by the foyer, not looking at each other, but rather, at our beverages, exactly the same.

'Wasn't it stupid of us to come all the way back here just to go out again?' Haris ventured.

I smiled. 'Maybe the exercise will help my blackened lungs.'

He grunted as he walked past. I wanted to stick my foot out and send him to the floor, busting his face against the dirty tiles. But if I did that, he'd fight back and I didn't know whether Haris could knock me down. Why not think happier thoughts? Like coming out of the elevator one day and finding an astonishing Egyptian girl waiting outside our building. For me.

I liked that one a lot. I made it up right about the time we moved in, though each time I lived through it it had a different and more fantastic ending. Still, the most fun was thinking about the girl herself and not the story surrounding. Other than head-turning beautiful, she'd have to be an Eastern Westerner, externally Islamic but internally secular, dividing the two with a hot-headed hypocrisy that excellently complemented my own. Which always made me wonder: How had my parents' piety produced a person made content by deodorant, water bottles and fairy-tale beauties?

For now, though, all I had was Haris. Not just an imam but a husband and a wife, too. The two of us could have been a society. Then one of us would agitate for Islamic law, and ruin everything.

Haris jangled his keys and made his way to the door. 'Let's go.'

Where?

the waitress nobody wanted

Gamiat al-Duwal al-Arabiyyah, the Avenue of the League of Arab States. An eight-lane beast that starts at the western edge of Mohandessin and slumps all the way to its eastern edge, right north of our Agouza. This mighty boulevard plays host to most of Cairo's Western restaurants and resources including the indispensable Metro supermarket, where we often stopped for good reason or none. This Friday, it was to use their ATM. And to rest, after a long walk, in an air-conditioned environment.

I asked, 'Do you want to eat anywhere in particular?'

It was a stupid question, considering both of us knew there was nothing worth it. A long time ago, back when nobody took pictures of masjids, when cities lived in their walls and there was no such thing as Old Cairo, nobody asked such questions. Questions are for the dead. Answers are for the living. My ATM card caught the light and the hologram sparkled.

To anyone walking by, the two of us were just perplexed tourists huddled at an ATM machine without a clue. I wouldn't have been surprised had some nice Egyptians walked over to inform us that we were, in fact, very far from the Pyramids. Actually, we'd come to Cairo to study Arabic, though that wasn't going so well. Our intention to study was lacking in every respect. We had little or no desire to look at a textbook, let alone study out of one. Neither did we feel any urge to approach a masjid, aside from my room-mate's occasional interest in prayer, or the obligatory rolls of film which were taken to impress relatives and friends back in America.

'That's a beautiful masjid,' they'd exclaim. 'Did you pray there?'

'I can't remember,' I'd say. That is, I'd rather forget.

Off and on, I'd experience a spike in my practice, the result of an impulsive burst of piety, with negligible long-term effect. Soon enough, I became afraid of the wave and did everything to crush it, till they were insignificant murmurs in an otherwise flat existence. That was why I had come to Africa for the summer: to find a way to rejuvenate my Islam. Yet the daily exhaustion that sapped my spirit in New York, where I went to school, continued to affect me.

My fault, really. To give myself hope, I had come to a region where hope had long since given way to conspiracy theories, Zionist plots and Mossad plotters, CIA assassinations and sinister organizations planning people's mistakes for them. Shouldn't I have known better? And then, in about a month more, I would go back to America not having improved, but more likely having been made worse: sitting in my new Upper East Side apartment, kicking myself for not having done anything more productive with my precious months abroad; always looking back, wishing.

But where did wishing get anyone?

Haris made eye contact, frightening me. 'Why don't we go to Chili's?' he asked. 'We've never been there before.' I looked at him with uncertainty, so he finished the discussion. 'Can you think of anything else?'

I scanned the hipper half of Gamiat al-Duwal, opposite us. No, I could not. So I whizzed through blue ATM screens, bounding from one menu to another, withdrawing sixty gunayh, my maximum daily allowance. About $15 at turn-of-the-century exchange rates. While my room-mate was hailing a cab, I stuffed the money into my wallet, unnoticed. Better we hide our comparative wealth, lest we end up spending lunch money on cab fare. Cairo cabbies were like school yard bullies.

To assist in this regard, I kept my eyes focused on the distance, away from the immediate sights and sounds. Perhaps this would affect our driver's opinion of his customers: We'd long been residents of this city, clearly not interested in anything around us. I craned my neck and looked higher up, noticing something altogether unexpected. There was a hideous yellow billboard, placed where only a select few might ever catch sight of it. Decorated with unimaginative square letters in black block script, it read: THERE IS NO GLORY OR POWER SAVE WITH GOD. Tucked into the bottom right corner, in similarly trim if smaller script, mention was made of the government of the Arab Republic of Egypt, which had paid for the sign.

Our cab driver asked again, 'What is the restaurant's name?'

My room-mate replied. 'Sheeleez.'

Whoever propped that billboard way up beside the second star to the right must have also picked the location for the Chili's outlet, presuming it'd be a good idea to put a restaurant behind a set of thick, obscuring trees and a large electronics store whose shadow veiled the establishment. The builders, I decided, had to have been Muslims. As if to indicate his displeasure at such incompetence, our driver let us out in front of the Mustafa Mahmud Masjid, which would've been a much better location for the restaurant. I indulged in a cigarette, smoking it to smooth the path to Chili's.

An eager young man named Hussam escorted us in, opening the door in an awkward manner, nearly knocking Haris over. Of course, I visualized the same, but worse, happening to me. Good thing my glasses were shatter-proof. That way, the whole piece of glass would be shoved into my eye, as opposed to the discomfort of several jagged shards.

'Keep away from Hussam,' I smiled.

My room-mate laughed. 'As long as he's not our waiter.'

He wasn't. Rather, we were informed that we had a waitress. Which led to the inevitable conjecture: Was she attractive? Would she marry us? Which one of us? If we fought over her, would the loser still have to pay rent? And, worse yet, would he get the uglier bedroom? But such speculation was inappropriate. She wasn't ugly. She wasn't pretty. She was either one or the other, but never in-between. With the help of her overly emphatic expressions, our waitress was pushed ahead of, or behind, the mottled line that separates adorable from reprehensible.

Bored with scrutinizing a repetitive menu—Chili's turned out to be expensive fast food that made it hard to preserve my ablution—I began to describe, to my room-mate, the sum of our waitress's engaging features, hoping to get him to flirt with her. But my attempts at advertising backfired. If she was as beautiful as I claimed she was, then it would've been ridiculous to allow Haris the opportunity to win her. A pointless jealousy emerged from within me, urging me to charm a girl I wasn't even interested in.

On her first visit to our table, just as my room-mate was about to ask for more time (he was caught between the burger and the cheeseburger), I put on my most earnest face. 'Could I start with the cheese quesadillas?'

What a wonderful echo that made as she confirmed my request! A high-pitched, energetic Egyptian girl, with an Arabic tongue made muscular from the demands of her powerful language, trying and failing to soften herself for the sake of a light Spanish. After she left with my request, twice recalled and then jotted down, my room-mate cautioned, 'Won't the quesadillas make you sick?'

'I'll be fine,' I insisted. Besides, he was just jealous. Our waitress had focused all her attention on me, treating him as if he were only a little animal, albeit with money and an appetite, sitting across from a much more attractive client. When she returned with my appetizer, I shifted it up a notch. My shy smile evolved into a wide-mouthed, toothy grin, which quickly ascended to contagious laughter and good-natured jesting, though I ruined it all with my last action: a disastrous wink of my right eye as she walked over to get the third Pepsi that I'd ordered. She wasn't just a waitress, then, she was a Muslim one. My excessive flirting caused her discomfort, but at the same time it gave me a bit of optimism, though I am not sure why. Our old values—that is, old to me—might survive this dark time, emerging into a better one which I foresaw as the replacement of Chili's with an Islamic franchise operation, much the same as this one except for the flourishes above and below. That is, a gloss of faith over a cover of emptiness.

My room-mate was twirling his straw around in his cup, building a little Pepsi whirlpool, which amused him—and, I am ashamed to admit, caught my interest. He stopped and looked up. The straw jerked and twirled, quickly losing its momentum.

'I need a haircut.' He put his hands on his head, pulling the ends of his hair in a wonderfully comic manner, demonstrating how unacceptably long it had grown. 'We've got the afternoon free. Do you want to go to that place near our apartment?'

going places for faces

All of Egypt is a shade of brown. The buildings, the streets, the people and the Pyramids. Hell, even the camels are brown. From an airplane's approach, Cairo is a mud-baked, third-world civilization that expanded too fast—no more than a sprawling sandcastle. The barbershop on Shari al-Ghayth, a few steps from our building, was however poles apart. Half the shop was tucked underground—an abrupt series of unfortunately beige steps stops just short of the door. If anything ever deserved its own roll of film, it had to be the shop itself, smothered by a furious signal red, a colour that tasted like salted meat and burned my eyes like molten iron. And then the door! It was entirely glass and nearly the size of the shop itself, framed by an honourable Muslim spring green. This made perfect sense, too, considering that the friendly barber's fundamentalism rose to another level. Books like *Stories of the Prophets* lay on his only table, studying made more comfortable by way of a reliable air-conditioner purring smugly in the background.

But since I said nothing in response, Haris got worried. 'Do you not want to go, yaar? He's a good barber.'

He was right, too. The day before, I would've jumped at the chance.

It was strange, the way Haris could swing from one emotion to its complete opposite. One second he was sullen and depressed, at the end of his rope and not in the mood to ask if anyone had any to spare. A few breaths later, a thin and rectangular smile occupied his face, pushing the ends of it apart, so that every feature on his visage beamed with pure joy. This time, though, he was just puzzled. His eyes were puzzled. As were his mouth, nose, cheeks, chin, ears and forehead.

'You really don't want to get a haircut? It looks like you need one, yaar.'

Thanks. 'I'm really not in the mood to go.'

'But we have an afternoon off. What else are we going to do?'

Sit here and argue about stupid things. 'Look…' I wanted to be firm, but instead, my voice cracked. Good thing the waitress wasn't around. 'I really don't want a haircut.'

'Well, why not?'

Because I don't have a girl. Not a good answer, I know. But it was mine, and so it would have to do. But because I didn't say any of that aloud, Haris asked me once more. 'You're serious about this?'

His insistence was disturbing. But maybe my intransigence felt the same to him. After all, what sane human being in this rational and ordered era in which we live, when all of life is a regulated march into oblivion (as opposed to meaningful free fall, I suppose), would refuse something as useful as a haircut? Were this the Islamic Emirate of Afghanistan, I would've been refusing prayer: The effect on my room-mate's ministry was about the same.

The waitress dropped the bill on the table and I didn't give her a second glance. I checked the total, put the cash down on the table, and turned to my room-mate. 'When I left'—

actually, ran out of—'the apartment last night, I saw the barber in his shop. I mean, I went past his shop. And he saw me...'

'Okay.' One eyebrow went up. 'So why don't you want to go?'

'Because he saw me.'

'What?'

I stood up, motioning for Haris to do the same. As we walked out, allowing ourselves and not Hussam to open the door, I clarified. 'You know he's a fundo. What if he asks me what I was doing going out so late at night?' I paused at the first of several steps. 'What am I going to say?'

'You're the one who ran out.'

'Yeah.' But. 'He wasn't supposed to see me.'

'God!' Haris threw his hands in the air, which made it look—for a second—like he was going to start praying. I remembered then that I hadn't read my morning prayers. At least I'd attended Friday prayers. One out of two. In an American school, I'd fail. After the Day of Judgement, I'd go to hell.

'I think it would be awkward, you know, to explain why I was running so fast.'

Haris shook his head. 'Obviously, if you run out of your apartment like a moron, someone's going to see you. You're just lucky the police didn't.'

I responded to this shrewd observation by staring blankly ahead. On my right, a block away, was the Mustafa Mahmud Masjid, built by a famous scientist who returned to religion and then established a foundation to spread his fusion of empiricism and fundamentalism. On my left was a failed attempt at a rotary. There was apparently once a fountain in the middle, but it was no longer turned on. Slightly off to the side was the arterial Gamiat al-Duwal, still crowded with cars, all of them brown-shifted just like everything else here. I spent this observation time thinking what I should to do.

The barber would definitely ask me why I ran past his shop so late last night. He was such a nice fellow, always informing us about the cheapest restaurants, good grocery stores—and I'd throw a wrench in our relationship. Being the religious type, he'd lose respect for me, and probably consider Haris guilty by association. Perhaps he'd even refuse to see us. On the other hand, not going wasn't too promising, either. I really did need a haircut, and if I waited till the next time my room-mate needed one, I'd end up looking like a goofy Sufi. Plus, if Haris went alone, my absence would only pique the barber's suspicion. Nor could I have gone on my own. It was nearly impossible for me to understand our barber. Only Haris could help me navigate his queries.

He asked, 'What are we waiting for?'

'Nothing, really.' I feigned a cough. 'Ready to walk back?'

'Walk?' He was stunned. 'It's a July afternoon in Cairo. It's like a hundred and ten outside.'

Is it? 'Well...' Time for me to stare at something else. I chose the ground. Too bad my feet weren't very exciting. 'I spent all our money on food.'

Haris moved closer, as if to hit me. I didn't flinch, because I knew I deserved it. 'You're such an idiot sometimes. Why the hell did you have to order quesadillas?' He searched his wallet but that didn't help. 'I only have ten gunayh left. That's enough for a cab and my haircut, or no cab and two haircuts.'

Another way of asking the same question: Do you want to get a haircut?

'Let's take a cab,' I suggested. 'I don't need a haircut.'

He glanced at the ugly mop of aimless black covering my head. 'Shut up, yaar. I'll pay for you. Let's just walk back.'

My life has been a series of accelerating and interconnected failures, one mistake creating a problem, one problem forcing a dilemma, and one dilemma—well, on and on it goes, till I wake up on a Thursday morning, shivering in an overheated country, wondering what use there is to getting out of bed. And as bad as that question is, my inability to answer it is a thousand times worse. But yesterday, after one too many retreats, I made that one thing that so often eludes me: a decision. To charge headlong into destiny. Well, against it, actually. But that doesn't change the fact that, for once, I did something.

Late last night, in the middle of another melancholy Cairo night, I bolted out of our apartment without a word to my room-mate. I ran and ran until my sweat-soaked body braked hard outside the Hardee's restaurant on Batal Ahmad Abd al-Aziz Street. My gaze pierced through each of the massive glass windows, my eyes forced open despite the dust that was begging them to tear.

But she was long gone by then.

those who don't speak urdu

It was the thought of that candy-apple red and sour-green barbershop that lessened the heat's burden on me. Our faithful barber kept his shop cooled to a frigid exactness, a compelling case for the marriage of Islam and modernity to mutual benefit. Not just that, the very routine was heavenly. One of his two apprentices (who, by the laws of Egyptian probability, had to be named Muhammad) would begin by dunking our heads into a sink and washing our hair with an aromatic almond shampoo. The suds would be rinsed off with a refreshingly cold spray of chlorinated water—both before *and* after the haircut. It was the first Islamic utopia of the fifteenth century. So I smiled in anticipation of the event until I realized I was smiling in anticipation of a haircut. This, my life.

I was already exhausted by my dehydration, but it was about to get worse.

When we turned the corner onto our street, something heavy rushed down my innards, creating an ominous internal gargle. In other words, the Gastrointestinal Sphinx. The Pharaoh's Revenge. The Ruin of Ramses. The Diarrhoea of the Dynasties.

'Oh God,' I moaned, 'those damned quesadillas.'

Haris turned, but on seeing me clutch my stomach, he didn't laugh. He even forgot that I'd made him walk such a fantastic distance without even a bottle of water between us. Rather, compassion was the order of the day. 'Are you okay, bhai?'

'I'll see you in the barbershop,' I promised, rushing away from him. Towards our apartment. Haris, meanwhile, moved in the opposite direction, towards the shade of trees and the barbershop just beyond. I yelled, 'Please don't tell the barber about this, either.'

Nor did he mock that. I thanked him by not saying thank you. In my defence, there were more pressing concerns. I ran towards our building, praying to God the Most Merciful that the elevator would be waiting for me, sparing me even a second more of agony. Funny how suddenly piety promises salvation. And miraculously, the elevator was waiting in the lobby, as if it had been descended from above only to ease my trial.

I relieved myself in our bathroom, in a horrific ordeal that left me spent of all energies. That and the bathroom stank a rank odour, which I foolishly tried to ameliorate with twenty sprays of Haris's Armani cologne. But the solution was worse than the problem that called for it, forcing me out of the bathroom while stifling the urge to vomit.

In the kitchen, I took comfort in sugary Pepsi, hoping that the blend of caffeine and saccharine would inject sorely needed vigour into my wearied body. I drank it straight from the bottle, too, in no mood to find myself an intermediary for the sake of an urgent matter. After all, cups were like priests. Was I a Christian? No, I most certainly was not. I was a Muslim who'd just spent sixty gunayh on a meal that was now making its way through Cairo's plumbing.

Before daring to make my way to the barbershop, I

waited at least five minutes more. The barber promised to be embarrassing enough; but imagine if my upset stomach attacked. Right as he asked me what I was doing running past his shop in the middle of the night, I'd feel it rushing through my guts. With no answer to his urgent query, I'd have to bolt again, this time out of his shop, half my hair neatly trimmed and the other half still quite chaotic. In the meanwhile, my room-mate would explain to the barber how I had made myself sick in order to impress a girl I didn't want.

'He is very stupid,' the barber would smile. 'He reminds me of the Arab League.'

When I got to the barbershop, Haris was still getting his haircut. The barber turned to greet me as I entered, but he left his shiny, buzzing blade too close to my room-mate's ear. I saw him wince twice. Once in front of me, and then again in the mirror across from me.

'Salam alaykum wa rahmatullahi wa barakatuh,' the barber announced. Not only did he greet me with peace, but the love and blessings of God. How frustrating. Only a full reply was appropriate.

'Wa alaykum salam wa rahmatullahi wa barakatuh.'

My turn came in five minutes. One of the barber's apprentices, who may or may not have been the Muhammad of the two, sat me down before the pedestal sink, pushing my head down at an awkward angle. It didn't help that I was tall. He lathered his hands with that magical shampoo and began rubbing it in quite emphatically, washing out Cairo's grime. The rinse came with water only a shade above frozen: Was this the water I'd so desired? But it was. I'd only forgotten the excitement of getting over the initial shock.

Then Muhammad scraped away a layer of my face with

his towel. Things were less subtle here. My room-mate moved to a black chair in the middle of the shop, while I sat down and adjusted myself in mine. As he tied the apron around me, the barber continued the conversation he was having with my room-mate. Nearly all of it escaped me, though, because the style and the vocabulary in use were far and away from the formality I favoured. Like the rest of my life. I spoke English well, but I wished it were something else instead.

My father came from a village—not even a town—in a corner of the subcontinent christened Pakistan. In his little hamlet, only Punjabi was spoken, a crude and poetic language of rivers. Much like the little islands that form in the wake of a fierce flood, outposts of mud and dirt that endure, surviving as future farmland for future people, Punjabi is the language not of realization but of potential; not of modernity but of the hope for it; not of tomorrow but of the heralding sunset. Those who speak it have tongues like hands splashing puddles, soggy from the rains of the season, in eager wait for warmth to emerge, bringing energy to effort and endeavour. Hence, we Punjabis run along the edges of meandering streams in the meantime, such that lend this language its melodious offensiveness, daring and rhyme.

But Punjabi was not to be the language of Pakistan. Rather, the secularizing elites of this new national idea, who somehow concocted a blend of Islam and Atatürk, chose Urdu to be the medium for their paradox, fumbling, then fading, then failing. One can only sit and wonder why. Urdu is the language of the kingdom to come, having come from the age of the Taj Mahal when it shone in the night and not as a tourist sight. What possible use Urdu has, in this darkness before the dawn, is inexplicable.

But this was no consolation to my father, who never sat in a court or composed poetry. Rather, he sang, and only in Punjabi, while on the battlefield he had to defend those 'nationalists'—men who'd never lived in his land or spoken his language, but claimed his as theirs all the same. To him, and thus to me, Urdu was ever the soul-stealer, the life-taker, the back-breaker, the grim-reaper, a script symbolizing the anaesthetizing fantasizing ambitions that have always been Pakistan but that haven't been for centuries now. Little wonder my father fled, out of linguistic, economic, social and political dislocation, to where else but where the colonizers also came. And so, all of my admittedly short life I have had no tongue of my own but only many different languages used to connect me, never to places, people or even faces, but only to ideas.

The barber said something to me that I didn't follow. And then, to enhance my comprehension, he stabbed me right below my sideburns.

'No,' I mumbled, 'they're okay.'

Then I think he asked what style I wanted.

'Same,' I said. 'Just shorter.'

My hair was sliced off with devastating efficiency. But I wasn't sad to see it go. Like every yesterday, it'd come back. Whether or not my room-mate was there to pay for it was another question. Followed by a third question, the one I knew the barber was going to ask.

'Were you the one running past my shop late last night?'

I flashed a look at Haris, who tried and failed to conceal a grin. Please leave me to suffer this one, as bad as it is right now. And that's what my room-mate did. He buried his head in a book and pretended to go deaf. Nor did I suspect was he eavesdropping. He wasn't the type.

As I turned back to face the barber, I tried my best to smile. 'Yes, I ran past your shop last night.' I also speak ugly Arabic.

'Was he there?' He pointed to Haris with a pair of scissors.

'No. Just me.'

I was only exercising, I wanted to say. But the barber didn't ask any more questions, preventing me both from defending myself, as well as from lying—which is what I would've done, had he continued this interrogation. The events of last night were not much more than a discord trying to eradicate itself, through whatever action, no matter how sudden or strange. Late last night, I ran to Hardee's as fast as I could, seeking something that might put me back together again. It was not that I fell apart all at once, but that I'd been breaking, first slowly and then more surely, till I hit bottom and shattered so hard that my shards sent me flying away from me. For a few minutes, I was no longer myself, but watching myself through time, as if one could observe repetition and then return to right it. I left everything I never had in the hope of finding someone who looked, from several feet away, like rescue.

Last night, it was just me. Alone. Just me running so that maybe I wouldn't be.

the embassy of east pakistan

During our first week in Egypt, my room-mate and I gave up on local cuisine. Generally unimpressive options that, for no extra cost, were hard on our stomachs, too. Unfortunately, the best alternatives were those five-star restaurants that offered fantastic food at even more fantastic prices. So where were we middle-income, temporary Egyptians to go? West, of course.

Because America is powerful, Egyptian reasoning goes, American fast food is therefore tasty, healthy and fun. (It is rarely, if ever, those three.) Still, that's how defeated wheels turn. And that's also the explanation for the incredible profusion of fast-food places popping up all over Cairo faster than you can say Gamiat al-Duwal al-Arabiyyah. But, because the prices were low and the food pretty hygienic, we were condemned to eating at these places for our first month.

To relieve the monotony, we purchased a glossy guide to Cairo's many restaurants. However, since this guide was only bought by those in our income range or above, its listed options catered to Egyptians who by and large didn't want to eat like Egyptians. But then again, I can't blame them. If there is one weakness in their culture, it is a gastric one.

In Pakistan, the Badshahi Masjid is an excellent clue as to the quality of the country's cuisines. In Egypt's case, the Pyramids offer a similar analogy: simple, bland, crumbling and ancient, devoid of any and all ornamentation. In their defence, many Egyptologists state that the treasures are *inside* the Pyramids—but I have bitten into Egyptian food, and I have yet to find riches. Or flavour. Still, McDonald's isn't much competition. A smaller pyramid, maybe, with a tourist booth and laser light beams all trying to obscure the fact that the food removes days and months from your lifespan. It is a combo meal and also a tomb.

It was Thursday evening and Haris was leaning against the dining table, his eyes scanning the guidebook with impressive speed. He yelled 'Hey! How about Chinese?' as if I was twenty miles away.

Because he wasn't Punjabi, I couldn't forgive him this. 'Chill man, you're so loud.'

'So?'

'What if the doorman comes up?' I asked.

He laughed while sliding his finger to mark the page, so that I too could see. Wok-n-Roll, a Chinese restaurant but an American franchise: therefore, it was probably tasty, but not virulently poisonous. It was a bit expensive, which wasn't so good, but it wasn't too much for a Thursday evening. Which, in Egypt, was the start of the weekend.

'There's no phone number,' I complained. 'Only an address.' In Cairo, even if you have an address for an establishment, it doesn't mean you will locate the place: The numbers don't appear to go in any order.

'But it's on Gamiat al-Duwal,' Haris countered. 'It shouldn't be far from all the other nice restaurants.'

'I've never seen it.'

'Well, there's nothing else.' He sighed. 'Do you really want to eat fast food again?'

'If I have to eat fast food again, I'll kill myself.'

'Why would you kill yourself?'

'Good point.' I passed the guidebook back to him, still open to the right page. 'I'll blow up the restaurant instead.'

We decided on Chinese.

After a good twenty minutes of hurried back and forth over Gamiat al-Duwal, it became clear that we weren't going to find Wok-n-Roll on our own. The painful solution was to ask for directions. The first problem was the name of the restaurant—God knows what the average Egyptian on the street thought we were referring to. The second, and bigger, problem was the Egyptian character. Whatever else I might bemoan, Egyptians have one quality that makes them stand out in an otherwise brown world. They are generous, warm-hearted and inviting, a spitting image of the true Arab, in reverse to many Arab nations whose populations exhibit an open racism so common it ceases to be offensive but instead expected. Egypt is a still-glowing ember from a fire almost out in every other part of the Arab world. But the problem with such embers is that, in amalgamation, they get too hot and burn you. And seventy million of them inflame.

Even if an Egyptian has no idea what you're asking for, he'll do his best to help you. Foreigners commonly warned us: Ask an Egyptian for something that doesn't exist, and he'll help you find it. Ask for the embassy of East Pakistan and you'll get six or seven different answers out of six or seven actual requests. You can only imagine the delightful precision born of our query as to the location of 'The Chinese Restaurant'. Every man on the street knew where it was. And every man on the street was sure it wasn't where the last person had confirmed it was.

We must have covered a dozen blocks a dozen times. Half of that and the two of us were enraged, over an hour gone with nothing to show for it. Unless I counted the two cigarettes that had fallen victim to our aimlessness. But we had no idea who or what to blame for it. Hosni Mubarak? Ariel Sharon? Christopher Columbus? The Arab Revolt? The publishers of the guidebook? So I kept my anger in check, and probably Haris did, too, both of us praying that we might dissipate our lividness with a worthwhile dinner.

Which of course we didn't eat.

We surrendered at the busy intersection of Batal Ahmad Abd al-Aziz and Gamiat al-Duwal, where a Hardee's and a two-storey Pizza Hut rounded out the corner. Thousands of Cairenes passed on their way, some of them glancing out of the corners of their eyes, wondering why we were standing so paralysed. Please don't offer to help us.

'Fast food again,' I whispered.

'What else is there?'

'I hate this place.'

Haris weakened. 'But there's nothing else, yaar.'

'I really, really hate this place.'

'Let's just eat here.' And then he glanced at his watch. 'How much longer can we look?'

Here being Pizza Hut or Hardee's. What with the humidity and the heat, nothing was too tempting and fast food even less so. Either greasy pizza or a fat-filled sandwich.

'I don't trust the pizza here,' I said. 'Plus, we've never eaten at Hardee's.'

With the name of God, Haris relented. As he swung the door open, he smiled. 'Well, look at it this way. At least it's going to be cheap.'

Yes. But it's not going to be real food, either.

We stood in line behind clusters of Egyptian teenagers, their hands tentatively reaching for, and then pulling back from, their dates, not sure if it was okay to touch, not sure if a parent was watching or if God would really mind. The girls looked more inviting than everything on the menu.

'All these fast-food restaurants should merge,' I suggested. 'They sell the same thing, anyway.'

'Then you can blow them up more easily,' my room-mate laughed.

I ignored that. 'What do you want to eat?'

'Actually, I have to go to the bathroom,' he said. 'Been holding it in since we found that Casper the Friendly Ghost restaurant. Can you order for me, please?'

'What do you want?'

He took a second to look at the menu and then he shook his head. 'You're right. It's all the same. Just get me whatever you order for yourself.'

I had a grilled chicken sandwich, complete with a soda and an excessive number of fries, so that's what my room-mate had, too. Only one table was open and that was where I sat, not eating until Haris joined me. Very quickly, we agreed that the food was even worse than anything at McDonald's.

'You should definitely blow up this place first,' Haris said.

'Nah...'

'Why not?'

'You're looking at it all wrong,' I replied. 'If I blow up the better fast-food places first, like McDonald's, there'll only be really bad places left, like Hardee's. And they'll go out of business on their own. You've got to have a strategy for these things.'

My room-mate lifted his sandwich and showed it to me. 'They should have a strategy for microwaving these things. How can you possibly ruin a chicken sandwich?'

'Maybe it's a lot harder than it looks.'

Haris turned his sandwich all the way around. 'They've been doing this for years. And they still ruined it!'

Not only ruined, but pillaged and burned. The chicken tasted as if it had been left out to bake in the Cairo sun, the heat and light sucking all the flavour and moisture out. In total opposition, the fries were dripping oily sweat, the grease of a fryer that could've rivalled the Nile. It was even difficult to get ketchup to stick to them. The best part of the meal was the soda, but that was the worst part. Soda was the one thing we could've bought anywhere else, and for a quarter the price.

From my seat, I could see the entrance perfectly. There was nothing better for us to do than make fun of the many patrons who walked in. We pondered the possibility of trying to sell these customers our food, but that idea was swiftly and wisely shot down. Instead, we wondered who was who and what they were doing at a Hardee's, especially when their clothes indicated better means. As I was dipping the last of my French fries into a puddle of ketchup in the corner of my tray, the door swung open yet again. But such a beautiful thing walked in that I forgot my fry in the ketchup and slid forward so fast I nearly knocked my drink over onto my room-mate.

'Easy, bhai—'

I cut Haris off. 'Shut up and look behind you.'

An Egyptian goddess stood at the beginning of the order line; for the first time in a long time, I was sure of what I wanted. Her black hair dropped below her shoulder blades, caressing the top of a loose, cream-coloured full-sleeve shirt, cut low but not immodestly so. Such reserve came with exceptionally tight pants, a beautiful black intense enough to make the night sky outside shift its hue to a less impressive navy blue.

'Can you imagine having a girl like that?' I asked.

It took him a second to form an appropriate response. 'You can.'

I stared at him, though this seemed a sin while she was still in the restaurant. 'What are you talking about?'

'She's probably Muslim, yaar.' He smiled and then turned to look again, nodding to himself. 'Plus, she's all alone. What more could you possibly want?'

She was alone. I was alone. She was probably Muslim. I was probably Muslim. Thanks to Haris (unfortunately), everything fell into place. This was why we couldn't find the Chinese restaurant. This was why my weeks had been so abandoned and empty, every evening like a small-town diner minutes before closing. This was why my life had been so pointless. This was how I knew Allah loved me. Here, at Hardee's—of all places—was my chance to erase fearfulness and cowardice. My stunted Arabic would no longer be pathetic ignorance, but rather, the laudable efforts of a mind unable to operate before such wonder. I would tell her that I was not an Egyptian, not even an Arab, but a Punjabi from Pakistan (later, I'd provide clarification) who'd come from around the world to stutter before someone as lovely as she. It would be adorable. It would be remarkable.

In other words, it would be perfect. But if for all your life you've thought yourself nothing, you'll only accomplish just that.

myself and back

'What the hell is wrong with me?'

Haris knew I wasn't talking to him.

I slumped against the side of the cab, my head pressing up against the glass.

We'd left Hardee's a full ten minutes after she walked in and I hadn't said a word to her. On the ride back, I told myself that no guy could kick game to every girl that caught his eye. But this wasn't every girl. This was the most beautiful one I'd seen in all of Egypt—without a father, brother, boyfriend or husband anywhere nearby. So far my best chance and I'd squandered it. Would it have been too much to have walked over and said salam? Every single time it happened, I'd tell myself: Next time, never again. But for every next time, there was a never again.

Few things can crack a young man's back as irrevocably as worthlessness. I saw myself lying on the ground being kicked in the gut time and time again by another me standing over me cackling. I was vomiting blood and choking on my own saliva. But I kept kicking. I rolled over and tried to scream but it was helpless mumbling. Stop! But I wouldn't stop. I was giving myself what my hands had earned. In the small back seat of the cab, all my frustrations were overwhelming me, tempting and taunting me, a rage that could only be released by some violent and unforeseeable act.

I hoped it would be a violent one, to bring the world down on my head, as punishment for the absurdity I displayed each day. Had I been driving, I would've gone kamikaze into the nearest embankment, only slowing down at the beginning so that my room-mate, who hadn't the faintest clue what was going on inside my head, could get out and watch from afar.

I exited the cab, slamming the door so hard that our doorman woke up, rushing to the front of the lobby, scanning with his fish-tank eyeglasses in all directions.

'What's he looking for?' Haris asked.

I didn't know and I didn't care.

Minutes later, we were back in the apartment, though I still don't remember riding the elevator, walking through the door or even taking my sneakers off. I do remember snapshots, little bits and pieces of a helpless wandering. I was looking for something in the apartment itself. What that was, I don't recall. Anyway, I didn't find it. Instead, I ended up in the sitting room, standing right in the centre of that empty space, while my room-mate nestled himself into the love seat and pulled a copy of *Cairo Community Times* on to his lap. I'd become so angry by that point that I found it hard to breathe.

'We need to go on vacation,' my room-mate observed, flipping through a few pages. 'Look at this, yaar. We can go on a cruise and swim with dolphins.'

Haris turned the magazine around to let me see, as though the script was legible from ten feet away. Then he turned it back around, not caring for a response. Perhaps not expecting one. His fingers skimmed the different pages, but that damned smile of his—he was dreaming of dolphins, hoping to swim alongside them in the sea—had to go. Were dolphins carnivores? Inshallah. Eat him. Then me.

But I knew no murderous dolphins would come knocking on our door anytime soon. This was my own Chandrasekhar limit: The Pakistani family's solution to every problem, namely, that the problem is itself the problem, had wrought its debilitating hypocrisy for too long. My life was at last blowing up from behind my face. When my voice finally found its way into my mouth, it was as a pathetic whimper: 'Why didn't I say anything?'

Haris looked up. 'Did you say something?'

'It was like I was just watching myself...' I mumbled. 'I should've said something.'

But he couldn't hear a word I was saying. So he looked back down, much more excited by his idiotic vacation plans. Nor did he have any idea of the depths of my fury. How could he?

I felt my legs shake so I grasped at the table hoping to steady myself. But before my hand had gotten even halfway there, the air was sucked out of me. Like someone had hauled a brick onto my chest. My skin burned in pain, but my mouth was so dry I couldn't scream. It was as if I could see my tongue—not with my eyes, but with some other vision—and I could only watch it loll helplessly in my mouth, no longer under any rational command. It took a few seconds for me to realize that I was being pulled out of, and away from, myself, so that I could see something I'd never seen before: Me.

I was the Muslim missing link standing in the middle of the room, his arms—my arms, actually (I had to remind myself)—dangling stupidly at my sides. My room-mate was a few feet away, turning pages. Backwards. On examining further, I saw something astounding. Haris was moving backwards, too. After a few seconds, he made his way, backwards again, towards the door, opening it in reverse and then shutting it behind him. In an instant, my body vanished as well. Was it because I couldn't remember how I'd entered the room? Was I a distended mind floating in the middle of an empty room, my gaze caught on the body I once inhabited? I heard a key being pulled out of a lock, and then I was alone.

If only I could trace my body's progress backwards and follow it, to wherever it was going. Perhaps there was something I'd see the second time around, something God meant me to know. How, though, was I to move myself without any arms or legs, hands or feet? With all the strength that I had I focused my mind on moving in the direction of the door to go after my departed body. But absolutely nothing was accomplished. I remained with the sight of a panoramic camera, my gaze limited to a vacated room. Somewhere, my room-mate and I were going back to Hardee's.

I'd left the apartment far behind. Instead, I was in front of the large glass windows of Hardee's, able to see myself and Haris. It was horrible. I begged God to stop this, for I could think of nothing worse than watching me squander such an opportunity a second time. There I was, munching away like a brainless, spineless dolt, awkwardly reaching for fries, clumsily sipping my soda. Good thing I didn't talk to that girl. To think myself deserving of her when in fact I was a repulsive presence who probably sent every girl fleeing on his approach. I wanted to pass through the glass and enter my body, to occupy it and transfer it, to spare me the humiliation of a task beyond my capacity. But I could come no closer. The glass knocked against my mind, causing an odd pain, entirely different from and yet very similar to the physical variety.

And then it was gone.

Haris was back on the love seat, while my body was accelerating towards me. Out of something like fear—that I'd strike myself and fall over—I blinked, but my body held fast and kept going, some queer glue welding me together again: my arms, chest, legs, face, eyes, ears and tongue to my mind. In a second it was over, and I stumbled back a step, so softly that not even my typically perceptive room-mate noticed. What the hell was the point of all that? That my fury at hesitating, delaying till a chance was gone, could propel me into a mood so disturbed that I saw things move backwards.

A thought emerged from somewhere and stuck, an urge too strong to be dismissed. I took my keys off the dining table and slid my feet into my sneakers. My room-mate turned his head towards me, so slowly that I could slip aside before we made eye contact. Dashing towards the door, I swung it open with such abandon that I nearly struck myself clear across the face. But I didn't let my clumsiness slow me. By the time our door slammed shut behind me, I was down to the third floor. Then, at last, the door opened again. Haris screamed something, but I didn't try to hear, nor did I care to answer. I picked up my pace, charging out of our building and bolting left, thinking that was the shortest way to my destination.

returning dervish

The night sky was dark, stuffed toxic enough to drown out the stars. I felt myself processing an energy that was coming from somewhere outside of me, supplying me with an explosive and liberating ferocity.

As I neared the barbershop, I foolishly peered in, only to see our barber standing smack-dab in the middle of his shop, his head tilted up so that he saw me go by—as if God put him there only to notice me go by, and nothing else. My tearing hurry brought confusion to his calm face, but I paid him no immediate attention. I was out of sight in a second, gaining speed, emerging on to an unfamiliar main street. No more thuds against my chest. Only the pounding clap of my feet against black pavement. I was running away from me, bloodied, bruised and beaten, but going somewhere, to return with someone who would finally prove to my tormentor that I was worthy.

Ten minutes more and I was there: face plastered against the glass, hands outstretched, eyes searching. I looked in every direction, towards the counters, the dining booths, the shortened queue and the benches all the way to the left, even the bathrooms. But she wasn't there. In the time in-between, while I'd been beating me for being me, she'd gone. She had, after all, come alone. Most likely she was ordering takeaway.

I pulled my hands off the windows and walked back a few

steps, all the hope and promise that had shot me out of our apartment leaving me a spent bullet unable to shatter even glass. Behind me, Pizza Hut delivery boys were laughing, their busted Hamitic and rushed Semitic wading in and out of my ears. Hopefully it wasn't me that was so funny. Reflections of Cairo's taxis bounced across the Hardee's windows, their headlights turned off for the night-time, horns blaring in more than adequate compensation. All that was left for me now was the return trip. And I had no energy to run as I'd come.

I could only think: Outside our apartment, my tormentor would be waiting for me, emboldened by my failure. Would I return not only injured, but worn out? He would point and laugh at me as I came up the steps and into the lobby, but eventually his laughter would have to cease. Because Haris would fix things for me. Though I'd feel the sting of humiliation—as indeed I was already beginning to—that would be mitigated by Haris's unconditional concern for me. In fact, he was probably sitting on the love seat right now, anxiously anticipating. The Hardee's girl hadn't bothered to wait for me, but I'd still stormed after her, ignoring the good friend who'd been beside me this whole time. How stupid I'd been for hating my room-mate! And thus I warmed to my return.

Haris would offer me something to drink, force me on to the love seat and do his best to cheer me up. But what would I tell him of this embarrassing episode? I needed something to tell him and something to tell the man who hated me, abiding forever inside of me; a story that satisfied the three of us, a story that made me capable and acceptable. So I couldn't be running after the Hardee's girl. At least, not entirely. There would have to be more. Maybe my running after her had awoken some new spirit in me. Somewhere on Gamiat al-Duwal, between Thursday night and Friday morning, the broken, hopeless person that I was had perished in a blaze of finality, born again a stronger, more purposeful man.

With each step, I reviewed each part of my unfolding story. If I gave it a simple beginning and end, then my room-mate would soon notice that I wasn't really a new person. Rather, I'd construct a narrated arabesque, revolving geometrically around an unchanging core. Here and there, the pattern would fling itself outwards in stunning flourish, capped by whispering circles and whirling dervishes, but, soon enough, it would have no choice but to fold back in on itself—before being hurried away again, a pattern pushed inevitably to infinity. There would be no conclusion. Only the dazzling and baffling varieties of repetition. Once I was back in the apartment, comfortably on the love seat, I'd begin, painting my pattern over every wall as my room-mate watched with addicted eyes. He'd even touch his fingers to the paint, smudging its newness a little, enthralled by what he saw before him. And then, when I was tired—for such a pattern cannot finish but can only be left hanging, waiting for more of the same—he'd watch me march off to bed, unable to sleep, staring at those eight-pointed stars, all of them part of one greater whole, invisible and yet inescapable.

haris

'My name is Haris,' I said, as I extended my hand.

'Salam alaykum,' he replied. 'I'm Wanand.' He released my hand, touched his heart and pointed to the young woman behind him. 'That is my daughter, Zuhra.'

The man stepped through a maze of suitcases, turned his back to me and began looking for something. 'Do you live in this building?' he asked.

'That's why I stopped to talk to you,' I said. 'I wanted to introduce myself.'

Wanand and I had a brief conversation; of course, it would have been inappropriate to include Zuhra. She appeared distracted, anyway. Wanand mentioned he was part of some kind of Sufi order, apparently quite a demanding one at that: His Ustad had instructed him to move to our building at this very awkward hour, for which I'm sure he had had some arcane spiritual justification.

When I added that I had a room-mate, who was also a student, I must have made a face, which Wanand took as a sign of disapproval. Nor could I think of a way to correct this impression: What could I have told Wanand about my room-mate that would not be undermined by the fact that it was very late, and that my room-mate had just raced out of our apartment, with no Ustad who compelled him?

On the cab ride back from Hardee's, my room-mate had been

oddly quiet. (He's otherwise often glib.) I suspected he was frustrated, but I didn't understand how infuriated he really was. I, who gets sick in Cairo every other week, never complain as he complains, but perhaps he has his reasons to.

Shortly after we returned, he walked to the middle of the apartment, hurriedly stuffed his feet in his sneakers, ran out the door, down the stairs and out of the building. Momentarily thinking it the right thing to do, I gave chase, but then stopped on the third floor. It was probably better he go off alone, to let off whatever steam he needed to let off. As long as he didn't do anything stupid.

I came back to the apartment, at a loss for what to do next, when the phone rang. It was our friend Rehell, who wanted me to go over to his place.

'At this hour?' It was past midnight.

'There's a great—what do you Americans call it?— soccer match on. My friend Mabayn is here, and he has a car. If you want, mate, he can pick you up, too.'

Not that there was anything or anyone in Cairo to be afraid of at night. 'Don't be stupid, Rehell, it's only a block away.'

Rehell lived with some other European students, most of whom I never got the chance to talk to. Their apartment was everything ours wasn't: slick, contemporary marble floors. Appealing modern furniture filled without creating clutter. There were no walls between the dining room, the living room and the kitchen, allowing a friendly openness that encouraged conversation. The cosy bedrooms were separated from the other rooms by way of a heavy mahogany door that kept out the noise.

Mabayn introduced himself as a South Asian who'd been

in Egypt since he could remember, and then returned to the television, his jaw hanging open in embarrassing expectation. At this, Rehell grinned and then invited me to share one of their grey leather sofas with him. His eyes lit up; he vanished into the kitchen and returned with two tall glasses of peach iced tea.

'Where did you get that from?'

He was proud of himself. 'I made it, mate.' Then, 'I mean, I bought the mix at Metro, and I love it. Try it, you'll agree.'

As I took my first sip—yes, it was lovely—Mabayn received a call on his cell phone. He looked terribly worried, then excited and then paralysingly uncertain. And then he hastily apologized. 'I have to leave. If you want a ride, Haris, let me know.' Did he think I'd come over only to leave? I politely declined, to which Mabayn said, 'It was nice meeting you. Maybe we can meet again sometime.'

I took Mabayn's departure as my cue. 'I came alone because he ran out of the apartment,' I confessed, dumping my concerns on an unsuspecting Rehell. 'He was so upset this evening that he refused to talk to me, and then he just ran out of the apartment.'

Rehell put his iced tea down on the floor and folded his right foot under his leg. 'Do you think this has something to do with his Islam?' he asked. For Rehell, that wasn't a strange question. He had to connect everything with his interest in Islam.

'It has everything to do with Islam.' Or, rather, the demands that Islam placed on its slaves. We Muslims have always been obligated to hold ourselves to standards that we knew we could not, and should not, meet; we held ourselves to these standards precisely because they were unattainable. This is the Muslim's most characteristic question: Why aim for that which is within reach? Then, when the West came, it was only natural that we would begin to obsessively compare ourselves with the West. I explained this to Rehell as best I could: 'He doesn't want the world to be the way it is, and he's furious with himself because he can't change the world to the way he thinks it should be.'

Rehell dithered. Maybe he was uncertain of how to phrase his question. 'Don't you think that's too much to ask, Haris, to be able to change the world?'

'But he's so dissatisfied,' I replied. 'Muslims know what everyone else suspects: We're bigger than the universe, and we know this—'

'Because nothing in the universe can satisfy us!' Rehell concluded. Then he disagreed with his interpretation. 'We might not be bigger than the universe, mate, maybe we're just better than the rest of the universe. That the universe can't satisfy us, maybe that's an indication that it's beneath us. In that case, we shouldn't worry so much about the way things outside us go, whether good or bad.'

Rehell's reliance on hierarchy made me think he'd become a good Muslim. 'I'm an optimist, Rehell.' What I see, I see the best of. 'Still, that's very hard to do, and I think it's much harder for him. Because for every positive out there, you have to admit that there are so many more negatives. Being a Muslim these days is like crying in the dark. You don't know what hurts more—the fact that you're crying, or that no one can see you crying.'

Rehell grabbed the remote control and switched off the television. 'Mabayn, too, mate. There's something wrong with him.' And on he went, explaining Mabayn's predicament, which sounded a lot like my room-mate's: A staunchly religious upbringing burdening a painfully divided and inadequate personality. Rehell looked like he was going to cry. I was so astonished by this that I also wanted to look like I was going to cry. 'Mate, sometimes Mabayn looks so hopeless. He just sits in front of the TV all day, or stares at the walls, or looks down and doesn't speak.'

'Are you trying to cheer me up?'

'I mean to say that your room-mate, at least he's trying. We need to talk to him, but don't get too down about him. Because there's a quality in him, even if he's dissatisfied all the time.' Rehell was no longer talking to me but to himself.

But who can live without satisfaction, which stems from realizing what is worth realizing, and we who are of multiple minds, our only realization is that we cannot say, with any confidence, what would be worth realizing, except for the incompatible aims that we pursue. A man at war with himself cannot rest. 'I just pray he comes back okay,' I said.

'Well, regardless, I'll pray too. In the meantime, maybe you need to rest, mate. We don't want you to get sick again, worrying about him, do we?'

'How can I relax when my room-mate's out doing God knows what?'

Rehell leaned over to pick up his iced tea. 'I think you're not as worried about him as you say you are. He's a good person, with a deep understanding of his religion and his place in the world, and that's a gift, mate. There's something in him that makes people want to listen to him and know what he thinks about things and be near him.'

'The only problem, Rehell, is that he can't stand being near himself.'

Rehell grinned. 'So what happens when he can?'

enharda

today

No matter how far you have gone on a
wrong road, turn back.

—Turkish proverb

ending with wendy

I slowed down only when I reached the stairs to the lobby, surprised by agitated voices. Going up the steps, I found myself amidst a crowd of people beside bulging suitcases from which bits of fabric poked out. Some of the men were movers, but not the tall, almost regal man, wearing a robe and a fittingly lengthy beard, barking orders. For a moment I thought it odd. Had I not gotten back just now, might I have missed them? But as I was tired, impatient to see Haris and eager to empty a bottle of water down my throat, I walked past. What did I care who moved in?

Our doorman, a dark-skinned, Upper Egyptian village nerd, was alone, sitting where he always did, on the bench farthest from the elevator. It took me a minute to remind myself not to stare at him, as enjoyable as it was to observe him. His was the face from which all other faces were made. Like Mr Potato Head. Two eyes, a nose and a mouth, with sprouts of hair on top, big ears on the side, and an inadequate body on the bottom. In his hands, he always held a set of folded papers, probably receipts and bills, which he flicked between his fingers like a pack of cards. He dealt them out, too: Every week he'd hand me a bill. On rare occasions, I'd know what I was paying for.

As I made my way towards the elevator, one of the movers shifted position, revealing behind him a beautiful girl perched on top of a suitcase. Her skin was an Aryan white; too soft to be Arab. Her eyes were intoxicating, like pillow clouds that surrounded an endless blue sky, only letting the most awesome portion through. And she tied an honest hijab around her head, a humility that only drew further attention to her face. Though I was notoriously bad with ages, I guessed she was about seventeen. Maybe eighteen, if I was generous, like Muslims were supposed to be.

This girl was an angel, a sign from heaven of all that I could still have, maybe in compensation for that Hardee's lovely that I'd missed. Had I been able to see myself, I'd have seen a statue, again unsure of where to plant his arms: swinging ape-like from my sides, or better yet, on my hips, like Peter Pan? After all, we had much in common: Both of us were lost and it was doubtful either of us would ever grow up. But on seeing me, my veiled beauty crumbled. A kaleidoscope of confusion mottled her previously serene face, turning her lips inside and out, her eyes around and her nose upside down. Not daring to lose sight of me, she tugged at the tall man's robe, as if to say, 'My father, Captain Hook.'

Not ready to face the wrath of a jealous Muslim man, especially not one as aggravated as this one—though it was his fault for moving in so late, wasn't it?—I rushed to the elevator. In the hope of continuing the nonchalance charade, I planned to hop over the two steps into the elevator lobby, but my body refused me. A sore left foot (mine, though it didn't feel like it) jammed against the edge of the top step. I flew forward, one leg kicking the air after the other, until my right foot finally landed, crashing against the floor. The resulting howl tore through the lobby, even echoing a few times for painful unnecessary emphasis.

Little Miss Perfect Face and her Big Giant Fundamentalist

Father had surely heard. The silence laughed and then, in a case of superfluous insult to very undeserved injury, my keys fell to the floor. I hurried to push the 'up' button, so hard that I might have fractured my finger. But the damned elevator took its time, languishing at the third floor. After a minute passed, I stepped back and grabbed my keys, shoving them into my pocket. When the elevator arrived, I sprinted through the doors, trying to disappear.

Before putting my key in the lock, I jangled the bunch, to alert Haris. Then I waited, expecting to hear him walking towards the door. But nothing. Thinking he might be in the bathroom and unable to hear, I unlocked the door and shoved it open with both hands, announcing a bold 'salam alaykum!' The door came swinging back and collided with my right foot, the second assault on my feet in the last five minutes. Mercifully, no one noticed, because Haris was nowhere in sight. So I walked in, slammed the door behind me and kicked my sneakers off against the wall, leaving little skid marks on the nauseous yellow paint which belonged in a hotel not a home. Since there was no response to this racket either, it could only mean one thing: My room-mate was already asleep. I tiptoed into the bedroom, my eyes trying to gather as much light as they could and shower it on to his bed, to reveal his dozing form. But he wasn't there.

we all need a bath now and then

I woke up staring into the cheap analog clock we'd bought from Omar Effendi a few days after our arrival, 09:00. Friday. I looked across the room and saw Haris on his bed, wrapped up in his scrappy blanket, fast asleep. But at least he was there. I climbed out of bed, sighing His name, either for hopefulness or out of hopelessness. After ten minutes in the bathroom, I was in the kitchen sucking half-baked fake Oreos and guzzling Enjoy apple juice which came in a square canister that made me believe Nasser hadn't died. Afterwards, I went to the sitting room and fell onto the couch. There were no classes on Friday.

Egypt was a Muslim country, even if it wasn't.

I spent about an hour on the BBC website, reading stories I'd read a week before, and soon tired of the weight of my room-mate's laptop on my lap. Then Haris walked through the hallway, one eye almost shut and the other twitching to resist the brightness.

He raised his hand, much like Imam Khomeini might have. 'Salam alaykum. I'm going to the bathroom.'

Five minutes later he was back, his face dripping wet, totally transformed. He, too, looked like Mr Potato Head. Except he was Indian and intelligible. With his right hand, my room-mate pulled one of the lemonade chairs towards me and sat down, his lips still smacking against each other, as they always did when he wasn't sure if he should be up.

'When did you get back last night?' I asked.

'Three or so. You were snoring.' He sniffed. 'I went to Rehell's. One of his friends, this guy Mabayn, was there—'

I had to interrupt. 'His name is Mabayn?'

'He's desi,' Haris explained.

'What do desis do, open up the Qur'an and pick the first word they see?'

But Haris was upset by this. 'He's a nice guy, yaar. You should meet him. We stayed up and watched a soccer match on TV.'

Bastard. He stood up to grab a bottle of water from off the dining room table, then sat down again.

'How's Rehell?' I asked. Why was I asking so many questions?

'Good, alhamdulillah.' He paused and cocked his head, so that he looked at me at an angle. 'What the hell happened to you last night?'

This was not how I imagined telling my story, with an overheated laptop scalding my legs and a drowsy room-mate looking ridiculous in a dwarf chair. 'I don't know,' I admitted. And I didn't any more. Nothing makes sense after you sleep on it. 'It's like, when I got back last night, I was so angry with myself for not talking to her. I couldn't take it.'

'Yeah.' He smiled, but kindly. 'You seemed pretty upset.'

'I was.'

'So where did you go?'

I tried not to blush. 'Hardee's.'

'Hardee's?' This amused him. 'You were going after her, weren't you?' As I began to nod, he got very excited. 'Damn, yaar. Did you get to talk to her?'

'No.' I let it sink in. More for me than for him. It hurt more. 'I ran all the way there but she was gone by the time I got there. I guess I could've... I would've told her how beautiful she was.'

He shifted to the little perch next to me. 'That would have been great. Can you imagine? She would've seen you rushing through the door, covered in sweat, having run all that way just to tell her you think she's beautiful.'

'Except the covered in sweat part,' I laughed.

'You could've asked her to give you a bath.' He slapped me on the back, his words slapping harder. 'Speaking of which, I'm going to take one. We've got to get ready for Friday prayers.'

I didn't want to go. But I didn't want to tell him that, either. 'Did you see that new family that was moving in last night?' I hoped to surprise him with my exclusive and distract him from his mission.

'Oh, the Kurdish family?'

Thud. 'They're Kurds?'

'Yeah,' he replied. 'I met them last night, when I was going to Rehell's actually. The father's name's Wanand, and his daughter Zuhra was with him.'

He'd gotten their names, too. Why did he have the balls to ask the questions, while I only tripped up steps and made a fool out of myself? Because I was me. That was what I did: Trip up steps and thank Allah I didn't fall down them. 'What else did you find out?'

Haris ran his tongue over his lips. 'Isn't someone curious!'

'Just wondering.'

'About Wanand or his daughter?' The confident bastard was in a good mood this morning. 'Wanand's in a Sufi order. He said that his Ustad made him move into our building at exactly that time of night. How weird is that?'

'That is weird,' I said. 'Because if I had come back only five minutes later, I might've missed them...'

'It's a sign from God!' Haris jumped up, his hands leaping similarly into the air. And then he tranquillized himself. 'That is, that you should go for Zuhra.'

'I tried for the same girl twice last night. Nothing happened.'

'Change is good, habibi.' He stood up and pulled his T-shirt down, but it was still too short. 'She even lives on the first floor of our building. You've got a month to make something work.'

'But her father lives in the building, too.'

'Nothing comes easy, yaar.' He yanked at his shirt again, though he seemed much more frustrated by the thought of what he'd just said. 'Anyway, when do you want to go?'

Well, you see... 'I don't feel like going.'

I expected him to argue, to tell me why refusing religious ritual was akin to asking God to send His wrath upon me unceasingly. But at least my defence was sincere: I had no desire to go. How could I possibly be in the mood for a tortuous sermon performed in a language not my own, the topic of which was, at best, entirely irrelevant to me or, at worst, intended to focus on those things so Islamically unacceptable about myself?

Haris took a sip of his water. 'What are you going to do instead?'

A valid question. Were I to spend more than a few hours by myself, such despair would take hold of me that physical pain would be bliss in comparison. Eventually, even the compulsion to eat would perish, though my stomach would still rumble in anguish. In all things, mind over matter.

He warned me. 'Yaar, you're going to hate yourself if you stay behind.' He stared at me to emphasize this. 'You know there's nothing to do here.'

'I know. But...'

He looked at his watch. 'We still have some time. How about we go to Trianon for breakfast first? I'll pay for that.' A smile, to cheer me up. 'Then we'll both go for namaz.'

Just the thought of those puffed pastries, cinnamon toppings, steaming coffees, chocolates and toffees, and I was a believer again. Anyway, what other choice did I have? Either I walked with my room-mate to the Agouza Masjid, or I trudged back to our apartment in the blazing noonday heat, to sit by myself for God knew how many hours. I was trapped between two avenues, each of which went a great distance to nowhere. Was it better to go nowhere alone?

'Fine,' I grumbled. 'But only for Trianon.'

Haris grinned as he walked into the bathroom, thrilled that I was going with him, though not ecstatic enough to give me a shot at the shower first. Wasn't I the one who'd run miles and miles the night before? But that didn't make any difference. He always went first, not only robbing me of my fair share of grooming time, but he also left the geyser running for so long that by the time it was my turn, there were only three temperature settings to choose from: steaming, boiling and scalding.

Every shower was an exercise in hopping into, and then quickly out of, a stream of unbearable heat. Plus I found our shower pretty disgusting. The tiles on the top were rusted, and the tub on the bottom was spoiled, gone from its original milky white to expired cream. And there was one more reason for haste: that fear of missing things. I thought I might spend so long washing myself that I might miss the one worthwhile event of my life.

Haris took almost an hour, so I had to race into the shower and turn on the water, and ended up burning the skin off my feet. Not the kind of treatment they deserved after all the work they'd done for me the evening before.

liberation from the need
for liberation

The weekend had been one long spell of nothing, interrupted by sleep and forays out of the apartment for more boring food. Over three days, we ate Arby's, McDonald's, stopped by a Mexican place with booming music in the basement but no other customers, and a Turkish restaurant named after the alpha Turk which made my room-mate sick.

When Monday finally rescued us, we mobbed one of our teachers, Ustad Thabit, with the intention of finding something to do. (Other than eating out.)

He was at his car, unlocking his door, when we went up to him. 'Do you need a ride?' he asked, using the dual form. Always sneaking lessons in.

'No, alhamdulillah, we're good.' I smiled, waving my hands, though then it dawned on me that in fact we did. I felt Haris suppress an urge to whack me on the head. 'Actually, Ustad, we have a problem.'

'Too much homework?'

If an hour a week is too much, then yes. 'The thing is, actually, we really have... Well, what do you *do* around here?'

'I teach Arabic.'

'No, what I meant was, what do you do around here for fun?'

'I'm married.'

In other words, Cairo was not New York. It was part of the Muslim world that we were supposed to be parts of as well. Islamic culture doesn't cater to individuals as well as it does to families, because Muslims find liberty in bondage.

Did that explain the overpowering desire I felt to have someone and have her have me? I thought that my growing up in a Pakistani family, with all the identity of a post-colonial nationality plus the stability of a Pahlavi monarchy, had something to do with it too. I was so sick of the mirage that the desi family so often was. I wanted to be apart: I wanted romance and reality.

Ustad Thabit noted our gloom. 'You two need wives.'

It was an ugly moment for me. And for Haris, too. The comment's inclusiveness and implicit implication of neediness mocked our futile hopes for exceptionality, our aspiration to be more than just carbon copies of a routed people.

I blurted it out. 'So where do we go to find girls?'

By then, Ustad Thabit was in his car, his muscular right hand on the wheel. He wasn't really involved in the conversation. 'You want a good girl?'

'Girls, Ustad.' Haris inched forward.

'One at a time,' Ustad Thabit clarified.

'That was the idea.'

'I think you should go to Islamic Cairo,' he suggested. And then he zoomed off.

cab fare for the kabah

We returned to the apartment in haste to depart for Islamic Cairo, where the plan was: Find wives, get lives. We changed into more comfortable clothes, since the sun would be out for some hours, and took three water bottles, since we'd be wandering around a lot. We decided to restrict our sightseeing to the masjids of al-Azhar and Sayyidna Husayn. And, lastly, we asked Rehell if he wanted to come. Though he was grateful, he was also busy. But he asked us to call him once we got back, so that we could hang out with him and Mabayn afterwards.

The driver let us off near a bazaar stall, taking care to puff up his price. We didn't mind, tossing him the cash and focusing on the madness at hand. Our pictures recreated a chronological approach to al-Azhar, with photographs taken at each important juncture. Someone, somewhere, back home would enjoy looking at them. Once al-Azhar came into full view, though, even we cynics had to pause to take it in.

Haris was stunned. 'Can you imagine someone could build something like this?'

How could something so massive be so human—unless it was built by a race of giants who by contentment were made into creatures uncomprehendingly alive. A race of Egyptians who'd long since been driven from the earth. My heart ached with pride, while my hands shivered worthless: they'd never contribute to anything so awesome. The prayer area was topped with bulbous domes and framed by modest minarets shooting humbly into the sky, not with arrogance but in liberating subservience.

Arabic for 'the Most Radiant', al-Azhar is a masjid and university complex, the oldest still-functioning university in the world. Originally a bastion of Ismaili Shii Islam, a propaganda factory for the House of Fatimah, it reverted to Islamic orthodoxy when Salah al-Din conquered Egypt in the latter half of the twelfth century, making the country his platform for the military and spiritual revival of the Sunni world that he intended.

After an hour of prayer and idle wandering, we turned our attention to the masjid of Sayyidna Husayn, accessible through a series of tunnels that opened up opposite al-Azhar. In the early years of Islam, Husayn (the grandson of the Prophet Muhammad, peace be upon him) took a stand against the corruption overwhelming the Muslim peoples. The target of his fury was none other than the second Caliph of Umayyah's House, Yazid.

Husayn took a small band of followers to the town of Karbala, in the south of today's Iraq, where his supporters were to join him. But Yazid dispatched thousands of soldiers prior to Husayn's arrival, in an attempt at psychological warfare. Husayn ended up with only a few dozen supporters, while his supposed partisans hid in their homes, refusing to face off against numerically superior forces. Husayn, however, like the minarets of al-Azhar, did not bend. On the tenth day of the first month, the day that God saved the Children of Israel from the Pharaoh, Husayn's army was massacred. Husayn's head, sliced off as a trophy, may have come to

Cairo. It may be buried in an area near the masjid's prayer hall. Whether or not this is true, thousands of Egyptians visit the masjid every week, to pay their respects to the kind of man never to be seen outside of tombs and cemeteries.

We finished our roll of film with a particularly good side shot, and then found ourselves seated on a sidewalk halfway between the two masjids. We produced the water bottles we'd packed and drank freely, happy to have something to quench a persistent thirst.

And then, suddenly, 'Salam alaykum!'

There was no mistaking that accent. We looked up, but the stranger, his face plastered with an eager smile, reacted first. 'Are you from Pakistan? I'm Pakistani.'

I confirmed his suspicions. 'Yes, I am.'

Haris immediately partitioned himself. 'I'm Indian.'

The man didn't offer his name. But then again, neither did we. 'Where in Pakistan are you from?'

'My mother's family was from East Punjab, but they migrated in forty-seven,' I answered. 'My father's Potohari.'

The stranger was still beaming. 'Well, I'm Lahori!' Punjab zindabad.

Haris wanted in on the ethnic action. 'My family's from Avadh,' he said.

Finally, the stranger gave us his name. Zaheed. And without any invitation, sat himself down beside us and accelerated in speech. It soon became obvious that his smile wasn't in anticipation of camaraderie, but only his regular resting state, a basic jubilance that I knew would fast become irritating. Then Zaheed explained that he too had come to Egypt to study Arabic. 'I just got to Cairo a few weeks ago,' he informed us. 'But I'm staying with another Pakistani friend, who's been here for half a year now!'

Nor did I only hate his oleaginous excitability. He was painful
to look at, too; though he was tall like me, and of a thick
build, he betrayed an upsetting resemblance to a slug. I had
no way to be sure, of course, not knowing exactly what a slug
looked like. But if someone asked me I would have promptly
suggested examining Zaheed. He had those absurdly drowsy,
almost amphibious eyes that too many desis are afflicted by:
they struggled to stay flush with his skin. Then there was his
posture. Up to his waist he was ramrod straight, but past that
point he arched forward as if he was breaking wind.

Surprisingly, Zaheed ended his own ramble. 'Tomorrow
night is the birthday celebration for Husayn. You know, the
Mawlid. Would you two like to come?'

'They celebrate Husayn's birthday here?'

Haris ignored me completely, directing his question at
Zaheed. 'Where's it going to be?'

'It's here at midnight,' Zaheed said. A little too fast.
Which made me realize the flaw in my analogy: A quick
slug was an oxymoron? Maybe if I combined his ethnicity
with his species, I might present a believable solution i.e.
Punjabi + slug = fast and stupid bug. Or maybe it was just
a learning disorder and I was being horribly cruel for mocking
him. It didn't matter. He showered all his attention on Haris
and none on me. 'So, anyway, yaar, you should come. The
Sufis will play music and perform their zikr.'

My room-mate pulled a pen out of his backpack. 'What's
your number? We'll call tomorrow.'

'I'll be out all day,' Zaheed said. 'Give me your number
and I'll call you.'

So Haris scribbled our phone number on a small receipt
I prayed Zaheed would lose. The fellow shook our hands and
merged into the crowds.

'He was so annoying,' I grumbled.

'Well, at least he told us about something we can do.'

'So did Ustad Thabit,' I laughed. 'And did we find girls?'

My room-mate brushed me off. 'I think someone wants to go back home.'

mint tea (hot, with philosophy)

The Trianon Café. An establishment for Egypt's upper crust, catering to the few who could regularly afford a mango iced tea. On the first floor, wooden display cases brazenly tempted with fine pastries, delicacies and delights, enjoyed over little round tables suitable for intimate and un-Islamic encounters. The waiters, dressed in tight black, darted from table to table as if the Scandinavian floor, polished to a mirror's surface, was water and they had no feet but only wings. This was where my room-mate and I met up with Rehell and Mabayn.

Rehell, being short for Rehellinen, had come to Cairo from Finland a month before we did, with similar plans of studying Islam and Arabic. Unlike us, Rehell was actually studying.

Mabayn was sporting energy from his shoulders to his shoes. He looked like someone with a lifetime gym membership. His sturdy presence, however, was marred by his lower jaw, which stuck out too far. He was always on the verge of drooling. Mabayn was definitely an improvement over Zaheed, but once we got to talking about religion, as we usually eventually did, he shut off. Just as Rehell lit up. I tried to answer Rehell's serious questions, but then Haris took over, rightly sensing that my enthusiasm for replying was waning.

Theology grew trite, my mind began to drift and my eyes

were not too far behind. Two callipygian Egyptian women approached, but their endless legs carried them swiftly past. There was nothing about them that wasn't worth following, no reason not to drop down and commence grovelling: Be my two wives. Then: Can you cook and clean?

Noticing my distraction, Mabayn roared with laughter he'd suppressed all night. I think all of Egypt heard him, which was neither exaggeration nor distinction—whenever an Egyptian spoke, every other Egyptian could hear.

'I see there are more important things in the world,' Mabayn said.

'Like her.' Rehell, not bothered that his question session was interrupted by someone's wandering lust, smiled, too.

'Don't forget her friend,' Mabayn added, still chuckling.

The two girls caught our stares and smiled in response.

'There, my friends, is an argument for polygamy,' I announced. I nodded in their direction. 'Or at least bigamy.'

'This place makes you proud to be a Muslim,' Haris admitted, though he immediately regretted it, unsure whether Rehell would be offended.

Rather, Rehell was perplexed. 'What do you mean, mate?'

I tried to explain it to him, taking the heat off of Haris, who busied himself with a napkin. 'Take two girls, right? Pretend that both of them are physically exactly the same. Like clones. If one of them is Muslim, she would be more attractive to us than the one that was not Muslim.'

'How do you mean?' Rehell asked.

'Well, the truth is beautiful. And people who believe in the truth become more beautiful. Because faith means the presence of God and the presence of God shines like light: light in the heart, light in the mind, light in the face. It's a kind of glowing radiance. While a person who sins becomes uglier for every sin: her outside, her face, her actions, her speech, her movements, they all betray inner—well—dirtiness.'

Rehell began to nod in understanding.

'You know,' my room-mate said, recovering his bravado, 'it's not too weird if you really think about it. Like in movies, the evil character has ominous features: the good character has bright features. From a person's face, you can understand a lot about them.'

I grinned. 'It's even worse when they wear hijab. Then none of that radiance can spill out the sides, so it just shoots out straight towards you.'

Rehell leaned back, waiting a minute to absorb our explanations. 'The more I learn about your religion, the better it sounds. You guys have so much to be happy for,' he said.

But Rehell was absolutely off the mark, strange for someone otherwise so insightful. We could only feign gratitude. And Muslims didn't fake things very well. There was nothing for us middle-of-the-road Muslims, caught between yesterday and the potential—not even the guarantee—of tomorrow, to be happy about.

Mabayn's face was especially soured. He stood up so fast that he knocked Rehell's fork to the floor. Worse, he didn't bend over to pick it up. Even worse, he didn't apologize. 'I have to go,' he stated.

Then he offered his hand, but Rehell refused. 'Is everything okay, mate?'

While signalling the waitress for the check, Mabayn mumbled, 'It's late. I have to get home.'

'All right. I'll go with you, then...' Rehell was aware that something was wrong, he just didn't know what exactly. If only I had a pen, to write it on a napkin and swing it around so that Rehell could read: Reality. That's the problem, Rehell. One can only be happy if one feels one belongs. Two pretty girls on the street, gone two seconds after they arrive, are nothing to be happy about. The world is horrible, but we are worse, because we not only let ourselves drown, but drink the water, complaining the whole time about how much we hate it.

My room-mate and I remained, diagonally across from one another, a little shocked by how quickly Rehell and Mabayn had left.

'Do you want to go, too?' I asked.

He shook his head, initially with hesitation and then with conviction. 'My stomach isn't doing so well. Actually, ever since we ate that Turkish food. Would you mind if I had another mint tea?' I asked him to order me one, too. Though why we were obsessed with a hot beverage in a hot country was beyond me.

When the waitress came with our teas, Haris grew puzzled. 'Have you noticed how we always come to Western places?'

'Because we're Western?'

He pulled his tea closer. 'Speak for yourself.'

This made me quite upset. Just like that. Snap your fingers and I'm pissed off. 'Well, sorry, but just look at you.'

'What about me?' Haris actually looked himself up and down. 'Just because my clothes are Western?'

'Well, yeah.' Two teaspoons of sugar for me, even though it was mint tea. Soon enough, I'd added two more. 'I mean, look at the girls we like. The places we go. Ever notice how we always go to Trianon for fun? And never the masjid?'

Haris stared into his steaming beverage for a few seconds. He fiddled with the mint leaves. And then he looked very, very sad. 'Maybe we just don't care to be Muslim any more.' Another pause, as he surveyed the place. 'It's like, from birth, the world is trying to twist us around, and eventually, we're sick of resisting. Maybe all of us are sick of it. Maybe it's all over, right now.'

'Over?'

'For us,' he stammered. Then he caressed the cup but refused to take a sip, letting the heat waste away. 'In a hundred years, is there going to be anything left of Egypt except Trianon?'

'Don't forget the Pyramids,' I added.

'Oh, great. One foreign civilization and one dead one.'

We had become faithless men worried incessantly about faith. We were increasingly unable to come together and more and more plagued by panic precisely because we could not. And we also felt a deeper, harder fear, which came at random hours of the day, just after getting into bed at night, during a newscast, walking down the street, or stopping at an intersection: the sense that everything was going wrong all at once. Still, my room-mate and I stood apart because we didn't want things to be this way. In this time of trouble, we viewed the lowest of the low the man who betrayed the cause, those supporters of Husayn who fled the camp at Karbala on the final Friday of the siege, choosing hellfire over martyrdom when the latter was so close. Many sins which would offend the traditional Muslim were no big deal to us. Unless they were those sins whose acceptance took one out of the community and into some weightlessness, neither properly here nor fully there.

Haris got out of his chair, unconcerned with whether or not I was following. Leaving our share of the bill secured by a salt shaker, I hurried to catch up. Out on Gamiat al-Duwal, our conversation had to compete with chaos. Perfumes, Little Caesar's pizza, noxious exhaust fumes. The bright lights above the shops oozed fluorescence into the black sky. Saudi men wore thobes the colour of snow they never saw, trailing above the marble—it was like these Wahhabis had learned to levitate. Egyptian teenagers stormed up and down, their voices competing, though there was nothing irate in their giddy banter. Beautiful babies pointed up at the gaudy items in store windows, yanked at their mothers' clothes, hugged their fathers' legs or streamed across the sidewalks in patterns that obeyed no laws, though their parents tried to make sense of them, all the while.

'Maybe Egypt isn't Western.' I faked a laugh. 'For one thing, there are too many kids.'

'Yeah,' Haris replied, his voice rising. 'That's a good point.'

There. Feel any better? For a moment, I felt the elation I'd meant to pass on to him. If youth promised hope, even far-fetched, impossibly distant hope, then hope even outperformed Cairo's pollution, leaving me wondering: Could there be too much of such a necessary thing?

'You can't be both,' I said.

'You don't think so?'

'When the going gets tough,' I remarked, 'you have to choose. Not that there aren't many Westernized Muslims.' Like us.

'But one day they'll have to decide what's more important to them, being Western or being Muslim. That day will come soon.'

'You think?'
'No. I hope.'

To understand the difference between the Islamic world and the Western, one need only examine their masculine idealizations of women. Much more can be understood by way of truth-telling fantasy than is visible through deceptive reality. The Muslim man is marked by his penchant for possession, for more than one wife, for multiplicity and diversity bonded to a single and strong axis. Thus, the Muslim idea of the world: The kingdom of ends rules over various regions of the world, all of them veiled—protected or exploited, depending on your perspective—by the decrees of belief.

The Western man goes trying woman after woman, letting them walk free so he can use them easily—liberation or exploitation, depending on your perspective—but the poor women are too slow to catch on. Some of them even think that the more they reveal, the more they're emancipated. When finally the Western man settles down with a woman, it'll be someone he took from someone else. Like America, Australia or Israel.

But this doesn't mean that the Muslim and Westerner have nothing in common. Rather, what they have in common is precisely what makes them so incompatible: Masculine idealizations, feminine subjugations. If it were only a question of gender relations and no more, I highly doubt the world would have come to such an impasse. While the superiority complex is in and of itself nothing bad, it does pose a problem for cohabitation. On one planet, both Muslim and Westerner desire the triumph of only their system—others can exist, only if properly tamed. Which poses a bigger problem for me.

I've spent all these years wanting so many things but finding myself without any of them. The source of the problem was not outside, but inside. For the last two or three years, I wanted only to know that I was brown, Eastern and Muslim, and I refused to admit that there was within me an equally relevant white man, Western and suburban, desirous of a house on a road named after some type of tree, a two-car garage, a few kids, a blonde-haired, blue-eyed wife and a boring, stable, income-generating job.

To accept the Muslim in me is to accept the imperialist, who not only conquers but erases, denying the validity of anything outside itself. Not surprisingly, the first target is my other half. But my other half fights back—it too wishes to live—and forms an ideology for its own defence, much as a people create a nationality around which to rally when their homes and lands are taken. What else would it choose but my Western childhood, my Western hopes and dreams? Then the Westerner expands, seeking colonies to exploit and abuse, to draw from and use.

Haris tilted his head to look at me. Since he did this while he was still walking, I was quite impressed. Part of me was afraid he'd hit a light pole. But at least that would be funny.

'We're not Western,' he insisted. 'Because their culture isn't alive.'

Like a man who built himself a rocket, shot himself into space but died on the way up, his body unable to handle the acceleration that his own mind had devised. Would his corpse escape gravity and go forth into the universe, on and on for no reason but momentum? In other words, half of me. There is such a thing as friction. On the other hand, my Muslim half was preoccupied with its descent. We'd reached too high and we were not meant to; God cast us down, careening towards the earth at deadly speed.

'Muslims have so many kids. It means we're still alive, you know? We're not Western.' Haris looked at me for confirmation.

'But we're dying, too,' I said. 'Just not in the same way.'

'We don't go quietly,' he laughed. 'And we take others with us.'

'Not me. I only want to blow up the fast-food restaurants.' I felt I shouldn't have been smiling. 'If some of us have to die so that we're not so heavy, then that's what has to be. Better that than all of us down and out forever.'

'You think people should die?'

I shrugged. 'I don't want people to die. But people will have to die. Look at these countries, Haris.' Then I quieted. I was in one of them.

'But we don't even know how to swim yet,' Haris pointed out. 'And we've already got people talking about the islands and the beaches.'

'But you can't ask people to only live to breathe,' I countered. Though I knew that that is what so many of us have done. 'There has to be a reason for them to swim. Otherwise, they'd be so obsessed with why they're swimming, they'd forget to swim and end up drowning.'

Indeed, if you are so apart from yourself for that long, you will no longer be able to tell the difference. Westerners searched through each and every philosophy till they separated their sacred from their secular, their souls from their bodies, their individual from their social, their meaning from their language and their life from their death. They have long lives, but short fuses. Clean cities, but sick hearts. Great governments, but evil armies. They champion human rights, but they are the greatest warmongers in history. So what of me, the contradiction of Cairo, the hypocrite? I had come here because it was a Muslim city, but I spent all my time assiduously avoiding anything that reminded me too much of Islam.

I spent my formative years in a town that was white and painted Christian. As a born Muslim, with a theology based on Semitic simplicity, Christianity was just too much mystery. So for four years of high school, I chose to be white like everyone else, blind to and from the fact that I was not actually white on the outside. I didn't realize how deep the hole was that I carved, for the carving there had made me feel more amongst everybody. But within months, with the promise of New York and the whiff of college life, my friends went their separate ways, each stealing moments from those days and pulling in different directions, leaving me in a timeless place. All that was left was the fake face I'd planted to belong in that nothing-place.

Having little else to cling to in New York, I thought I might fall in love with my reflection. (Beware, then, the many sins of sight.) With only a mental shove, I cleared years from my life, regretting the many days I had spent as one thing (white) instead of another (brown). Voilà! What I did not take into account, however, was that I was like the many other desis on the outside; I was not actually brown on the inside. Rather than accept this, I redoubled my efforts, trying harder and harder to be accepted, doing more to diminish those parts of me that didn't conform. My fellow desis confused my keenness to belong with ill-willed hypocrisy, a muddle my small-town mind was unable to work out. Did I mix up their similarity with me, with me? I did, and these were the rules for doing so:

1. The mother country is called Pakistan/India.

2. Partition was necessary/a tragedy.

3. The mother country is more than the place where winter vacations pass, more than the food we eat and more than the clothes we wear at festive and thereby exclusive occasions.

4. There is a language called Urdu/Hindi; though I don't speak it, it is my mother tongue and more beautiful than any other language.

5. Punjabi, too.

6. Because we're desi, we have our own cultures and values.

7. In order to be different, one must use special offhand expressions, dress differently on certain holidays and choose, for ethnically exclusive gatherings, an exclusively ethnic restaurant.

I'd uprooted myself from my Connecticut childhood, the only one I'd ever had. Adolescence was an ending sunset, abandoning me to sand-dune boundaries and Karakoram peaks. Mine became a desert, jungle and mountain country, spliced by the mighty Indus. Here and no further! There and no less! We'd gaze at the red, white and blue, and shudder. We'd gaze at the green and white and erupt into patriotic blindness— the type that only a person who never knew the country, never fought for it or suffered in it, could. I was a Zionist in this, pretending I'd found home and no one else could have had a more indigenous claim.

We revelled in humiliation, an odd sensation Muslims are prone to seeking. But beware self-pity: inside her womb lies the graveyard of those gone before. For example, when my friends slowly but surely crossed a line they claimed to have erected, blurring the boundary between Muslim and Hindu, upping the heat in their ethnic orgy; as much as I raised the volume on a booming Punjabi beat, or focused my eyes on the latest Bollywood bombshell, there was no silencing the sad song of separation. There was more to this world than its flattering untruths and its obsessions with youth. And so here I was in Africa.

the mere adherent

There was a loud rap on the door. It took me a second or two to figure out what to do. I rushed to the door and opened it without bothering to ask who it was. If ever I involved myself in anti-government activity, I noted, it would be wise for me not to be so reckless. This time, though, it was okay. It was only Mabayn.

He slid past with a slippery salam, finally facing me once he'd gotten to the dining table and turned the tables on me. It was as if I'd just entered the apartment and he was waiting for me. I decided I really didn't like Mabayn much. He displayed astonishingly insensitive behaviour—especially for someone who'd been raised in Egypt.

'Where's Haris?' he asked. As if he had the right to know. In his manners, he was becoming a typically intrusive Pakistani. Was that where he was from?

'He's washing up.' Seeing as this would mean nothing to him, I spread my arms apart, as if to indicate something of great size. 'He takes a long time in the shower. He won't be out for a while.'

'Oh.' He looked confused, his left hand dawdling at the edge of the table, a finger rubbing against the polished finish.

Why was I forgetting Muslim protocol? 'Come in, sit down. Would you like a drink?'

He bit his lip and looked me hard in the face. For a

second, I was afraid. He was a heavily built man. 'Do you drink?'

'Alcohol?'

'Yes. Do you drink alcohol?'

'No, I don't.' I tried to be more serious. 'I don't want any here, either.'

He nodded. 'I just wanted to make sure.'

As he made his way to the sitting area, I went and poured him a glass of Pepsi. When I came back with the drink, though, I was surprised to see that Mabayn had taken the love seat, leaving me to the little lemonade chair. Was it rude of him? Then again, had I been present, I would've forced him to take the love seat. If anything, Mabayn deserved pity. His shoulders sagged towards the floor. His robust arms trembled, their bulges but unsteady stuffing.

'Did you mean what you said to Rehell?' Mabayn looked at me closely.

'You mean about the girls?'

'You said that people are more beautiful if they have faith.' He didn't seem amused. 'Do you think that's true?'

'I think so, yeah.' I thought about it some more, lest I lead him astray. 'I mean, I see pretty girls in New York. But they're nothing compared to the girls here, even though the girls here don't dress so immodestly. Actually, that's part of their attractiveness.'

I think he wanted to disagree, but he didn't know how. Instead, he took a long sip of Pepsi. 'My problem, my brother,' Mabayn sighed, 'is that there's no one for me to talk to.'

'Talk to?'

'My friends are all from away. For the summer, they go home. Now I have a problem, but I have no one to talk to. Unless I can talk to you.'

Hmm. This meant he wouldn't be leaving anytime soon. 'Why do you want to talk to me?'

'My parents can't understand. They just pray all day, and they pretend I'm not there. But you are different. I know you care about Islam, alhamdulillah. But you're from America. You understand how hard it is to be Muslim. You were looking at the girls.'

Was that an insult? 'Okay, then. What's your problem?'

'I am in love,' he whispered, blinking as he revealed his dark secret.

'Excuse me?'

His head jumped forward, as if someone had kicked it from the back. 'I said,' with more force this time, 'I am in love.'

And this was a bad thing? Unless Mabayn was in love with a man, which was too much for 1 a.m. on a Tuesday morning. 'Who are you in love with?' Notice my carefully constructed gender neutrality.

'That's the problem.' As he said it, I felt as if someone had kicked me in the back of the head, too. But then, mercifully, 'She's not Muslim.'

I wanted to fall down to the floor, praising God Almighty for making Mabayn's beloved female. But that wouldn't have gone down too well. 'Well, what is she?'

'Her parents are Christian.' His voice cracked.

Seeing how much closer his shoulders had gotten to the floor, I did my best to fight gravity. 'I know it must be hard for a Muslim man to be in love with a Christian girl, especially if his parents are really religious. But there are many good Christian girls out there, who have good hearts and minds. There is a difference between a person who doesn't know faith at all, and a person who has a different faith. You know what Islam teaches. Of all people, the Christians are closest to us.'

'That's the problem...'

'Islam?' I was now very confused. If Mabayn was going to convert, I didn't want to hear about it at this hour. Or any other, for that matter.

'She's not Christian.'

'But you said her parents—'

'Yes.' He stammered. 'Her parents are Christian. She is only born Christian. She celebrates Christmas, but who doesn't? She drinks too much, she's not modest in her dress...'

That immodesty was probably what made Mabayn fall in love with her. I'd thought that living in a Muslim country would have certain advantages. If you're going to fall head over heels for the easiest of reasons—what she looks like— at least the outward is outwardly Muslim. Unfortunately for Mabayn, he'd found himself someone who not only rejected Islam, but all the traditions previous. I wanted to kick that glass cup out of his grip, catch it in my right hand and bring it down on his skull, smashing every bone in his face, till his mouth welled into a bloody sea of teeth and Pepsi. Our faith was on life support and this spoiled pseudo-Egyptian brat had the audacity to yank at the plug.

But I was in no mood to argue with Mabayn. Rather, I pretended to be concerned. 'Is she Arab?'

'Syrian,' he replied, a little uncomfortable. Maybe he was having second thoughts about coming over and opening his heart to me, an almost complete stranger.

'That's good,' I said. 'She's an Arab. Don't you see?'

He bought my fake interest. 'What do you mean?'

'If she's Arab, she can understand Islam. It's not like

you're marrying an atheist from God knows where.' I wanted to say Iceland, but then I thought what if Mabayn knew someone from there? He was, after all, friends with a Finn.

But my comment didn't help.

'I don't know what happened. I always said I would marry a good Muslim girl. But there was this party. I did not want to go but my friends made me. I met her there and we spent time together. I'm twenty-three. How long am I supposed to wait? I might wait five years and never find anyone.'

In other words, you mean you might be like me. 'I don't mean to discount your feelings, but down the road, in twenty years, when she's not bothered by your daughter wearing a bikini, dating a guy or going to a dance, what are you going to do?' Come complain to me again?

'It's not lust,' he insisted. 'It's more than that.'

It might have been. It might not have been. But it no longer mattered. It was too late for Mabayn. God had given him his chance and he'd squandered it. Something had blinded him, not her body, but something deeper, past his ribs and inside his heart, a plague that spread till it had seized all of him. Perhaps he caught it at the party when he first saw her. His body said yes. His hormones said yes. His heart said no. So he silenced his heart. With that one choice, he lost every year of his life. It was that simple, and that was the most frightening part of it all.

When we began college, many of my fellow Muslim students and I started out on about the same page. A handful found a faith that remains difficult to understand or even appreciate. Islam dictates their whole lives. Some of our group eventually lost themselves: They claimed that religion was nothing but hypocrisy, a veil for what wasn't underneath. But they never did anything constructive; all they did was harp on the negatives while refusing to embody the positives. In other words, because I'm a hypocrite, you're one, too. What they couldn't understand was that one could sin but still feel a deep attachment to the faith, a refusal to let it slip entirely out of reach. Their death was a slow suicide.

But others were swiftly crushed. The world is heavy; we have to lift our hands above our heads to keep it from falling on us, but we have to keep our hands up all our lives—even after the blood drains and our arms go numb. Some of these students demanded feeling and so they threw off the world, feeling momentarily lighter, until divine gravity returned with its justice, quashing the brief thrills of sex, drugs and alcohol. Their bodies were destroyed in a second, the ferocity of the moment putting to shame anything I could do with a glass cup. Yes, if you looked at Mabayn casually, noticing the way he was sipping his Pepsi, studying the floor as if it was about to explode, cracking the knuckles of his left hand against his thigh or chasing an invisible fly with his eyes, you'd think him alive. But just a second more and you'd see something that had escaped you before. Mabayn was dead.

And if it was so easy for Mabayn to die, it wouldn't be that difficult for me. I was sure that once, a long time ago, Mabayn had felt as I had a long time ago: I'd been a wall of faith, impervious to any assault. Until I made the mistake of engaging reality in battle. Now Mabayn was sitting before me, too small for the love seat that his body dwarfed. He had not only died, he had actually killed himself. I doubt that's what he'd set out to do, but in any case, that's what he had accomplished. Failure is achieved through many half-steps, compromises and mental negotiations, all of which bring us to a line, and when we cross it, we are done. We might as well die and receive judgement before we go down any deeper.

But dead men can still speak. 'I guess I find her physically attractive because I find her mentally attractive.'

I seriously doubted that, but I didn't say it. 'We're guys, Mabayn. We're physical.' I knew, because I was the expert on the subject. Good thing he couldn't ask Haris, who was, unbelievably, still in the shower.

'My brother, I hit rock-bottom.' Though he addressed me, it seemed like he was talking to himself. As, indeed, he had stopped listening to anything but his own desires. 'I know I do anything to be with someone. You know? I wanted a girl like the MTV girls.' He sighed, finishing off the last sip of his Pepsi. 'For every person, there is a test. I think I failed mine.'

'Why would you accept failure?'

'I did not accept. I met her, we talked so much, and then so fast, she's with me. I don't know if that is victory or failure.' He wanted to take another sip of his Pepsi, but the glass was empty. So he looked at his watch instead and then he panicked. 'I am sorry; I did not know the time. Sorry to keep you awake so late.'

'No problem,' I lied.

And Mabayn left more politely than he'd come.

I fell on to the bed and stared up at the ceiling, imagining for a second that we lived in an Ottoman Empire without conversations or situations like this. There were no more passports between us either. A Caliph on a throne, too, ruling over a society of believers, nothing like the world was today. Not only was Mabayn dead; we all were. Fools like me only pretended not to be. Everywhere, everything was falling apart, the ruins of Islam picked up and blown away, for the third or fourth (and worst) time in history. This time, maybe it was just for mockery's sake. That is what we'd become, the laughing-stock of the powers that had been and would be for quite some time longer.

I could look out our window and see Cairo, but I could not see Cairo, despite all her youth, rising to change the world. But it was one thing to see defeat in the clothes we wore, on the channels we watched, in the dreams we sought and on the products we bought; it was an altogether different thing to see that defeat envelop me, such that my Muslim half had been overrun and colonized by my Western half. How could I let such darkness invade my mind till I could no longer present anything—not even resistance? Though, if I were to spend the next few years of my life failing and flailing, I was sure I'd end up a second Mabayn. I knew then that I'd do anything to escape that fate.

I reached up to turn off the light when Haris stepped in, finally done with his shower. Tomorrow we'd wake up and the Nile would be gone, thanks to him.

'Going to sleep?' he asked.

'Just wanted to relax,' I said. 'I'm not that sleepy.'

I switched off the lights and it was silence, except for my room-mate reading his prayers. Since he knew me so well, he knew that my quiet meant there was much on my mind.

'Is everything okay?' A pause, to make sure I'd heard him. 'You've been acting weird these past few days.'

'I'm all alone.'

It took Haris a second to think of a reply. 'You won't always be, yaar.'

'Well, in that case, it's an excellent illusion.' And then her face came into my mind. Not the Hardee's girl, not

Zuhra, but her, the one who had ice cream with me at that little diner by a main road whose name I should know. 'I think of all the crap I've gone through since then and I wonder why it couldn't have just stopped back then.'

'Were you even in love with her?'

'It was a long time ago,' I replied. 'Besides, I don't even know what love is. But I do believe that if you're with someone, you don't let them go.'

'But she said no.' Haris shifted in his bed. I knew, because his bed creaked. 'I mean, if you haven't accepted that, you're living in a dream.'

'All our lives are a dream,' I countered. 'And when we die, we wake up.'

'That's not what I meant.'

I pulled the blanket up—the air-conditioning was making me terribly cold. 'There are some things we cannot and should not accept, because if we did, they'd destroy us and everything we hope for. It's better to dream inside a dream than to die inside it.'

'But what would you get out of that?'

'I can't accept that the past is gone. I can't accept that she's gone. It's not that I don't know. I can see her with another guy and understand that. But deep down, I refuse to believe that one day she won't be with me again. Perhaps it's stubborn stupidity. Perhaps it's noble and romantic. I guess, either way, it's pathetic.'

My room-mate chuckled. 'Pathetic isn't always bad.'

'The world is so strong, Haris. Everything goes in one direction and we just watch it go. Either I accept that I can't change its flow, or I fight it.'

'But why fight it?' He wasn't impatient, but only compassionate. There was a heart in this man bigger than our building. 'Why fight this battle if you know it's already lost? Go after someone else.'

'I'd still be fighting.'

'You keep saying we keep fighting the same battles. But that's only because you want to keep fighting the same battles. At least, if you moved on you'd have a chance of winning.'

'That's not why I fight.'

'You fight to lose?' He laughed, but softly, because he wasn't sure if he was supposed to.

'I can't accept that when I die I will have lost what was once mine.' Tears made an appearance. 'I don't want to believe that the world is more powerful than me. Even though I know it is and I can't imagine how that could change.'

'You know what the world is really like,' he countered. 'So why not accept that if you can already see?'

'So many of us live in order to die.' As I said that, the tears spilled, moistening the pillow. 'I think there's something so beautiful about those people who don't let the world dictate things to them. Anyway, we're all dead. All that matters is if we fought or not.'

'If we fought the world?'

'I want to die fighting something stronger than me.'

I think Haris heard me crying. 'Like fate, which you can't escape?'

'Maybe.' I closed my eyes, pushing more tears down my face. 'But then all my life, no matter how long it lasts, is only an act of suicide.'

'You want your life to be a suicide?'

'Either we die fighting or we die hiding.' I did not want to die like Mabayn died.

I swung my legs out of bed and searched for my slippers.
'Where are you going?'
My hand wiped the last few tears away. 'The bathroom.'

Leaving the bedroom, I turned left and headed for the
balcony instead. I found myself absorbed by rows of small
sedans below me, packed in a tight diagonal pattern, their
rear ends taking up the space where sidewalks should've
been.
'Don't tell me this is where you pee.' My room-mate
smiled and slid the balcony door shut behind him.
'I didn't want to keep you up,' I said.
'The last time you left in the middle of the night, you ran
to Hardee's. You seemed a little more down this time.' He
moved in closer. 'I have to keep an eye on you.'
I approached the edge again, thinking of that girl and the
world that always turned me down and the distance from the
balcony to the ground. One jump, the joy of freefall and then
no more doors sliding open and people telling me they've got
to keep an eye on me.
'You know...' I put my elbows on the ledge and relaxed
against it, the concrete scraping my skin. 'I would've really
been good with her.'
'It isn't just about her. It's also about you.'
I shook my head, 'I don't aspire to that any more.'
'You would've changed for a girl that you don't even
know if you loved, but you won't change yourself for yourself.
I don't understand you.'
'Welcome to the club.' I nodded. 'I've never been able
to forget the past, Haris. Not in my whole life. The more you
remember defeats...'
'But why remember what you don't like?'

Good question. 'Because I keep failing. But I don't believe I should.'

'Sometimes there's a sign in failure.'

Haris came so close to me that I could feel him breathing. It was calming, but that was the wrong feeling for the moment. I lunged forward, kicking my right foot against the cement. The pain shot through the insides of my leg. 'It's not over!'

Haris let that echo for a few minutes, until it seemed to him that all my energy was spent. 'We can't go back in time,' he whispered. 'You know that.'

'If the past is dead, then we're dead, too. If we look behind us, we see youth and promise. If we look ahead of us, what do we see but death?'

'I see what you mean...' But I don't think he did. 'I just don't think I can look at things the way you do. I'm sorry to say, but I think it's impossible.'

'It'd be like jumping off this balcony and coming back to life.'

Haris turned and started walking into the apartment, his back to me as he talked. 'Don't think I'm too weird,' he begged, 'but do you ever come out here and want to jump off?'

'Like right now?' I asked.

He swallowed. The two of us barrelling towards a conclusion neither of us wanted to face. 'We came halfway around the world and for what? Cairo hasn't changed a damn thing.'

'What can?'

'There's got to be somewhere I can go,' he said.

'Where?'

'Tomorrow.' Haris was reaching for the balcony door. 'I

know you're having trouble forgetting about her. But you have to move on. Why not consider Zuhra? Why not focus on all the things you can still do? For God's sake yaar, you're twenty-one.'

Zuhra lived on the first floor, I recalled. Were I to jump, I might catch a glimpse of her asleep in her room, a last glance before I smashed my head on uneven cement. For that second, I could pretend she liked me, and maybe even that if she was looking out her window just then, that she would rush outside and call for help, crying before my broken body. But if that was so, then I didn't know if I would still want to jump.

getting up to go

When I saw what time it was, I nearly fell out of bed. 11:00. I was very late for my first class. My only class, but still. Hopping over the bed, I tripped on the end of the rug, caught myself with the help of a bedpost and then I spotted Haris. I hadn't noticed him, sitting on the edge of his bed, quietly reading the Qur'an. 'Not quite awake yet, huh?'

I nodded a blank. 'You didn't go to class?' A stupid question, I realized.

'I couldn't leave without you.'

'Why didn't you wake me up?'

He closed the Qur'an and set it gently on the bedside table. 'I thought you might've gone to sleep really late last night. So I thought I'd let you have your rest.'

'Well…' I rubbed my eyes and found them blurrier still. 'Thanks.'

And then I fell back on to the pillow, staring up at the ceiling. Till the afternoon, we didn't do more than watch a BBC News special over the Internet, check e-mail with unnecessary regularity, guzzle bottles of water, stare at furniture and comment on how inappropriate it was. Only after Haris prayed the mid-afternoon prayer did we decide to go out for lunch. Our choice was the McDonald's in Mohandessin, a restaurant designed for tourists, albeit located in a neighbourhood where tourists rarely tread. Unless they want to see how really ugly Muslim modernity can be.

For most of all its thousand-year history, Cairo has been confined to the east bank of the Nile. It was only in Nasser's time that the city grew to take in the west bank, too: the Egyptian urban population was booming, and all those people had to be put somewhere. Like the socialist he supposedly was, Nasser then designed several boroughs to absorb the demographic boom, each of which reflected his proletarian mythologies. Mohandessin, or 'Engineers', was one. Sahafayeen, or 'Journalists', where our classes were held, was another. Unfortunately for Nasser, Egypt woke up to a strident 1967 Overture. With the failure of pan-Arab socialism, and Nasser's passing in 1970, Anwar Sadat reversed course. Today Mohandessin is everything it wasn't supposed to be, the capital of Cairo's concrete capitalism, a mess of a place popular with the rich, dynamic and affirmatively unaesthetic.

Take McDonald's, for example. The walls are covered with pseudo-Pharaonic patterns and murals displaying busts of long-dead kings, ancient temples and the mighty Pyramids of course. The pictures are painted in a luxurious matte brown, evocative of a stability that has nothing to do with the boisterousness of a McDonald's. But the worst is to come. Painted over these murals are cheery McDonald's characters in the most vulgar poses: biking down a pyramid; running through a temple; screaming near a statue of Ramses II. I was shocked, but soon found that nobody else cared. It's as if the defeat is so great and the present so discouraging that Egyptians have accepted McDonald's as shock therapy. This is where parents bring their children while they're still bite-size, exposing Egypt's future to its future. Egypt's children swallow the bitter pill of our super-sized disaster, dipped like Chicken Nuggets into a condiment of domination.

Because it was a Tuesday, the line was pretty short. When our turn came, it was a fish fillet combo for Haris and a cheeseburger combo for me. (They give you two burgers, which makes you feel like you're getting more for your money.) The total should have come to twenty-two gunayh, but instead it added up to thirty-three. Unless we'd forgotten how to calculate or, more probably, the economy—and the currency with it—had taken a recent, unnoticed nosedive. Another reason one should never be without a television.

Haris was visibly annoyed. 'Why thirty-three?'

Cashier Ahmad blinked. 'Because of promotion.'

And then he explained: If the customer ordered any combo meal, McDonald's added 'fine china plates' (his words) for only eleven gunayh extra. In other words, the much-vaunted promotion—the way Ahmad said it, it sounded like an angel sent down from the heavens to save the Arabs—increased the price by fifty per cent. And there was no way around it. The Arabs would be saved, damn it, whether they liked it or not. If you purchased a combo meal, you purchased the plates, too. They offered three variations on the same pattern: white, with different coloured bands on the edge (bright red, blue or green), and a yellow pattern zigzagging through this band. The way I saw it, it was cheap imitation Aztec. An allusion to McDonald's designs on Latin America, too, and yet another reference to a vanished civilization. The choice of defeated nations was, to say the least, unnerving.

Haris tried to explain to Ahmad that the promotion was supposed to be optional; we didn't want—or need—'fine China plates'. We were students. We didn't have guests.

Hell, we barely had friends. But the argument went over Ahmad's head. So far over, in fact, that it caused the manager to turn around and come over to our register. Though he was good enough to try to reason with us. We told the manager that we didn't have the money to spend on the plates and, on top of that, we wouldn't want a so-called 'fine China plate' from McDonald's—who would? But our forceful haggling didn't produce results. So, while the manager was still addressing me, to convince me of the benefits of fast-food ceramics, I turned to my room-mate.

'I really think we should eat somewhere else. How about Hardee's?'

And that did it. Aware of our desire to choose another, competing franchise, the manager gave in straightaway, cutting out the plates and even bringing our food up to the second floor, where we'd decided to sit (just to make him walk up the flight of stairs). There, in relative peace, we enjoyed our meals, making the occasional observation about the pedestrians beneath us. So much hassle for such simple bliss. The lesson: All you have to do is inform the manager you're going to walk away, while (pay attention, this is the most important part) beginning to walk away. The masses only have to stand up, preferably all at once, and tell their leaders, 'Either you rule with justice, or we're going somewhere else.'

But where can they go?

And why would the managers care—unless they also lose some business?

even dragons have their demons

Haris headed for the bathroom as soon as we got back. I figured it was for ablutions and maghrib, the sunset prayer. He prayed by himself. I fell onto the lemonade chair and despaired for the rest of my evening. Then the phone rang.

'Hey!' It took me a second to recognize Zaheed's voice. 'Tonight's the Mawlid of Sayyidna Husayn, remember?' I didn't. 'Can you think of anyone else who might want to come?'

Haris, Rehell, his European friends, and probably Mabayn. Zaheed was excited, but despite his overflowing cheer, he cautioned us—we were planning to bring non-Muslims to a very traditional Muslim festival. Good sense and discretion were called for. I hung up after we decided on a convenient meeting time and place. It was my job to spread the word.

Calling Rehell was easy—he'd jump at the chance both to attend as well as lecture his friends on the sensitivities appropriate for such a festival. The second call was harder. I found Mabayn's number after going through the little mess of notebook paper we called our phonebook and wished just as soon that I hadn't found it.

Mabayn's weary voice answered the phone. I could hear him struggling to get the receiver to his ear, and I broke into a petty smile. I never thought I'd call a dead man.

'Izzayak?' he asked, sounding exhausted.

'Alhamdulillah, I'm good.' And before he had the chance to bemoan the defeat of Islam from Morocco to Indonesia, I announced our plans. 'We're going to the Sayyidna Husayn festival tonight. It starts at midnight, I think. Do you want to come?'

Suddenly, Mabayn was alive again. Or just faking it really well. 'You don't actually observe that crap, do you?'

'What's so bad about it?' I asked, though I knew his reasons. Sometimes, they were mine.

'It's not allowed,' he sighed. Mabayn the Wahhabi. But the virus was dormant inside me, too. Where was Rumi with his dragon-slayer? 'We're not supposed to celebrate those kinds of things, you know...'

I wanted to ask him if it was wise to marry an irreligious woman when Muslims had enough trouble holding on to their faith in their own countries, but I held my tongue. Precious me and all my hypocrisy. For if Zuhra was non-Muslim, and she liked me, I would've thrown my religion out of the window and chased after (her, and not my faith). 'I don't think it's right to celebrate his birthday, either,' I admitted. 'But we're going just to hear the Sufis play their music. It's not like we get to hear this stuff back in America...'

Mabayn was quiet.

'Look,' I said, 'I understand why you think it's wrong. In fact, I agree with you. But give us a break, man. There's nothing we can do around here for fun. Better we go where people are actually talking about godly things than go...' To a club? To meet a Syrian girl?

I imagined Mabayn sitting in his room, rubbing one foot against the other. Because Mabayn had betrayed his principles for a girlfriend, he didn't want to put them aside for this, too.

Fighting after you've surrendered—that never works, does it? But how fiercely and stupidly we struggle after we've unmoored ourselves.

'Come on,' I urged. 'We're not going there to worship Husayn.'

the second battle of karbala

From the moment I arrived, and saw the size of the gathering, I knew it'd been a mistake to bring non-Muslims. The many believers in attendance, already under assault from a battle that put Helm's Deep to shame, were sure to spot alien Uruk-Hai at one of the last festivals still within their weakened hands. Little surprise, then, the rage that gripped each Egyptian upon seeing the white faces in our fellowship. Defeat leads to resentment, and resentment, revenge.

That was why, in front of the masjid of Sayyidna Husayn, the crowd went from a calm sea of individuals to a vicious stampede, a collective alive and possessed of only one purpose: eliminating the foreign bodies. From every direction, their anger rushed towards us, sending us smashing into one another and then down to the ground. I wobbled and tried desperately to regain my balance, but I could barely keep myself on one foot. Until a swarm of police officers descended on the crowd and opened a clearing straight towards us, their batons batting Egyptians away with an efficient brutality. I loved the moment I saw it heading towards me. My mistake.

While our white friends found themselves surrounded by a protective curtain of uniformed men, Haris and I were lashed by their canes, mostly against the back and once or twice on the arms. Two police officers grabbed us from behind and tried to throw us into the horde of Egyptians retreating to the safety of the masjid's walls. 'No!' I yelled, pointing to Rehell. 'We're with them!'

Their heads swung to Rehell—whose quick confirmation granted us our release. A minute later, Haris and I were back, part of a police-escorted group, embarrassed and enraged that we'd been punished so swiftly, while the police had rushed to protect the Europeans. But even the sting of baton blows began to diminish. Drums kicked in, fuelling a maddeningly addictive beat. Haris smiled the biggest smile I'd seen all summer, the beaming exhilaration of a city man realizing that he was still a Bedouin. It remained somewhere in our genes, though mutated by now. It was recessive, hidden, not expressed phenotypically. We were homozygous recessive: failures in all senses of the word.

And we had also failed to get any closer to Sayyidna Husayn. Because we had some good-looking white women in our group, who tantalized many a coffee-coloured Egyptian man, we suffered unwanted and slowing attention no matter where we went. To have even attempted approaching Husayn's tomb would've been a death wish. Thus Rehell, Haris and I— the Muslim trinity—decided that, rather than continue with a clearly futile task, we'd do better to find a place to rest our feet. The police proposed we stop at a nearby café, and we agreed, also eager for something to drink.

Behind the masjid and to our right, there started an alleyway entered by way of a broad ramp. But because the masjid was so festively decorated, with bright lights, fluttering banners and hanging lanterns, the alleyway appeared to disappear into blackness after a few yards. Lucky for us, the café emerged while there was still light on our path, an establishment occupying all of a three-storey building struggling not to fall on its face. The front of the café was filled with chrome seats and red umbrellas soiled to a maroon. Inside was a dingy sea green all over the roof and the walls, bottomed out by a white-tile trim running halfway up, except where they were obscured by obese Egyptian men who dwarfed their little chairs and wrapped their sweaty hands around old shisha pipes. The owner, sure he was going to be rewarded with our foreign currency, invited us up to the third floor.

'It is the best café here,' he assured us. And he might've been right.

The third floor was a lazy balcony, open to the sky but still air-conditioned, combining the comfort of modernity with random gusts of warm summer air. Over my shoulder I could see streams of Muslims emerging from the stark black of the alleyway, feeding into the sea of believers thronging the grounds. The Sufis had pitched tents around the masjid, banging drums and singing with voices loud even by Egypt's standards. Everything in me wanted to be down there and not up where I was, staring at a few Europeans blowing smoke out of their mouths and comparing the resulting patterns. Most of them were unable to speak Arabic, let alone understand it, and still less capable of appreciating Islam—or any other faith, for that matter. I began to hate the strange people that they were, the puncture in time that they represented: a hollow and fake race, no more than post-imperialist flotsam. Why was I up here taking care of them? I belonged, rather, to the disordered crowds below which made chaos look gorgeous.

I leaned in to Haris and whispered, 'I haven't prayed maghrib.'

He smiled because he had. This also meant that he wouldn't come with me. Nor would he want to. The crowd, combined with the heat, was too much. So I faced the table and announced that I'd be venturing down for prayers, alone, and that I'd return in ten minutes or so, inshallah. I remember being looked at as if I was deranged. What idiot would dare risk going out into that? Undeterred, in fact motivated, I rushed down the stairs, nearly banging my head on the low ceiling, so happy to be away from the pathetic, frightful glances of people afraid of anything beyond them, terrified of any reality that might impinge upon their escapist artificiality. I wanted to find a rock and hurl it into the balcony, maybe to smash someone's head in, but I decided not to. What if I hit Haris or Rehell?

Turning to accommodate an aggressive older woman, I felt a hesitant hand on my shoulder. It was Mabayn and he was trying on a smile. 'I haven't prayed, either.'

So the two of us went together, not a word passing between us. There I was, going to pray, and I was letting my pride ruin my worship. Rather than talk to him, I fumed over his interruption. He could have just as well gone to prayer without telling me—then it wouldn't have been showing off, which would have meant his prayer would have counted.

Getting into the masjid was a jihad in and of itself. About three hundred women and men were trying to enter through a door wide enough for two. After a good deal of shoving, I found myself not just inside but several feet forward, handing my shoes to the fellow at the door, a tall man whose left shoulder tilted forward too far. The masjid was packed with countless worshippers, reading Qur'an, praying, crying, sleeping, littering. The stench of a people who could not afford deodorant filled my nostrils. Finding a corner relatively free of refuse, we began our prayers. I read through my own in a hurry, hoping not to get sideswiped into a pillar.

I think Mabayn wanted to leave the minute we were done, but I forced him to wait: some commotion at the front of the masjid urged me to linger. He shrugged and told me we best be off, but I refused. Maybe to get back at him for tagging along. Reluctantly, Mabayn followed me to the source of the sounds, produced by a circle of upset young men, all sitting quietly now—except for the youngest one, who was standing and yelling.

'Four Palestinians, your brothers in faith, were killed this week. By missiles they could not see and tanks they could not stop. And what have you done for them? Swirling and twirling while they were weeping and dying, you are here tumbling about like a bunch of drunken fools.'

The room fell silent, the name of Palestine echoing from chamber to chamber. Palestine. There was a potent magic in it, a sadness inherent in its awkward, stretched and painful name. Its last syllable was too long, as if God was warning the Palestinians that their demise would be dismal. And the drunken fools had nothing to add, nothing to defend themselves with. In fact, I smiled at our humiliation, even though someone finally found the courage to cry out, 'We are here for Husayn!'

It wasn't enough. 'You've cried and danced, but Husayn did not cry and Husayn did not dance.' Words that hurled daggers of doubt into us. Did Husayn and I really share the same belief? If I had lived in his time, would we really have stood in the same lines to pray the same prayers? The man screamed again, 'Husayn fought! So why do you cry and why do you dance?'

The young fellow's comrade nodded and prepared himself. For a man sitting cross-legged on the floor, he spoke as if his voice was artificially amplified: 'No one loves Husayn any longer. They only come here because they love themselves, Muhammad.'

Muhammad agreed. And repeated. 'They come here because it makes them think they have faith. Then they go home and they do nothing.'

The comrade replied, 'But remember: They have cried and so they are pardoned!'

There was no doubt his words were infuriating the crowd, but not enough to make them attack back: We understood that what he said was true. Then it struck me: I was in Egypt, a country that took pride in oppressing whoever got a little too autonomous. Their heated words would quickly alert the police, engaging them in what would probably be a brief and hopeless battle. But perhaps that was the point. I turned to Mabayn and then to the back of the prayer area, thinking foolishly, helplessly, romantically, that I might urge my brothers to bar the masjid entrance and at least slow the policemen. At least so that we could hear them out, let them say whatever they wanted our congregation to hear.

Another man from the group stood up right after angry Muhammad sat down. There seemed to be a system to their venting, as if the outburst had been planned long before. This new speaker did not yell like Muhammad; instead, he cupped his hands above his face, to catch the rain spilling from the heavens. 'O our Lord!' he thundered.

Without a thought, we were the chorus in resounding echo. 'O our Lord!'

'We seek your mercy and your assistance, our Lord. Unite us, and bless us, and bless all those who stand against those who stand against the truth.'

'Amen!' the crowd raged. I wondered if my friends could hear any of this. And if so, what in God's name did they think was going on?

'Our Lord, wash away these governments of ineptitude, ignorance and inefficiency! Our Lord, bless us instead with governments of wisdom, foresight and courage! Our Lord, make us like light, to cast out this nightmare of darkness! Our Lord, help us save all that is good in the world!'

But all he received was silence, as still as Husayn's tomb. We all wanted to scream amen. Of course, we didn't. We had neither wisdom, nor foresight, nor courage. Instead, we ambled, flushed and humiliated, back to our previous positions, focusing on the masjid's sullied floor, dirtied by the waste of a people who could do no more than beg a dead man for help. And right on cue, a soulless team of police officers streamed in, running with remarkably quiet hurry, such that the full effect of it was fantasy. They came from three sides, with helmets, body armour and assault rifles, but no shoes. No usurper is so crude as to upset the whole project. But rather detract from it, bit by bit, till there is nothing left. The upstarts were arrested with a dazzling efficiency that the government was unable to display in almost any other endeavour.

Mabayn looked at me. 'It's time to get out of here.'

And he left, without even waiting for me. Wasn't I the foreigner in need of protection? I watched him go, his fat head retreating, quicker and quicker towards the door, eager to depart from the scene of another loss. Poor Mabayn had come to pray, to connect with God, and all he had seen was futility in repetition. What his heart must have been thinking, I could not imagine. I wondered if he'd go back to the café. I wondered if I would.

An old man, seated on the floor, began an uncontrolled scream. He had no teeth, I noticed.

'All of you, out!'

But there were no police left to receive his venom—they'd gone as swiftly as they'd come. No matter, for they were not his targets.

'Animals! Take your beastly souls and leave!'

Someone screamed curses, 'Shut up, old man!'

'Leave now!' His reply cracked like lightning. Then he jumped up, much too fast for someone his age. 'Leave as you left Husayn! Only one of you deserves to stay in this masjid. Only one of you tried to stop the police when they came in. And he—' pointing to the front of the masjid now—'lies asleep in that tomb.'

He kept jabbing his finger into the air, as if the motion would return Husayn to life. Then he burst into sobs. And then we all did, letting upon the floor of the masjid all our sorrows and all our frustration, the fights in our homes, streets, cities and countries, till the masjid could've grown a forest of melancholy from our tears. I rushed to the exit, stuffing a gunayh into the hands of the doorman, who thought this more than necessary. He gave me my shoes with a smile, which greatly offended me.

'What are you so damn happy about?' He leapt back, because I'd screamed. 'Yazid won. Again.'

prayers for liars

I tried to step out of the masjid and was shoved off the bottom
step. Though the café was to my left, the force of the crowd
urged me right, and I accepted, allowing myself to be led
towards the many little alleys spat out of Khan al-Khalili. Past
some tourist shops, hanging rugs, prayer mats and calligraphy,
I spotted Zuhra at the end of the street, her tiny body
fantastically out of place in the frenzy of heavy Egyptian men
and women, donkeys and overburdened fruit carts. I moved
sideways, ejecting myself from the crowd. She was just as
beautiful as before and just as before, she didn't notice me.
Her unforgettable eyes peered in every direction but mine.

I looked around for Wanand, a mother or a sister—
someone who could contact a male relative who'd emerge
out of nowhere to beat the hell out of me. But there was no
one in sight. With all the strange men here, many with
unnecessarily forward claims of righteousness and similarly
forward hands, why would she risk being so vulnerable? So I
walked towards her with a familiar gait. As though I was
approaching my wife. And what would I say to my wife?
Were my tongue able to walk, it would stumble down the
street, a drunken lovelorn coward just hit by a truck he'd
been pushed in the way of. Still, saying something badly
would be better than saying nothing at all. Which is what
happened, again.

The force of a family bulldozing through the swarm of people—and me—spun me sideways. I ploughed back into the crowds, but I was too tall and Zuhra too small. She was reaching for something, then it looked like she was talking to someone, but all of this was concurrent with her acceleration away from me, though likely not deliberately. For a good ten minutes, I ran up and down the length of the alley, but I couldn't find her.

Back at our exclusive third-floor balcony, empty Pepsi bottles littered the tables. The smell of shisha hogged the air. The obscuring smoke, and its pungent odour, turned everything ugly. There was nothing small here, no frail delicacy, no beautiful Zuhra, only the stench and the many strangers who savoured it.

Of course, Haris was the first to notice me. 'Are you okay, bhai?' In other words, I looked as bad as I felt.

'I'm fine.' I wiped my forehead. 'It's really crowded out there.'

'What took you so long?' Haris looked at Mabayn for an explanation, but what could he say: 'I ran away'?

I spared Mabayn the embarrassment. 'I stopped to watch some of the Sufis sing their zikr.'

First I went to pray, with my heart feeling resentment towards my brother. Then I lied about what I'd done. Not to mention standing there watching the police haul away the few Muslims who still spoke the truth. Haris, meanwhile, was inflamed with jealousy: he'd come here because he wanted to see the Sufi groups engaged in their intoxicating worship. Better to watch them than watch Karbala all over again, I thought. But before my room-mate could engage me with any more of his questions—which would've demanded more deceit—one of Rehell's female friends stood up, adjusting her temporary hijab.

'I'm bloody tired,' she moaned. 'Shall we call it a night?'

So much for wanting to watch the Sufis.

Though I'd just come back in, on our way out it seemed that the number of people had doubled, while the walls, buildings and stores hemmed us in tighter. At the exact time we needed them, the police spotted us and swarmed towards our group, smacking off the good Muslims who had the misfortune to stand in their way. I flinched. And then I bit my lip. Now would not be a good time for any Egyptian to miraculously turn into Husayn. But probably none of them present here could—they were here, after all, worshipping a dead man. What kind of life could that create?

One of the girls said, 'We need to call a cab.' And then she stared at us, the Muslim/Arab crew, expecting us to do it for her.

However, it was the police that answered. In a bold, unexpected—and rather suspicious—display of foresight, they found us freedom from the masses in the form of three taxicabs, parked and waiting on the side of the road. The drivers were leaning against their doors, smoking cigarettes that had grown very short. At least Karbala wouldn't be a financial loss: nothing would bring down their ridiculous fee of fifteen pounds per cab.

Not surprisingly, Mabayn was the first to give in. And I hated him again. 'We have to take these taxis,' he informed us. As if we didn't know.

But Rehell was in no mood to yield. 'Let's go down the road and try to find some other cabs, mate. I'm sure we can get a better deal.'

'No, we can't get a better deal, Rehell.' Mabayn was avoiding looking at me. Was there something in his eyes he didn't want me to see? 'Where can we possibly go?'

'We can't pay forty-five gunayh,' Rehell insisted. 'That's a bloody rip-off.'

I saw Rehell converting and becoming a Wahhabi, escaping to a madrassah in some small village, ever dissatisfied with the pessimism of his new-found family of faithfuls. He would even do something to change things. What that was, I didn't know.

Mabayn countered, 'It's going to take you half an hour to find another cab, Rehell. I don't think the police are going to wait around the whole time.'

'So what?' Rehell was yelling, and at Mabayn. 'They don't have to wait!'

'What about the girls?' Good Haris, interjecting. Making things make sense. 'We can't make them wait. The crowd doesn't look so friendly, either.'

'Nothing's going to change their minds,' Mabayn repeated. 'The price is set. I mean, look at them. They think we're human dollars.'

Once we accepted the fare, Zaheed left us, walking to his nearby apartment. Rehell, Mabayn and Haris divided themselves between the cabs. But no cab for me. Was it the men who failed to triumph? Was it the look on their faces as they were carried away, with Palestine still unsaved and Jerusalem still enslaved? I would not be emptied so easily. I would not trudge back into our lobby, after so many hours, only to ride the elevator back to hell. I was not going to be like Mabayn, who told strangers of his defeats in the late night hours.

Rehell looked up at me from the cab he was in. 'Everyone's in a cab, mate.'

'Yeah.' But Zuhra's not.

Haris leaned out his window, cutting short some small talk with the driver. Probably a last attempt to get the fare lowered. He asked, with some concern, 'Are we waiting for something?'

Rehell stuck his arm out the window: 'Him!' Indeed, I remained standing by myself. So Rehell became more serious. 'Mate, the girls are waiting. Everyone's quite tired. We should go.'

'You should. I'm not going.' And to emphasize that, I took some steps back, into a crowd of Egyptians who'd stopped their worship to observe us—or the brief argument we'd just had. Or they just wanted to see us leave. 'I have to go back to Sayyidna Husayn.'

Haris swung his door open and pulled himself up.

'I have to go back,' I smiled. 'I promise nothing stupid this time.'

He nodded, slowly. 'Do you have cab fare?'

I pulled forty out of my wallet, and then realized it was a stupid thing to do in front of the cab drivers. There went their last chance for any renegotiation. But that was their problem, not mine.

'Do you just really like running away?' Haris asked.

'It's different this time,' I insisted.

aladdin's ladder

I was brown again, just another of the numberless native sons, sitting on the edge of the sidewalk, where a few days earlier my room-mate and I had met Zaheed. Did that make it a blessed place or a cursed one? I leaned back against the wrought-iron railing, staring up into a sky splotched by festival lights. Little candy wrappers and crushed walnuts clumped up on the pavement where they rustled against the ceaseless traffic of feet and often fell victim to it.

This was Cairo, not the Cairo that had been, nor the Cairo that would be. Wrinkles on the faces of the old men that passed by, many of them with bumps on their foreheads for the many times they prayed, the only time they willingly bowed to something more powerful. Proud young men, too, shoulders broad and backs erect, marching this way and that, with dreams, purposes and hopes, but in this poor and decrepit place, devoid of any fantasy's realization, what would become of their eager gait? Bumps on their foreheads. Of all the sadness I felt, none of it was connected to a lack of opportunity. I could have sold my soul to the West and made all the money a man could dream of making. I was many things, but I wasn't stupid.

Nor, it seems, was I blind. A familiar figure caught my eye. Her hijab bobbed to the left and right, and then it was gone. In my haste to meet it, I slammed up against a small

Egyptian who looked a lot like our barber, but there was no smile connected to this discovery, much like the present you're asked to unwrap when bigger and better ones await. So I shoved him to the side, discovering in the process that I had some physical strength, and charged towards her.

I thought only of pursuing her, not about the consequences of burrowing deeper into a city without street signs. There was a messy neighbourhood after the masjid, in whose direction I stormed. Going right, on to a long, lantern-lit street, lights suspended out of glassless windows. Didn't anybody have electricity out here? Ahead of me, greedy Egyptian men, bored with their unattractive wives, longed after Zuhra's body. Arms reached for her but she was always out of their grasp, darting left and then right, her little feet pounding pavement and hopping over almost invisible ruts and bumps in the road, which slowed me down and dealt my feet painful blows.

My eyes squinted in the darkness, trying to preserve this frantic race. The celerity of the moment mottled any such possibility. Another right after the plaza, a long run down a concave lane, past a restaurant with dozens of benches arrayed in perfect order, something out of an elementary school cafeteria. Following that, we turned right again, past packed houses, swooning left and then needlessly left, and then what? The only person who could get me back was moving farther and farther away. Where the hell was she going? And how did she know the way? There was only one answer, and though I begged me not to whisper it, I did nonetheless.

She was trying to lose me; make me fall behind, a fitting punishment for the sick stalker she suspected me to be. It was cruel of her, but I kept on, refusing every voice that told me to stop. I thought for a few minutes that I had lost her, but then I spotted her form stopping before a masjid, its slender minaret more Anatolian than Egyptian though not very ambitious. Hoping to stay unnoticed, I scurried behind a wall, vanishing from sight. When I peered out a few seconds later, there was nothing but a long alley, ending at the outline of a masjid. It was like I was inside a postcard.

The road thinned out as I got closer, branching off into two little lanes, each of them much narrower than the path I'd been on. There was a hint of a door, too, and some light coming from behind it. I rapped on the entrance, but the huge door swung into me, hitting my arm and making me fall.

'I'm sorry,' the man who stepped out said.

From inside the masjid, I heard someone laughing. 'Wanand—' The rest was unintelligible. It sounded like Persian, but it wasn't.

I had picked up the name, though. Which meant I'd heard Kurdish. 'Don't you live in—?' I began.

Wanand's voice was bigger than him. 'Why are you here?' He pushed me again, literally swatting me out of the way. I almost fell. My heart was audible. I'd been chasing after the man's daughter and had almost admitted as much. Thank God he'd cut me off. Wanand looked to his sides, but he didn't find what he was looking for. The door still open, he went back in.

I peeked into the masjid, and was quite surprised by what I saw: it looked more a home of worship than a house of one, with mismatched carpets hiding the floor and loose sheets draped over the far corners of the wall, sloppy but comforting cosy. From the tiles on the wall, it was obvious the masjid had survived an earthquake: once masterpieces of mathematics the tiles were entirely distorted, starting in one place, cutting off abruptly and reappearing at the wrong height. All this was made visible by the strained effort of a lonely bulb, descending from the ceiling and making it halfway down. A bulb as a pivot; beneath, a circle of men looking like they'd just woken up.

In the midst of this silence, with strangers ahead of me and pitch blackness behind me, a voice boomed from beside my ear. I jumped on spotting a man, his right hand thrust forward to meet mine which slowly and stupidly took it.

'Salam alaykum.' He looked simply splendid in the darkness that framed him. Of my height, but wider, he had thicker shoulders and a barrel chest. His skin cracked in places, of age, sun or stress, but underneath that, he came in a soberer colour. He looked less South Asian and more Central. A stern beard wrapped his hard features, magnifying soft eyes, out of place on an uncompromising face—and a prominent line crossed his forehead, dividing it in half. It grew when he opened his mouth. 'My name is Rojet Dahati.'

What? 'Rojet—'

He cut me off. Leaning over me, he faced the circle, his eyes on one man in particular. 'Salam alaykum, Wanand. How are you?'

'Wa alaykum salam, Ustad. Bashum.' Wanand answered like an obedient child—obviously, Rojet was the Sufi teacher my room-mate had referred to, the man who made Wanand move to Agouza. And then move again. Wanand stood up, opening a space in the circle for his Ustad to sit. This left me alone by the door, though I was a step inside the masjid.

'Are you waiting for someone?' Rojet looked offended. 'Else you must sit.'

'No, I came alone.'

Then he smiled. It appeared nobody in the circle but

Rojet wanted me to sit, until I said salam to the circle and gave them my name.

A younger man snapped, 'Ta Kurdi?'

'No.' That was as Kurdish as I could get. 'I'm Pakistani.'

Rojet interrupted him. 'Azad!' Either he was commanding him to free himself of some burden, or it was some sort of reprimand. Or it was his name. But of course I didn't think that at the time. Rojet bowed his head. 'You must forgive these questions. We haven't had guests in a long time.'

The man—Azad?—waxed apologetic: 'Bubura, Ustad.'

'He is sorry,' Rojet clarified.

choice before chance

The others began whispering amongst themselves. I could tell it was about me.

Thank God, Rojet reverted to a pleasant Arabic. With his index finger, he singled out the first man on his right. 'This is Wanand.' And then, 'This is Azad. This is Kibr. This is Keyf Khoshi. Though we are five, we attempt the work of many more.' He paused there, so I might remember. Kibr, who had mocked Wanand a few minutes earlier, kept a disturbingly acute eye on me. Keyf Khoshi only wanted to survey me. And Azad was the man who had asked if I was Kurdish. He was also the only one wearing a skullcap, a neat, knitted white one.

Rojet continued, 'We are the Immortals of the Order of Light. We've come to this masjid to learn and thereby purify our hearts. Perhaps you would like to sit and learn with us.'

'I don't think I have the time,' I admitted. Unfortunately, it came out too abruptly, words that I wish I could have taken back. Azad looked genuinely disappointed.

'I was only asking.' Rojet was so relaxed. 'You seem upset.'

'I'm not.'

'Your tone would suggest otherwise.'

'Maybe I'm just tired,' I sighed.

'Why are you tired?'

Many pious men were blind, after all. 'For one thing, it's well past midnight.'

'You chose the time to come here, didn't you?'

All in the circle shifted to gauge my reaction to his excellent retort. But I didn't answer. Instead, I pretended as if I hadn't heard, looking past him and on to the cracks on the walls, hoping the architecture might consume me. It didn't. My chosen diversion became painfully tedious. I, who always wanted to improve on the silence, was being made to suffer it.

Finally, Rojet opened his mouth again. 'We remember God,' he explained. Though I didn't want to know, and had even said so, I had no choice now, a lone gunman surrounded by a superior army. 'We remember God so that we can enslave ourselves to Him.'

I nodded, hoping I'd sound interested. 'How do you do that?'

'By seeking death before death.' Rojet nodded exactly as I had. It was as if I'd been standing on one faulty, wobbling leg, and he'd kicked even that out from underneath me. Though I tumbled, astonished, towards the earth, the impact of flesh against gravity not even commenced, he persisted. 'We are the Immortals, awaiting Perfection. We make this choice before He takes our chance: that is our goal, to die before dying.'

'You mean...' Why was I so nervous? 'Destroying your baser self?'

'No, no!' Rojet waved his hands back and forth. He was either mocking me, or signalling an aircraft. But then he rested his hand on my knee. A shiver shot through my legs. 'If you take away the human's ability to sin, he ceases to be human. Thus, if you take away the baser self, you destroy the self in its entirety.'

'You can't do that...' I was trying, very hard, to complete a thought. Though we all want to express ourselves well—false hopes born of too many English teachers—few statements ever come out whole. 'I mean, you can't do that to yourselves.'

'Of course we can.' He nodded. 'We can kill ourselves.'

'You ... can ... kill ... yourself?'

Rojet burst out laughing, so hard that I was afraid he'd bring his dilapidated masjid down upon our heads. 'I can kill myself?' he repeated. 'That sounds like a job!'

Kibr jumped in—didn't he need permission?—'I have a job, I heal people. I have a job, I kill myself.' He glimmered with glee. 'Does that make any sense?'

'It doesn't make much sense, now that I think about it.' I let myself grin thinking they were only jesting with me, a complete stranger. For the police state that Egypt was, wasn't this a little too intimate: a band of Kurdish Muslims in an out-of-the-way masjid calmly discussing suicide so late at night?

Rojet understood my hesitation and squeezed my knee. 'I can only kill myself once,' he said.

I drew back. '...If you wanted to...'

'It cannot be a job, then. It can only be a goal.' Rojet stood to begin a cycle of prayer, inserting an afterthought just before he raised his hands, his dark eyes set on mine: 'There is no compulsion in religion. Everyone here came of their own free will. Even you.'

in my dream i see mujahideen

Haris and I were waiting in line at the infamous Mohandessin McDonald's. The sun streamed through the large street-level windows, reflecting the white marble outside back into the restaurant, creating an irrepressible haze. To lower one's gaze was, quite literally, to risk blindness.

The restaurant was filled with young Egyptians, heads bobbing to top ten American pop. Their very presence was unsettling. I'd been to McDonald's in many countries, but only in America and Israel did it ever feel like it really belonged. Because those two countries worked together, they matched each other, like fire and lava—one is never sure if they are the same thing, or if one is born from the other. The United States and the Zionist State: glossy societies constructed over the remains of tattered, ravaged, native populations. No matter how hard Egypt tried, it simply couldn't be that bold, that colourful, that artificial.

Haris pointed up to the menu. 'I feel like having an apple pie.'

I laughed with victory. 'And you're the one who keeps saying he isn't Western.'

'They're good, yaar.' Just then our turn came, so he ordered for the two of us. 'Ayz combo wahid wa itneen.' Combos one and two. For some reason, Haris chose not to order the apple pie. 'Maybe next time.'

Ahmad punched through the menu with robotic ease. 'Thirty-three gunayh.' Somehow inserting an 's' into both 'th's', without ever making it one letter—a specifically Egyptian talent.

'Thirty-three?' My room-mate cursed.

'It's the damn plates.'

Ahmad was perplexed. 'You want more food?'

'No, we don't,' I explained. 'We don't want the plates.'

'But this promotion,' Ahmad began, his English an Iraqi scud, falling apart before it got off the ground. But Ahmad persisted. 'You order combo, yes? So you have plates.'

Except this time, his dull, programmed monotony lit a fire in me. It was that rarest of moments, when my anger overcame my timidity, rushing from my inside to the outside, a torrent bottlenecked solely by the width of my mouth, too narrow for what the occasion called for. 'God curse you!' I was screaming. 'To hell and back!'

Haris was so taken aback he actually jerked back really hard. The employees and patrons around us froze, then whipped around to look at poor Ahmad, who by this point was turning red. In all his working days, he'd probably never expected he'd be the centre of such attention—a possibility the training manual had skipped.

'This is a promotion,' I thundered. 'Do you even know what the hell that is?'

Ahmad shook his head, though his hands shook faster.

'Of course you don't, you idiot.' I seethed. 'You don't even speak English, but everything in this stupid restaurant is in English.'

By this point, Ahmad's lips were twitching. 'You do not want promotion?' he burbled, hoping his intervention might restore the restaurant's reassuring regulations. But his words only made things worse.

'No, we don't. Are you deaf?' I must've been yelling loud enough for them to hear me at Trianon Café. And then, it roared out of my mouth: 'Indana ikhtiyar!'

Silence. Except for the air-conditioner, which didn't understand how provocative my words were. Instead, it hummed on, fitting background to a moment that could only properly be rendered in whitewashing nothing, the thick lull of a blizzard that simultaneously deafens and awakens. The great conspiracy to sell Egypt's soul for bargain basement prices was being resisted at register three. By me. A Punjabi. Living a Karbala dream in his dream.

Ahmad, meanwhile, was approaching cardiac arrest. The pathetic man took a step right, fumbled left and then nearly flipped over backwards, in desperate hope that Big Brother Manager might find him and fix things. Ahmad turned only to return a few minutes later, inviting us to sit upstairs, in wait for more fulfilling service. Then he handed us our drinks and apologized for the delay. Slowly, everything was returning to instruction manual ground zero.

Haris slapped me on the back. 'Good job, yaar.'

We sat down at a little table crushed up against the big glass window. (One shove and my room-mate and I would've crashed down on to the molten sidewalk.) The manager showed up after a few minutes, a stumpy plump man who reminded me of a thumb, albeit one dressed in navy blue pants, a periwinkle shirt and an intrepid red tie.

Out came his hand, first to Haris and then to me. 'Salam alaykum,' he greeted. 'My name is Muhammad.' But of course. He sat down beside us. It was his restaurant, in a way. 'I must talk to you about what you said to Ahmad downstairs.' His face as pale as a brown man's can be, perhaps a muddled vanilla. The analogy reminded me of our food.

'I'm sorry for yelling,' I confessed. 'But I get so damn angry dealing with all this incompetence. In truth, I'm still mad. We should have a choice.'

Muhammad treaded carefully, sensing my upset. He darted his eyes left and right, making sure no one was listening to us. Who would spy on a conversation in a McDonald's, I wondered. 'The problem was not your yelling,' Muhammad clarified.

'So what was the problem?' I asked.

'You cannot speak of choice so casually,' Muhammad replied. 'Imagine what will happen if people think about it too much. Our country will turn into a Western country, where people only have rights and no responsibilities, thinking they are equal to their God. They make money so that they can buy things. Then they die. Then the same will happen to our beloved Egypt.'

'I think you're going too far,' I said.

'I am looking at the future.' He was watching Egypt being overrun by storm-troopers while I was thinking of a cheeseburger. 'You are looking at quarterly profits, my brother.'

'I don't see what this has to do with a combo meal...'

'It has everything to do with a combo meal! Don't you see how your reaction to this meal could ruin everything? It could even lead to secularism.' I admired the restraint, for he was as angry as I had been just a few minutes ago when I'd let everything loose. 'Soon, it will be like the West here. I choose this, I choose that. I don't want to do this and I don't want to do that. I only listen to me. I only care about me. What about God?'

Ahmad dropped the food off at our table and vanished just as soon. The fries before us smelled delicious, but

Muhammad's worries were in the way of our satisfaction. To get to our food, it would be necessary to get rid of him. A few simple twists and turns and I'd make him cannon fodder, to be ground down and processed into the next hamburger he sold. That's really how they invade, you know. Inside sandwiches. While our leaders fight to make bigger missiles.

'But what if there was a Muslim choice, different from the Western one?' I asked, getting Muhammad's attention very quickly. Most Muslims want the progress and development of the West, without feeling that they've been secularized. 'You see, in secular societies—most of which are Western—choice is a right. That's why Muslims are so afraid of choice, because we think it'll make us godless. But what if choice was not viewed as a right but as a responsibility?' I leaned towards him: 'That, my brother, is how I see it: I have a choice, but it is my duty to exercise it.'

Muhammad's closed eyes were beginning to dissolve into an opening, through which my thoughts might flow. 'Please, my brother, continue,' he said.

'In the Qur'an, God tells us He created humanity to worship Him. But He also tells us that there is no compulsion in religion. Are these two in opposition or cooperation? For if they were in opposition, as the opponents to choice argue, then we would be saying that there is a contradiction in the Qur'an.'

'May God forgive us!' Muhammad whispered.

'Consider, my brother, that God has asked us to follow Islam. All of us, not some of us. Therefore, we all have the responsibility to exercise choice. If something is a responsibility, it is a duty but also a right. To deny people the responsibility given to them by God is to challenge God.'

'God will destroy those who challenge him,' Muhammad noted.

'And have we not been destroyed, my brother, for refusing to grant those responsibilities that God demands of all humanity?'

'But what if this leads to secularism?'

'It may or it may not.' I grasped his hand. 'I only ask: Would you accept what I have to say?'

'Only if it is good for Islam.' And then Muhammad began to glow, radiating with the promise of throwing down dozens of shahs. 'Because I must consider if this idea is good for my obedience to God. I would ask the scholars whose learning I respect. But I would also read the Qur'an and hadith, because I cannot make a choice unless I think about it very much.'

Flawless victory. 'And why is that?'

'Because on the Day of Judgement, God will ask me...if I made the right choice...and I could only make the right choice if I considered all sides of the issue.' His head was bobbing up and down, in fact to the rhythm of a pop song on the speakers. Which meant my work was done. There was no going back for Muhammad. He was all but a fry in so much ketchup, out of the container and drenched in something better. Shaking our hands, Muhammad left in a hurry, tearing his cellphone out of his pocket and almost dropping it in excitement. I wondered who he'd call.

A good ten minutes later, we were done, and made our way down the stairs and past Ahmad, who waved hesitatingly in our direction. He pointed, cautiously, to the exit.

'What is it?' I asked.

Haris clutched my arm tight enough to cut off the circulation. 'Look...' His voice faded away as he saw my eyes move towards the door.

We rushed out in excitement, finding ourselves stuck in

a crowd that ended only a few feet from the door. There must have been thousands of Egyptians, their fists like minarets held up to the sky. A giant poster was draped over both sides of the al-Nabila Hotel, screaming populist might: 'Maak Ikhtiyar?' Got Choice?

The crowd was marching for Mustafa Mahmud. A smaller contingent made north, while rumours circulated of mobs on the bridges, in Zamalek, Doqqi and even Khan al-Khalili. But the view to anywhere was obscured by hundreds of flags, for Egypt and Palestine together. Our voices joined a swelling chorus. This was going to change all of Egypt, I understood, and from Egypt outwards, till an obscure fast-food restaurant incident consumed the Ummah.

We spotted a crowd of Egyptians huddled around several flat-screen TVs, broadcasting updates as soon as they came through. The common soldier was establishing justice, arresting members of the corrupt elite—the criminals who'd hidden behind the trappings of power for far too long. Some of the aristocrats even arrested themselves, an event enjoyed by all. Mubarak conceded defeat, stepped down, and elections were called for the coming month of Muharram. A new year. A new Egypt.

'Because Allah has given us ikhtiyar,' the rector of al-Azhar announced, in his address to the country. He then ordered the formation of a council to draft a constitution for the Islamic Republic.

To this, cheers went up, but even these were fast lost in the general roar.

'Let's go back for that apple pie.' Haris smiled. 'Maybe I can get one for free.'

who knew abd al-bari?

I woke up from my dream just as they were forming the rows for fajr prayers. I joined in, but only because I wouldn't leave a good impression slumped halfway over myself while they prayed. Unfortunately, action meant purification—in their bathroom, which stank like a stable, making me tiptoe to the sink, afraid to touch anything, even the water, which rivalled ice. I performed the swiftest ablution in Egyptian history, returning to the prayer area just as Rojet cried God's greatness. I thanked God for making the morning a few hours away. I'd stay up with them after prayers, feign some more helpful interest, and then leave. I could sleep away the day once I got back to our apartment.

Scratching gunk out of my eye, at the same time fascinated by how fast it accumulated, I joined their circle. While they praised God, I wondered if I had bed head. What distressed me much more, however, was Rojet's animated speech. How anyone could be so motivated at such a fantastic hour eluded me. He talked like a cartoon character, big eyes bouncing around, hands waving this way and that, like he was flying through the sky and calling home to tell someone about it. But of course he wasn't. He was in a masjid, with several other followers, right before the crack of dawn, discussing what I imagined they discussed every day. Suicide.

Rojet leaned towards me. Gliding from Kurdish to Arabic. 'You're not tired?'

His speech was a time-delayed grenade, only slowly exploding—the shock wave boomed well after the echo bounced. This caused me, and probably everyone else around, to feel like we were perpetually lagging behind. Hit by the bullet before you heard the gun go off. 'My body's tired,' I said. And it was. My head was heavy, my eyes hurt and my right leg ached. But, 'My mind's not.' It was bright as day in my mind. Because of Rojet.

'And?' he asked.

'And what?'

'And why are you here?' His disciples enjoyed the moment at my expense. Not a very Islamic attitude, was it? 'You are sitting in our circle, though no one asked you. A tent has four pegs, not five.'

'I thought that since I prayed with you, I could maybe listen, too.'

'You had no choice but to pray with us. If there is a congregation and a man can join it, he must.' He shook his head. 'But you do not have to listen to me. You may get up and leave.'

Was that a dare? He must have thought I was weak, emasculated, a fake and fraudulent. Worst of all, tolerant. 'No, I want to listen.'

'What if you could not?'

I took care not to sound too angry. 'Why not?'

'Because,' he said, 'I'm asking questions now.'

'I can answer your questions,' I nodded.

'Are you sure?'

'You don't believe I can answer them?'

'I believe you can.' Rojet straightened his back and asked the first. 'So, my brother, tell me. Tell us. Why did you come here to see us?'

I'd rather have washed myself with more of their ice water than have answered. Especially with Wanand so near and so eager to hear what I had to say. Thus mine was a roundabout approach. 'If you mean to ask why I came to Cairo, it was to study Arabic for the summer. But if you're asking why I'm here in your masjid, I came for the Mawlid. But I got lost and—'

'You were lost?'

A fake sigh. 'Yeah, sort of.' Deception comes in many forms. 'I was really just sick and tired of America. The place burns you out, you know?' Maybe he didn't know. 'I thought that being in a Muslim country would be different, that maybe coming to Egypt would make it easier to improve myself.'

There were murmurs of approval in the circle, brief smiles and burning eyes, looking relaxed, relieved, a little vindicated. Though Rojet was silent, measuring his mouth with his thumb and index finger, much as thinkers do.

He finally spoke. 'So, let me understand. In order to improve yourself, you came to a festival where Sufis dance around a dead man's tomb?'

Every lie has its fallout. I tried another tack. 'Well, I got lost at the festival and...'

'You lie!' He leaned forward like he was going to pound into my head but he retreated just as fast as he'd burst forth. A calmer anger took hold. 'You were lost long before the Mawlid. You came here because you had gone everywhere else. What else would make a person travel halfway around the world, from a flourishing civilization to a faded one? You watched people who expect their mourning for a dead man to represent Islam, their collective guilt violating our belief in individual responsibility.' His pace didn't allow me a second to gather myself, to even prepare a response. 'Anyone with ears can tell you what they heard. A man running, becoming louder, slowing and then, finally, stopping. When I first spotted you, your expression revealed everything. These words you offer now, they are nonsense.'

'I don't—'

'Quiet your useless tongue.' He slumped his shoulders, so that he looked a little bit more like me. Not very flattering. 'This is how you appeared. A man who ran to the end of his rope, found that it ended at our masjid door, but could not understand why.'

Though I was terribly afraid he'd call me out on it again, I tried ducking his argument. 'I don't know why you're so angry with me. I told you I was looking for something.'

'What were you looking for?'

'Maybe I was running after myself.'

And that was all it took. A happy laughter overcame him. 'You ran after yourself?'

'Figuratively speaking...'

'I understand.'

'So why is it funny?' I asked.

'Actually, it's beautiful.' Rojet sat back, resuming his previous posture. 'If God loves someone, He brings their inside outside so that they can see more clearly—the better to fix their problems. He makes them hurt, He makes them fall apart, He makes things unravel till there seems no chance of repair. So you were lost, running around. But you couldn't find what you were looking for, so you ended up here.' Rojet raised his arms, pointing to the dome, which I hadn't noticed before. That wimpy bulb fell from its centre. 'This is as obvious a blessing as they come. That you ran so fast and so hard and then, when you finally gave in, it was here. Do you not see a sign in this?'

I suppose I did. But I didn't dare say so. Rather, I stared about for several seconds, as if I was looking for the sign he mentioned. The other members of the Order, Immortals as Rojet called them, broke from their places in the circle as my silence continued. I heard the sounds of a village awakening to another day. Light spread into the masjid from the high, slim windows, revealing carpets an old, muddied red. They looked Mamluke and as if they hadn't been changed since then, over five hundred years ago. The walls alternated between dirty grey and puke green. The prayer niche was off-centre, closer to the left end of the wall and tilted slightly.

Did Rojet expect me to answer every question he asked, for the rest of the day? I'd stopped here during a failed task. I did not intend to live with him, and certainly not stick around to amuse him. 'I should get going.' I paused. 'My room-mate's going to be worried about me.' This time, I'd been gone the whole night.

'What are you going to do when you get home?'

'What am I going to do here?'

Rojet's smile began as he tilted his head downward. For the first time, I wanted to smack him upside the head. Turning his head away from me, as if something in me demanded such distance, he said, 'We can teach you about Islam.'

'I don't know what Islam you follow, Rojet.'

'We give our lives to God.' He tapped a finger on the carpet. Did it believe him? 'We will be martyrs in His path.'

I shouldn't have, but I laughed. 'A martyr gives his life for a cause.'

'If you march into battle and you know you will not come back, and in fact you do not want to come back, is that not suicide?'

No. 'Because you're giving your life for a higher cause. I mean, you're a martyr only if the act you undertake and the reasons and intentions behind it are pure and proper.'

Rojet smiled. 'If I give my life to God, and do not unjustly harm any others, am I not a martyr?'

'But you'd be harming yourself,' I countered, 'if it was a suicide.'

'I don't harm myself in battle?'

'It's not deliberate.'

'It isn't?'

To that, I had no response. Rojet, however, did. And how he gave it to me. 'You have never lived the answer, but you can produce it when called on to do so. You tell me what Islam is about, but you do not believe in the explanation you give.' He inched forward and placed his right hand along the side of my head, with just enough force to make it sting. I was afraid he might slap me, hard, but he didn't. Instead, he examined my skull, as if I was dead specimen of something understandably extinct. 'This head of yours,' he said, 'has led you astray.'

When one is afraid of the truth, one cannot answer it. When one sees someone who so believes in his words, he is made helpless. Rojet knew as much. 'Before this Ignorance returned to the earth, before these Humiliations that plague us, the world's peoples sustained themselves with the sacred. But in this day and age, whenever we are, that is absent. The body has conquered and the flesh has triumphed.' He let go of my head so I could face him again. I did so with some embarrassment, though I wasn't sure why. 'Why did God send Jesus, upon him peace, with such a spiritual message, while Muhammad, upon him peace, received a more balanced message?'

'The Children of Israel had become too worldly,' I said. Rojet's eyes forced me to carry on. 'Jesus came to emphasize the spiritual because it was being abandoned. Since Muhammad completed Islam's final cycle, his message was more balanced.'

'But now, the world is becoming too worldly, saving no space for our faith.'

'No space?'

'Islam is the ultimate truth.' He was happy with these words, or made happy by them. 'Would you say, let us give the truth some space? Let us accommodate it?'

'So instead you just say, give up, let's kill ourselves?'

I saw Kibr move in closer, keen to hear. He almost relished the aggressiveness I directed towards his master. 'Tell me,' Rojet said, 'if your enemy is a snake, what good is it becoming a snake? The only way to save ourselves is to give up on the world—'

'But what you're proposing is that we take our lives,' I interrupted.

'Is your life really yours?' And when I hesitated, he pounced. 'What is today's world based on?'

Frustrated for falling behind, I mumbled, 'Secularism.'

'On making every man a god. At times, he becomes his own god, though most men are weak and worship other men. Is that what Islam is based on?' Of course not. But Islam was not the world. 'Muhammad preached that he was returning people to their original religion, the religion of Abraham. Should we not be like Abraham, if he is in this way our father?'

'Abraham didn't kill himself.'

Rojet smiled condescendingly. 'This body, and the mind it holds, is the standard by which all things are judged. It is the idolatry of this day and age, and thus it must not only be resisted. Resistance is for the weak. They must resist us! We must be strong like Abraham. We must take our axes into our own hands and strike the idols down. After all, we do not worship what they worship.'

I didn't know what to say. But everything in me told me to contradict this, to introduce an opposition, to prevent him from having the final word. 'Why does this have to be a fight?' I didn't let him reply without explaining myself first. In other words, I spoke just like he spoke—and it charmed him. 'Why can't this be about us and not about them?'

'They have made it so. They practise divide and conquer, with us as societies and then with us as individuals. First they separated God from the political sphere, calling this political secularism. Then they separated God from the economic sphere, calling this economic secularism. They did this, bit by bit, till we became entirely deconstructed, told that we could still cherish our belief in God, though without any way of realizing it.' Rojet was not angry, nor even frustrated. His tirade was a measured, rehearsed one. 'We are the pitiable victims of a bloodthirsty comedy. A dark light from out of our reach invades our homes—beaming missiles, naked grenades, gunshot televisions, prancing bombs and smirking tanks. They have poisoned our oxygen and then they ask us why we are choking. They have hidden the sun and then they accuse us of blindness. They have locked the exits and then they tell us that we are free to leave. Are we to bang our heads against the world which we could never break through?' He met my eyes with a stern rebuttal. 'That is all you have ever done.'

'That's not fair,' I protested. 'You don't know me. You don't know anything about me. I've done much more than that.'

'You ran here, for one thing,' he offered. 'And then you told me that you were sick of it all. So you tell me. What have you done?' Not surprisingly, he heard nothing in response. 'For centuries, we have been fighting fire with fire—and we only burn faster. The more we learn, the stupider we get. The tougher we talk, the harder we are hit. It is worse now than it was twenty years ago, and believe me, twenty years from now, it will be worse than it is now. Finally, we have come, a promise fulfilled from ages previous. Though we are five, we are alive. Honour the Lord, for an answer is mightier than a thousand questions.'

Then came the glow that comes bouncing on the heels of a raging storm, a sudden, honest peace that muffles every distracting thought. I'd always been a coward. I would rather run than stand, argue than listen, ask than answer. But there was something about Rojet that begged me not to take my immediate distaste for conclusive difference. In other words, I wanted to know if he had the answer I'd fathomed existed somewhere out there. An Islam that made sense. To me.

So I asked him. 'How do you know when to go?'

'We are not equal,' he replied. 'As men we are, but as believers we are not.' He pointed to Kibr. 'He will be going third. Before Azad and myself.'

'What's the point of giving your life?'

'He is our goal, may He be praised.'

Well, I thought, at least it sounded orthodox. 'And who taught you this?'

'Abd al-Bari, may God have mercy on him, was the pole of poles. I was but a peg he drove into the ground.' And then he paused in honour of the man. 'What he taught is what I teach: We must die before dying. The world tells us that death should be fought against, hidden from or only whispered about, whereas we are taught to celebrate death. Ask yourself, do you disagree with this? Or is it only that you fear it? For if you disagree, it is for you to walk out this door, and no one here will think any less of you for it. But if you fear this path, then ask yourself, what is the worth of cowardice?'

'You think I'm a coward?'

He shook his head: 'You are quick to judge, and rather arrogant, but no more so than is the lot of your generation. In your heart, I know you care for this religion more than for any counterfeit reality.'

'How would you know that?'

'For years you were lost.' It was just barely more a sentence than a question. 'And now, you are here. If, in fear, you hide from the path, then not only do I offer you my pity, but my warnings. Turn away and you shall spend the rest of your life as you spent the first half of this night—running.'

I wanted to know if I would forget everything Rojet was saying to me after a few days, whether the brightness of his words would lose colour as all other reminders inevitably did. Or had he brought me an insight that would spark some change? Perhaps if I spent my life learning from him I would become another, but I thought my life too great a sacrifice. I wanted to ask him: Could I return?

Instead, it was Rojet who asked me, 'Do you not have somewhere to go?'

Surprised, and in fact offended, I shook my head. 'I thought you wanted me to sit and learn...'

'Does this look like a time for learning?'

And indeed it did not. Azad and Kibr were preparing themselves to leave the masjid, with bags wrapped around their shoulders. 'We have only a short time here, and then we are to leave. We must find places and people; we must know the possibilities of our actions and then ensure they are realized.'

'I can help.' But I felt myself the type of little horror who isn't really a horror, except that no one wants him around.

'Are you Immortal?' Rojet stood, reaching to gather things. 'Or are you as physically alone as you are emotionally?'

'Well, my room-mate...'

'Then go to him.' Rojet was barking out orders. To the others, too, but in Kurdish. 'What kind of a Muslim would you be if you cared only about yourself?'

I would be me.

It was fair to think that Kurds were, like Egyptians, kind people—so what had Rojet shown me but mandatory hospitality? It was not extraordinary, after all, for a good Muslim to invite in a tourist lost late at night with no other place to go. And then he had talked to me for some time after prayers—a time of day men like him were awake anyway. He hadn't even offered me food, unless I considered his talk a kind of nourishment. I was a fool for thinking a man of Rojet's stature could be attracted to me. Me, who was down and depressed, had seen in him some spark of something other, higher, upper or elsewhere, yet of course I was not to him what he was to me. I had nothing to do but go back to the apartment.

A man had lit a fire inside of me and then abandoned me to the flames.

no time for games

Outside were brown buildings and brown grounds, relieved by the dinginess of children in blue or grey gallabiyahs. Unfortunately, both directions looked the same to me—I couldn't figure out my return. Thank God Keyf Khoshi came out the door just after me, a thick cloth wrapped around his head, dangling down the sides and brushing his beard, and a bag over his shoulder. He looked a little strange for the summer.

'Salam alaykum.' Keyf put his hand out, dropping his bag in the process. I tried not to laugh but I couldn't help it. To defend himself, Keyf spoke perfect English. 'I knew that was going to happen.'

Rather taken aback, I asked, 'How do you know English?'

He was so pleased with himself, he avoided the question. It seemed one of their talents: personal contentment legitimated the imposition of exclusive rules for conversation. You ask, so I ask, too. 'Where are you going now?' Keyf asked.

'I'm going to my apartment. I didn't seem too welcome back there.'

This made Keyf shake his head. Later, I would learn that everything made him do that. 'Nonsense, nonsense. You're always welcome here. We were all very happy that you came and talked to us, and we will be happier when I tell everyone you want to come back.'

'You're happy I came?' Maybe they didn't get visitors. Maybe Kurds felt lonely. The last century had been pretty ugly. Which made me think: What were Kurds doing in Cairo anyway? And why hadn't I wondered about that before? Unique among many Muslim countries, including the Pakistan that could have been my home, Egypt was pretty homogeneous.

'Why do you speak Kurdish, Keyf?'

He smiled. 'Because I'm a Kurd.' Then he looked at his watch, exhaled and agreed with himself. 'Time is short for us, and so it's short for you. But still, we wouldn't want to overwhelm you. You can't learn everything in one day.'

Again. 'Why are there Kurds in Cairo, Keyf?'

'We saved this city once,' he smiled. 'Remember?'

'You mean a thousand years ago?' And then it dawned. 'You're still here?'

'Well, not me, exactly.' Keyf scratched the back of his head. 'You see, we're some of their descendants. Salah al-Din chose us to come here to wait for something to happen, and that's happened. So now the Order of Light begins its mission. We're going to do to Egypt what would have been done to her enemies.'

I was ashamed to ask questions, because his story embarrassed me. So I justified it: When I was back in wealthier circles, at some posh dinner party, we'd share stories, laugh over them and remind one another how lucky we were to be in the sensible, rational West. 'So you're going to save the Muslim world,' I asked, 'or just Egypt?'

'We've already lost the Muslim world. That's why we're here.'

He was skirting something, but he didn't want to tell me what it was. Either that or he didn't know how to keep the conversation going.

'Where are you going now?' I asked him.

'I have to check some addresses.'

'Are you going anywhere nearby?' In other words, help me get out of here.

'Not so far,' he said. 'Which way are you going?'

'Agouza.'

'Great.' Nod. 'You can come with me.'

Keyf's head seemed loosely attached to his neck. It would start to wobble, and he'd jerk it back into place. I wouldn't have noticed it except that during the length of our walk, he kept doing it, leading to abrupt ruptures in an otherwise casual conversation.

As we turned the corner on to a larger, cleaner street, he pointed to his bag. 'You remind me of me.' Better him than the bag, but still quite surprising for someone who'd just met me. Thankfully, he explained further. 'We may have very similar backgrounds.'

'How so?'

'It's a strange story,' he admitted.

'I've got time, Keyf.'

'Well…' He looked away. 'Have you ever watched the movie *Good Will Hunting?*'

I couldn't help but stop. 'Yeah, I have.'

Thank God we were having this conversation in English.

'I know it sounds funny.' Not really. Just inappropriate. 'I grew up in a wealthy family. We had many conveniences, including a satellite dish. Me and my brother, may Allah have mercy on him, first watched the movie some years ago. But we caught it about two-thirds of the way through, watching the end and feeling mystified. And then they showed the film again.' He wanted me to react to this, but I didn't know how to. 'What I meant is, well, we watched the conclusion and then the introduction. It was like knowing the answer before hearing the question. You can imagine what that does.'

'It certainly kills the plot,' I mused.

'We knew what William was doing, but we didn't know why.'

'This made you join the Order?'

'This was well before the Order. It was the way that the movie kept getting replayed on that channel.' A snap of the head and he was back on. 'I thought to myself, why am I hesitating in accepting something I believe is true?'

'I think that sometimes.'

'Exactly!' He patted my chest with his hand. 'I'd listen to Rojet and think, he's got something very important to say, and not just for us Kurds. But then I'd come back to my comfortable life, and I'd want to forget—until forgetfulness failed me.'

'It failed you?'

Another snap. 'Watching that movie made me realize that I'd want for more things, all my life. The movie ended and then it began again. But death chooses us and then what?'

I thought I got it. 'No second chances.'

'Either you understand by the time the end comes.' Once more, his head cracked back. It looked mighty painful. 'Or you die and there's no chance for comprehension.'

Keyf pulled at his bag again, bringing it to the top of his shoulder, and gestured with his hand, showing me the way home. As we parted ways, I began to think over what he had said. Because Keyf reminded me of me. Why did Muslims dismiss the outwardly Islamic and embrace the externally Western? Keyf was someone I wanted to trust, even if he was claiming far-fetched mythology. Some of his story I could make myself believe. But his last revelation was simply too much. Did he think all of this was a game? And even if he did, why would he play it with me?

the undying might of the west

Were anyone to have asked me the time, I would've guessed it was eight o'clock in the morning, precisely the time I'd normally be staggering to the bathroom. But not this Wednesday, negotiating as I was a maze of dirty, cramped streets, unable to pinpoint where the mud ended and the buildings started. My ankles cracked with every step, till I was afraid they might snap off and stay behind, not willing to return to modernity with me. Then there was that burning in my stomach from not eating or drinking for so long. Most of the Egyptians I passed either ignored me or looked at me curiously, confused by the paradox of my clothes against my circumstances. And I wanted it all to go away.

Maybe I could make it go away. Maybe, with a long nap, a meal and a hot shower. In comparison to the severe stench of animal faeces, softened only by occasional gusts of diesel fumes, I remembered our bathroom as the best place on earth. How wonderful that paradise of soft grey tiles and shiny mirrors, one behind the sink and another just above it. Tearing off my sullied clothes, I would toss them into the washing machine, I'd throw in a box of detergent—yes, the whole box (we'd go to Metro and buy another later)—and climb into the shower, relaxing under its drizzle. But if Keyf hadn't been lying—and I assumed for a moment that he hadn't—then there would be no Metro. And the people who shopped there would likely be lynched.

I had skipped Sayyidna Husayn, walking on to a main street that ran alongside al-Azhar. I hadn't spotted it because my hand had been running against its wall for a good several metres. Were my feet endowed with speech, they would've thanked me profusely. I'd cut out a considerable number of blocks and reached the primary avenue where a dozen taxis gathered next to Egyptian commuters battling over who'd gotten there first. My clothes were gross, but they were Western. This would be very easy. I stepped to the edge of the street, well past the crowd, and watched with amusement as each and every cab slammed on the accelerator and raced towards me, in their haste for my foreign cash. The commuters behind me were aghast. How quickly they'd lost what seemed a sure thing.

I picked the newest cab and fell into the backseat.

'Masrah al-Balloon,' I whimpered. 'Agouza.'

A worrisome U-turn and we were on the elevated highway, speeding past light traffic, blazing towards the Nile, and then beyond. I craned my head out the window to the crowds of Egyptians filling the streets below, congregating on the sidewalks as the morning gathered steam, clumps of them busy on every sidewalk, waiting for something or nothing. But none of them appeared to me as they would have yesterday. I felt enormous sadness for them. Seeing rundown, broken Cairo, I understood the possibility of Keyf's claim. How could this place survive any shock? How would its people function in the event of tragedy?

Their leaders—our leaders—were either too stupid, or too cruel—depending on whether I wanted to be an optimist or a pessimist—to help them. Nor was that material. It was terrible under colonialism, but not unbearable. Back then, the people had a cause to fight for, a leadership to rally around, and a visible enemy to oppose. But having fought under the banner of imitative ideologies, and suffered the direction of self-serving despots, the Cairenes found themselves here. Nowhere. One theory after another is first lauded, then implemented and finally discarded, futile hopes of doing more than surviving, but perchance thriving.

Nationalism, secularism, socialism and the promise of pan-Arabism. And then 1967. BANG! Four digits like bullets. After which a respite, the happy consequences of the big oil boom, with the Arabs temporarily resurgent. In Afghanistan's mountains and valleys, over Communist cannon fodder and artillery volleys, a rag-tag army defeated the fearsome Soviet Union. We'd slipped to the right, but it wasn't real: it was a charade. The people were not more Muslim, but only looking for that which made them somehow different— Islamic movements, as if moving was all that mattered. They reduced Islam to the here and now, and now it's later. Allah Hafiz. We started left but ended West. The paralysis of defeat. The confusion after retreat. So where did we go next?

Right before we parted ways, Keyf had made an unforgettable offhand comment. He made it under his breath, in Arabic no less, but it was straightforward enough: 'There's so many kids.' Had I just arrived in Cairo, I would have said the same. But having lived here for several weeks, the number of children—indeed, the enormous population—appeared ordinary now. So what about Keyf, who'd probably lived here his entire life?

'What do you mean, Keyf?' I'd asked. 'There's always been this many kids.' I turned in bewilderment, only to find him looking guilty. Why?

'I didn't mean that. I don't know what I was thinking.'
He put his hand on my shoulder, which only frightened me.
His hand was trembling. 'If you want to get out of here, go
straight till you spot a restored Egyptian house with a big
yellow construction sign on it. Turn left at that alley and
you'll see Sayyidna Husayn. From there, you can make your
way.'

For the love of God! 'Keyf!'

'Yes?'

'Why did you say that?'

He looked through me for a few minutes, but he couldn't
hold: he wasn't the teacher, just a peg hammered into the
ground. 'Rojet tells us certain things, but not everything.'
Keyf was appraising his bag's strap. It was dark blue. His face
was deepening red. 'Just a few weeks ago, everything changed.
This was the Cairo I was too young to remember. I mean, this
is the Cairo I was too young to remember.'

'What the hell does that mean?'

He looked behind him, and down both alleys, away from
me as he spoke. 'I'm thirty-five years old.' He dropped his
shaking hand from my shoulder. 'I was born three years ago.'

'That doesn't make any sense.'

'I know.' He cleared his throat. 'About six weeks ago,
there was almost nobody in Cairo. Now, the city is bursting
with life. Like it was when I was a child.' Then he was
shaking his head. 'No, not like it was. It is as it was.'

I coughed to suppress my laughter, but I ended up
laughing anyway. Because his explanation was so bizarre.
'Keyf, this is the dumbest thing I've ever heard. You want me
to believe that you're all Kurds from the future, but descended
from some hero from the past, and now you're going to go
take your lives to save Egypt?'

'I can't make you believe it. But then again, I can't make you believe anything.' He checked his watch, almost dropping his bag as he did. But the bag didn't fall this time. 'If God wishes to do something, who are we to say it's not possible?'

'There is one thing you can tell me though.'

'What's that?'

'Where's your brother now?'

'He's not born yet. He was four years younger than me.' There Keyf paused. 'But I'm still alive. I mean, I'm just a baby. Who hasn't watched *Good Will Hunting* yet.' Which was his way of telling me to drop the topic, I think.

'So what happened to your brother?'

'I told you, he isn't born yet. He was my younger—'

I cut him off. 'No. I mean, in that other—what is it—I mean to say, you did watch *Good Will Hunting*. You remember watching it with your brother. So that was real, which means your brother was real, too. Did you leave him behind in that other world?'

'He was martyred in the wars.' Keyf noted my confusion, but his intervention only made it worse. 'He died defending Cairo.'

a world for the worldly

The taxi driver cut off Gamiat al-Duwal before a gas station, turning on to the street before ours. When we were about to make the last right, I saw Rehell slumped at the edge of a miserable curb, his butt only barely above his feet, in his hands an almost emptied bottle of water. He didn't see me, but I ordered the taxi to stop anyway. I regretted it almost immediately: what could I tell Rehell about what had happened to me?

The slam of the taxi door startled Rehell. He struggled up, with the help of a hand on someone else's car, and rushed forward to say salam. And begin another lecture. 'What the hell happened to you, mate? I've been waiting here for hours.'

For hours? 'I was at the Mawlid.' Sort of. I spotted Zuhra outside the masjid, and gave chase. But instead of catching her, I unearthed a small Sufi order preaching sermons of suicide. If I harmed myself, their leader explained, nothing could harm me again. And do you know what, Rehell? Part of me wants to believe him.

We were sitting between two old Toyotas. 'It's bloody nine o'clock in the morning,' he roared. 'Haris stayed up all night, worried about you. Poor fellow's stressed himself sick.'

It wasn't like any of this was intentional. 'You see,' I began, 'I was somewhere behind Sayyidna Husayn, and I got lost. There was this masjid with its lights on, and what was I supposed to do? It wouldn't have been smart to try and find my way back so late at night.' Rehell wasn't buying it, so I added, 'I fell asleep there, and left as soon as I woke up.'

'Haris called me at five this morning.' Rehell produced a bottle of water from somewhere. 'He thought maybe you'd forgotten your keys, or something terrible had happened.'

The keys were still in my pocket, next to my passport. 'I wish I'd been able to call...'

'You look like crap, mate.'

'Thanks, Rehell.' I tried to smile.

'Do you know why I'm up this early?' Obviously not— he asked just to emphasize his righteous wrath. 'Haris called at six, to tell me he was going to sleep. He asked me to stay up for you, just in case. So that's what I've been doing. Up and waiting for you.'

Wonderful, Rehell. I can barely hold myself up, and you make me feel guilty.

'I'm going to say some things,' he said. 'I hope you don't take them the wrong way.'

'How can I take them the wrong way if I don't know what they are?' I sipped at the water, but wished it was Listerine instead.

'There's something wrong,' he said. 'With you.'

'What's wrong with me?' Go ahead. Tell me. Everyone else has.

Rehell looked at the water like he was claiming it. (It was his water, after all.) 'You got back from a festival a whole day late. Don't tell me you got lost, mate, because that can't be it. And there's something else.'

'I'm a dork.' I tried to brush him off, but I only dismissed myself. 'I always get myself into the most ridiculous situations, taking the wrong turn, forgetting papers, dropping things. It's a wonder I don't kill myself.'

He didn't buy that, either. 'Mate, you weren't like this before, were you? I mean, I barely know you, I can't tell for sure, but I can tell that you're two different people inside— two people so different that they can't stand each other.' Rehell inched closer. 'Don't you know what you are? You say the most profound things about the world, about religion, about the people in this world who try to follow that religion, and we find ourselves thinking about it days later. Not just me, but Mabayn, too. We talk about it at night and sometimes I tell my other friends.'

'Even Mabayn?'

He ignored that. 'How does someone with that kind of impact on the people around him, how does he disappear at a Mawlid? How come he's always drowning, trying to pull himself out, but finding himself too weak?' He wanted me to answer this, but I wanted to fall down. Or maybe leave. 'You're seriously drifting, mate,' Rehell concluded.

What the hell was I, a log? But I supposed the analogy held. We were of a big brown tree, great and good. But worrying about how high we could reach rather than our relations with the forest we were a part of, we grew arrogant. In this blindness, we had missed the lumberjack with that thing in his hand. Call it an axe. He chopped us down and divided us up. We were shipped, by sections, then ground down and sliced up some more, made into perfectly white, blank sheets of paper, with little blue lines on each page.

'I do feel empty, Rehell,' I admitted. 'I go through most of my days only because I don't know what else I could do with the time.' Couldn't I just banish him from my sight? Though I knew what I said could also free me. 'Sometimes, I think about very serious things, but at other times, I don't give a damn about those things. What is depth if I'm afraid of it?'

'Why would you let yourself do this to yourself?' I wanted to give him a notebook and tell him to interview me later.

'I don't know how to do anything else.' I stole the last sip of water and then continued. 'This is who I am. You might not like it. Sometimes, I hate it. Actually, most of the time—' I tried to laugh, except he and I knew it was forced—'but I can't change what I am.'

'You can change, mate.' He became very excited. Was it time for his fajr? 'All these bad things that happen to you, these negative feelings, I think they're God's way of talking to you. Telling you that you need to change. Mate, He wants you to change.'

Maybe. 'So God makes us and then makes signs to change us?'

How fast his bubble burst. 'I suppose so. I mean, yeah.'

'Why doesn't He just make us change, then?' I paused. 'I mean, He gives us signs. He gives us clues. If that hadn't happened to you, you would've died—it's a miracle! That's what people say. But it's not. There's no such thing as miracles. Everything is just what God decided it to be.'

He paused to ponder. 'Is that what you really think?' Rehell asked. As I asked myself: How and why had I been taken in by a man as naïve as Rehell? Did he really believe that you only had to make the decision to believe, and then you were automatically enlightened, and everything made sense?

'Look, Rehell.' I sighed. 'Nothing makes any sense. You

can say, "Islam is rational," but it's not. It's just a leap of faith. People say, look, we proved it to ourselves, but you can't prove anything to yourself, and you certainly can't prove anything to anyone else. You can only make a choice—and that choice depends on a lot of things.'

'But Islam is so simple.'

'Islam is simple, according to what? Islam makes sense, according to whom?' I wiped the dust off my jeans. 'I used to believe them when they said people who believe, they're happy, blessed, content. I don't believe that any more, Rehell. People who believe are angry, cursed and confused. They often die in prison, or they're persecuted, oppressed and ridiculed. And what of Islam? If Islam is the truth, why is the truth such an awful failure?'

Defeated. But. There he was trying his best not to be. 'I thought your culture and your religion were so lovely, mate. The way things still made sense here, in a way they don't anywhere else.'

'I'd just learn Arabic and leave, Rehell.' I handed him back his water bottle, though all he did was place it between his feet. 'They say, in Islam, the most important thing is to believe in One God. And the unforgivable sin is to associate others with God. So by that measure, we Muslims are still better than non-Muslims. So why are we punished, while they live lives of wealth and prosperity?'

'This world is for those who love this world.'

'Whatever, Rehell.' It was a lame excuse. A coward's excuse. 'It might be for them, but why does it have to do everything possible to extinguish us?'

He tried one more time. He really tried. 'Nobody's better than anyone else, mate. Neither Muslim nor non-Muslim. So don't judge things that way, else you'll go mad.'

'We might all be equal,' I countered. 'But are our beliefs?' I checked my watch, making it clear he had nothing more to say to me. 'They're just choices, Rehell. People make choices and the world decides whether those choices are good or bad. And then we die.'

Rehell's hand was tempted to find a place on my knee, to exude hospitality the way Arabs did. But he kept his still-Finnish hand away from me. Most people can't see it, but it takes a lot to be an Arab.

'Would you like something to eat?' Rehell knew what I knew. And all he could do was grin, faintly. Helplessly. And offer a broken man breakfast. 'We've got eggs and—'

'I'm tired,' I said. 'I need to sleep.' I cannot stay and make everything be the way you want it to be. Poor Rehell had fallen in love with Islam and so he'd fallen in love with us Muslims. But each Muslim he met—myself, Haris, Mabayn—was a disappointment. He must've been wondering how such an immense faith could produce such pitiful followers. And then, of course, his questions would become mine: If the followers are pitiable, how can the faith be immense?

Eventually, we all surrender. 'You have your keys, right?'

'Yeah.' I nodded. 'They're in my pocket.'

i dream of khosni

Was it this apartment that my heart missed only hours ago? Our room was filled with a light that should have suggested cleanliness, but only drew attention to the emptiness. Haris's laptop lay on the dining room table, surrounded by water bottles and half-finished boxes of imitation Oreo cookies. I slipped out of my shoes and entered the bathroom, staring at the shower but finding that my will to take advantage of it had evaporated. Inside the bedroom, my room-mate was snoring at a mighty rhythm. I changed out of my dirty clothes and into my pyjamas, and collapsed on to the bed.

In the only dream I remember from that sleep, Hosni Mubarak was performing his annual State of My Nation address, using the monopolized opportunity to announce his hope for peace with Ariel Sharon. Most probably, Hosni was stuck with last year's S-Class. But while broadcasting his outline for dialogue live on every channel of Egyptian television Hosni made what in retrospect must be considered a fatal mistake. Rather than say, 'Hosni Mubarak has the courage and the foresight to see that negotiations based on the unfair terms dictated by the occupying power and its sponsor,' Hosni began his capitulation with an unfortunate, 'Khosni Mubarak has the courage...' 'Khosni', not Hosni. Because Hebrew, unlike Arabic, has no 'h'.

It took all of Egypt about three seconds to register that their president, never elected despite all those elections, was an undercover Israeli, probably a Mossad agent. What a horrid way for Khosni to have blown his cover. Israeli Prime Minister Ariel Sharon explained to the *Jerusalem Post* that while Mossad did have agents throughout Egypt, the State of Israel would never directly interfere with Egypt's illegitimate government. And if it did, Sharon noted, would it really display such incompetence? Al-Jazeera reporters thought this an intriguing point, but nothing was going to change Egypt's mind.

The children of the Mother of the World, heirs real but really imagined to an empire that once threw down Persia in two unimaginable battles, decided Khosni was so much flotsam in comparison. Earth-shaking riots erupted in Cairo, Luxor, Tanta, Alexandria and elsewhere. Though Khosni deployed troops throughout the country, he must have known that the game was up. For too long, he had stifled a gentle people, and now he would pay for it: stuck in the Intifada to end all Intifadas without even a stone in his hand. Shaban Abd al-Rahim, Egypt's horribly dressed working-class pop superstar, broke into a studio and got himself a live broadcast, using it to call for retribution.

Chanting 'nahnu nakrah Khosni', the masses made clear that a state of dual sovereignty had emerged. Shaban himself played the part perfectly. Like an Arab Imam Khomeini, except not quite so intellectually, physically or spiritually imposing, he marched to the Presidential Palace, all the eyes of the world on his ample body and garish red shirt, impossible to miss even as he was surrounded by thousands. He stood face to face with the army, but those noble young men only emptied their guns into the air, declaring that they too were

Egyptians. The people sided with the people, a part of my dream that, sadly, surprised me. Once inside, with the cameras still rolling, Shaban ripped off his shirt (I closed my eyes and sought refuge in God) and with it, choked Khosni to death. From Rabat to Jakarta, Abidjan to Kazan, cheers of exultation erupted.

A One State began its rise, to lead the Sacred Compensation in the Great Overturning of the Humiliations. The Zionist Usurpation would be defeated. After decades of unimaginable conflict, a Caliphate of Light would shine rays of justice and splendour from its heart in liberated Jerusalem. But I woke up disturbed. The heart was diseased. The light was not bright enough. The jubilation was artificial, the victories were unsatisfying, and the final conquests were pointless. The darkness remained, much as it had been, albeit hidden; I sat up, shaking. Haris was still snoring and I had no idea what time it was—the curtains were tightly drawn—knowing only that I'd rested for many hours. And felt much worse for that. Sweat poured down the side of my face, and my chest thumped furiously, as if my heart would do anything to escape. None of Keyf's warnings had come to pass, but even then. I was sad; I couldn't sleep. I just wanted to cry for hours on end.

as flies to wanton boys

I woke up lying on my stomach, my head to my right, my eyes staring at Haris, who gazed back at me, though only one of his eyes was visible. The other was buried under a pillow.

'Where'd you go last night?' He tried to sound angry.

'I'm sorry.' Not entirely, but it helped. 'I saw Zuhra after you guys left. I tried to follow her but I got lost—'

He coughed. 'Zuhra?'

'You remember…'

'Yeah.'

'I was looking for a place to rest, and I found a masjid.' I paused. How much did I really want to reveal? 'I must've fallen asleep pretty fast, because I woke up early in the morning. I left right away.'

Haris tried to smile but it looked like he was about to cry. 'You're telling me that you slept over in a masjid and you didn't wake up for prayers?'

'No, I did.' I looked at the headboard. Unhelpfully boring. 'I mean, I slept through the night.'

'That's weird.'

'Why?'

'All the masjids here close for the night. They only open for prayers.'

'This was just a small masjid,' I replied, uncomfortable. It really is that easy to say too much. 'There weren't too many people. I only spotted it because I saw a light coming through the window.'

'Well, didn't the people there ask you who you were?'

'They did.' I should've thought before starting this conversation. 'I didn't know what to tell them, but they figured I was lost. I mean my Arabic sucks.'

'They didn't care that a stranger was sleeping in their masjid?'

'They're Muslims,' I said.

He bought it. 'That's true.'

Haris started to cough again, a violent fit that heaved the upper half of his body into the air, his right fist dancing spasms before his mouth. When he stopped, he fell back onto the pillow and turned deathly still. Out of fear, I praised God. Haris had gotten sick several weeks back, sending us chasing after doctors, tests, injections and more medicines but the illness had vanished of its own accord. Maybe staying up for me had brought it back.

I stood up and made my way to the air-conditioner, pointing to it, to make it look like I wanted to shut it off to make him comfortable—which I did—but more to check if Haris was still alive. His eyes, almost shut, focused on me. For a minute, I hovered at the foot of his bed, beside the window and an old television set that never worked. He kept looking at me.

'Do you need anything?' I asked.

With his left hand, he waved me off, and then gave up, sending his raised arm crashing down onto the side of the bed, his fingers dangling uselessly over the mattress. With his right hand, he pulled up the knotted blanket and hid his head underneath, revealing his feet in the process. I snatched his prayer rug, hanging off the end of his bed, and spread it out in the sitting room, performing the asr prayer. Afterwards, I sat and stared into space, letting the knowledge of Whom I'd just spoken to sink in. But the nagging buzz of a nearby fly interrupted me. It was to my right. Then it wasn't. Then it was near the dining table. Then it wasn't. Seizing an unopened bottle of water next to one of the lemonade chairs, I lunged, swinging at the fly but missing by a few inches—a mile for the fly.

I strolled over to the balcony with the bottle in my hand. Pressing my face against the glass door, I couldn't make out much. It was halfway between day and night, with the light from inside our apartment preventing me from seeing anything outside. To my right and only a foot away, the fly skirted the glass, unaware that this transparent solid stood in the way of what would soon be a much-desired escape route. In a release of denied ferocity, I launched my right hand forward and smashed the bottle, big with the weight of liquid within, into that damned little fly. Badly bruised, the fly fell desperately downwards, losing altitude fast. I'd all but crushed one side of it.

But still, it bounced off the window while it descended, looking for a way out. Why was it so hard to kill such a little thing? Each of its attempts at escape produced a disgusting clicking sound, the fly further injuring its mangled form. This made me shudder and pause: its attempts to flee were only making it die faster. Soon, however, pity subsided and irritation returned. I struck again, trapping the fly between my bottle and the glass for a gruesome second. And that was that. To God we belong and to Him we return. Swollen with pride, I released the bottle, the fly dropping towards the floor. But I wouldn't end it there. A half second later, my bottle returned, slamming against the window, over and over again, streaking guts and chitin across the glass. The fly was not only deceased, but had practically vanished. I saw no sign of any lingering anatomy, except a piece of wing stuck to the side of my water bottle. Cocking my head back, just like Keyf would, I chugged huge gulps from it, all the while eyeing the fly's ruined little limb, only inches from my mouth.

Between the entrance to our apartment and the elevator, there was a fat hallway, almost as wide as it was long, stairs going up and down on one side. The floor was covered by a speckled grey concrete which ran halfway up the walls, overtaken then by a bland white that reached and overcame the roof. In the corner of this square hallway, entirely our own—no one else lived on our floor, if it was fair to call it that—garbage was deposited, taken away once a week by someone I never saw. In this heap, I tossed the emptied bottle, stopping a moment to watch it start to roll towards the elevator. Turning back to the apartment, I heard someone coming up the stairs. In all our days here, we'd never encountered anyone on the stairs, though people lived above us and below us.

It was Azad, and he threw himself at me. 'Salam alaykum!'

I fell backwards, crushing the bottle underneath my left foot, doing an unnecessary injustice to all that was left of a departed insect. Surprised himself, Azad slipped back down the stairs, falling into that dark landing. When he recovered, he gazed up at me as if I'd pushed him down.

'You scared the hell out of me!' I wheezed.

'I didn't think you were outside your apartment.' Azad spoke perfect Arabic, too. The kind I found easier to understand, though there was something odd about it. 'I came up the stairs but I didn't know you were outside so we both scared each other.' His Arabic wasn't driven by the logic of communication, or even the proper pace of punctuation. Azad didn't know Arabic so much as he had memorized it. Then he flung his right hand out towards me, snapping it into position with an audible crack of the wrist.

'What are you doing here?'

'Everyone had somewhere to go except me because'—he paused right there—'they were busy, there's not much time for us and I had nothing to do, so I thought it would be nice to visit you, to know who you are and you should know we want to see you.' A long inhalation. For a shorter sentence: 'Wanand told me where he lived and that's where you live.'

Peculiarities of language aside, I was touched by Azad's coming all this way to see me. 'How did you know which apartment was mine?'

Azad smiled. 'Muhammad told me.'

'Who?'

'I mean the barber.' If the barber was named Muhammad, then what were his apprentices called? 'When I got here I saw a bright barbershop and it looked Western so I thought you probably went there. Did you get a haircut recently, because I remembered you had short hair. I asked the barber if he knew any foreigners and he said there were two, one taller and one shorter, and the taller one liked to run and you like to run.'

My face turned the colour of the barbershop. Red, that is. Not green.

But the Order was on my mind. And I wasn't in the mood to have my room-mate step out, wondering what the hell I was doing talking to a middle-aged man in a skullcap. So I eased our door shut behind me. 'Do you like coffee?' I asked. 'I know a great place on Gamiat al-Duwal. It's not too long a walk, either.'

'If you want, we could run,' Azad said with a smile.

The length of the stroll, I stole glances at Azad, trying to discover his Kurdishness. Of course I didn't know what Kurds were supposed to look like. Azad's eyes were a little too Turkic, but besides that, he could have been Egyptian. Lost in analysis, I barely noticed that he had stopped walking and been reduced to observing.

'It's good to see that this part of Cairo is already so modern.'

Modernization is, apparently, in the eye of the beholder. 'It is very developed,' I concurred.

He turned around the other way, to look at the buildings, but I stood in his way. 'You need to tell me something, Azad.' And so I told him what I needed to. 'I don't mean to bring this up here, but I can't just walk around and act like this is a normal conversation.'

'You mean because of what you learned about us?'

'Are you really going to take your lives?'

'Whatever we have to do I will do'—again with the awkward pause—'because we have to leave because there's no place for us here.' He looked down the street, maybe for the café I'd mentioned. 'The government will become angry and begin to oppress the people even more, but it is better that they start now, because they will look for people to blame and they will find the people who started the wars and they will find them and slow them. Then maybe we will have a chance.'

Azad gripped my elbow and motioned for me to keep walking, which I did, at his ambling pace. We passed the usually abandoned Big Boy restaurant, foolishly placed on the bad end of Gamiat al-Duwal, and searched for a potential crossing. Cairene traffic surged in an endless stream, leaving me wondering where all these Egyptians were going.

'Was the Cairo you remember like this?'

'No'—Azad swallowed—'because it's gone.'

the coffee nobody wanted

At Trianon, I ordered an apple tea—ever since I'd visited Istanbul a few years ago, I was obsessed—and Azad chose the same. After the waitress left with our orders, he confessed he had no idea what almost everything on the menu was. So when our drinks arrived, I was thankful he enjoyed what he'd picked. Then he pushed his glass cup to the middle of the tiny table, looking perplexed.

He tapped the wood as he spoke. 'I thought you said we were going for coffee?'

'Oh.' I don't even like coffee. In fact, I can't stand it. 'It's just an expression, really. Do you want to go for coffee? It's like saying, do you want to go have a drink, spend the night talking with friends, relax somewhere outside the house.'

'So why don't you just say that?'

'It's a lot to say, don't you think?' I shrugged. 'Besides, it's just an expression.'

'That sounds American'—he was suddenly laughing—'you say one thing and do another.'

'But, sometimes...' Was I really about to defend America? Not too loud, I told myself. I didn't want to die at Trianon. 'You say you're going for coffee, because you might not know what you want to get. In America, there are so many choices, and it's easy to change your mind because there's always something new, so you just say, let's go out for coffee.'

That was too much for Azad. 'Why go somewhere if you don't know what you're going for?'

Well, I ran to your masjid, Azad. And I got a friend out of that, even if he's going to put a bullet in his brain one day. 'The point isn't the coffee,' I tried to explain. This really was frustrating. 'The point is to go out and spend time with friends.'

'So why don't you just say you want to spend time with a friend?'

'I don't know, Azad.' All this trouble over words? 'It's just more efficient this way.'

'That sounds even more American!' He slapped his hand on the table, attracting the waitress's attention. I waved her off before she could come over, distracting me with her figure. 'That's how Americans are, right? They talk about coffee because they don't want to admit they're not independent, because if they want to spend time with friends they think they might seem weak. But everyone would only think they are people and need friends.'

I, too, pushed my apple tea to the side. For everything it was, it was still my country, wasn't it? Besides, I was sick of hearing Muslims pick on America for their shortcomings, their brainless governments and backwards thought processes. Most likely, Azad didn't have a clue what he was talking about. Like an angry preacher, he was just experiencing verbal diarrhoea. I decided I'd be Imodium.

'Have you ever been to America, Azad?'

'No, never.' He smiled. 'I've never even left Cairo.'

'So what is it with you and America?'

'Aren't you from America?'

Not quite an answer, but perhaps it would lead to one. 'Yeah. I study at New York University.' Like he cared.

He did, though. He looked horrified, withdrawing his hands from the table. 'Don't you remember what happened there?'

'Where?'

'In New York!' Again I had to deter the waitress, while an ignorant Azad reached for his apple tea, in need of its steaming assistance. 'It was very sad what happened in New York, but then they became so mad they were bombing everywhere and sending their army after everyone, chasing ghosts and invading countries and establishing colonies.'

What could possibly make the world, already so bad, any worse?

'What's going to happen in New York?' I asked. 'Is that what destroys Cairo?'

He got choked up. 'After they went after Iraq, things got worse, because all the people became so depressed. A lot of people will lose faith in things, even in their religion, and then in themselves. America will be so angry and violent they will scare the whole world and turn the whole world away from them. One day they will be sitting in a café with so much coffee but no friends.'

alphabets and atoms

Wanting to play the good Muslim, I paid our bill and walked Azad to the service road, waiting patiently while he hailed a cab, a formal salam and a moving hug forming his generous farewell. And then I was all alone, standing at the curb, buffeted by Trianon's artificial breeze, thinking infuriating thoughts. Azad was going to take his life, like his fellow disciples, at the discretion of his master—who would depart with them. Burned many times in the past, by institutions and fraudulent friends, I reserved judgement. But they were good people, full of a frustrated light, steeled to their purpose, without a hint of deceit. And if they left, then what of me? I would return to the world I knew a few days ago, an existence in which everyone's solution was everyone else's disagreement, mentalities that associated spirituality with inconsistency, religiosity with insularity.

Rojet's masjid could be only an intermission in an otherwise interminable monotony: Go to sleep, miss prayer, wake up, go to class, walk back home through the heat, argue with my room-mate, debate the meaning of promotions, swallow two cheeseburgers, miss another prayer. Every now and then, I'd dream of those missed prayers and spot myself in hell. There were still two more months of that before I returned. And then what would I do in New York? All praise is due to God for His methods. Should He wish a path upon us, He makes it impossible for us to contemplate any other path, lining what we might have considered alternatives with only heartache and headache. Already, I was sick of expectation, in comprehension that it was an illusion. Soon I'd be disgusted with existence as well.

And then what? That the world was empty was a given. That I could find holes in every person, and thus every answer, was understood. But could I find holes in their attitudes? I was too scared to put a gun to my head, too scared to be the direct cause of my departure—but I saw little so upsetting in a leap off a balcony, a rushed descent out of here. Were I not to show up at Trianon in the next few days, nobody—not even the friendly waitress—would miss me. Perhaps they'd wonder what became of that lonely foreigner, questioning each other in sideline banter, but someone would say, 'He's gone home.' And then they would worry about getting their orders right. They were just like me: they were circles revolved around a self-made axis. They chose a pivot, drove it into the ground, and shackled themselves to it. Would I too keep orbiting?

But the Order didn't treat me like a random visitor, a chance guest. They treated me like someone who was supposed to come, who was good for having come, and better for answering in ways they wanted me to answer. They shared with me their visions of the future, which perhaps could have served as warning. But just me, alone, what would my reactions do for that future? Unless they wanted me to leave this world, frightened by the prospect of returning to an America that was soon to start foaming at the mouth. The war to end all wars—because it would end all nations?

Signs come to us, clues, suggestions, and some devastating warnings, but we gaze at them only briefly, passing to safer, softer things, like the sand in which we duck our heads. Most of the men of Karbala let Husayn die, because he was not important enough for them to risk interrupting their daily monotony. In 1945, humanity saw the worst a worsted species could propose. Fighting a foe that had, for all intents and purposes, already been rendered harmless, America added a bonus, a Fat Boy and a Little Man for two cities that vanished two seconds later. Yet were I to ask an American about this, he would find some justification for this act, so evil that the entire world still lives in fear of it. And if something similar happened in the United States? Then, of course, they were eternally innocent. The perpetrator: a genetically defective beast race that happened to resemble, from afar, Westerner humans.

--------------------------------- **A a** ---------------------------------

a·gain 1. Once more, a second time, anew **2.** Referencing a prior place, location or period

a·leph 1. The first letter of the Arabic alphabet, probably evolved from a pictorial representation of a cow or an ox, as is the case with Hebrew **2.** The letter that represents the beginning

all 1. The whole amount or quantity: *All of Hiroshima and Nagasaki was destroyed*

A·mer·i·ca 1. Refers generally to the primary land mass of the Western Hemisphere, which consists of the two continents of North and South America, joined at the Isthmus of Panama **2.** Refers specifically to the popular republic of the United States of America, a democracy established in North America on lands seized or purchased from various indigenous peoples,

most of whom were driven to submission and then extinction
3. The first modern constitutional democracy **4**. A nation that
emerged after a successful revolt against British imperialism,
precipitated by British refusals to grant popular representation
to the American people **5**. A country that, until the 1960s,
practised legally enforced discrimination based on a person's
colour **6**. The prime supporter of late 20th century sanctions
on Iraq, which in total killed nearly half a million persons (see
also, terrorism, state-sponsored varieties of) **7**. The first
developer of the nuclear and hydrogen bombs; the latter
alternatively known as the H-bomb

―――――――――――――― **H h** ――――――――――――――

Hy·dro·gen 1. The second element

Hy·dro·gen Bomb 2. The second bomb

Hy·poc·ri·sy 1. American reality

A is also for 'are'. Are Muslims any different?
    But there's more to it than that. There's E, as in $E = mc^2$

―――――――――――――― **E e** ――――――――――――――

E·gal·i·tar·i·an·ism 1. The assertion of social, political and
economic equality for all persons **2**. Along with liberty and
fraternity, one of the three themes of the French Revolution
3. Prominent strain in American social and political thought
(see also, H)

Eve·ry·one 1. Every person: *The A-bomb killed everyone,
indiscriminately: the rich and the poor, the male and the
female, the innocent and the guilty*

But unlike others, I have a knowledge that prevents me from ignoring those reminding flashes of light. Because I understood death before I understood life. Whereas most people experience their youth as a time of promise, or at least a good deal of potential, I had been a sick child, and had nothing to revel in but burst veins, scar-tissue skid marks, holes in my arms from IV injections, things like that. The first doctor said, 'I'm sorry, but...' The second doctor said, 'You know, when a child is born so sick...' And the imam said, 'Children go to paradise...'

When I was fourteen and the radiation from countless X-rays had permanently damaged my bones, my doctor told me I might never have children. I, for impotent. I am impotent. I am irrelevant. I is for Islam, too. And E, for evolutionary dead end. E is for etcetera as well. When I was sixteen, they told me I had stomach cancer and I was pressed for time. My parents cried, 'He's dying. Again.' But it wasn't again. I was born dying and I lived dying, every day only closer to the inevitable. I felt my death a part of me, as much as my arms, my legs, my eyes and my mind. In that way, I was different from almost everyone else.

I knew something they did not. Something Azad and his fellow seekers also knew, though perhaps in different ways. To live forever, to escape our mortality, this is the sick dream that inspires the tyrants of the world, not the beautiful few who somehow manage to find solace—unless I is also for imaginary and impossibility. We are cowards, afraid not only of death, but also of the life that will lead us there. We cause others to suffer only so that our illusions can linger, if even a few years longer. E is for Emerson, too. When you strike a slave—whether he's a slave of another man or only of himself—you must also kill him.

these sufis do groceries

It was almost ten. With Azad gone and my stomach filled to the brim with a mix of hot and chilled liquids, it was time to go home and do nothing until I fell asleep. I could have gone left, the longer but brighter route, or through the dark and confusing streets on my right, which would save me a few minutes but hid too many ghosts behind the unlit forms of parked cars. Metro's shiny blue sign caught my eye, as it must have been intended to, making me remember: I hadn't eaten anything substantial in some time. Nor had Haris. On a Wednesday night, it'd probably be empty, so I could do some quick shopping and depart.

I marched to the back of the store, towards the soft drinks section, thirsting for something other than just water or Pepsi. But right as I stepped into the aisle, I came face to face with Rojet, standing there as if fruit juice meant the world to him.

I cursed aloud.

'Wa alaykum salam.'

Laughter from the both of us, though his began first, and was genuine. I reached for Enjoy apple juice, which came in neat, rectangular cartons. In addition, I took two tropical blends. 'You're kind of far from home, aren't you?' I said.

'I was here to see Wanand,' he explained. 'Things are difficult for him.'

'Wanand doesn't live in a grocery store,' I countered. 'Or did he move again?' I looked away, as if I could see through the back wall. 'By the way, thanks for kicking me out of your masjid.'

'Sometimes you need to walk away from something in order to walk back to it later.'

I ambled back towards the bakery, but only one of the three bakers—each of whom always gave us a hearty salam—was present. Except this baker, already unlucky to be working all alone on a Wednesday night, gave me a niggling gaze. I recalled I hadn't showered in a few days, but what did he care? I was still paying. For cookies, pastries and some small, delicious pizzas, each the size of my hand, sprinkled with tomatoes, green vegetables and onions, my favourite.

'Is Azad going to get back okay?' Rojet asked.

'You were following him, too?'

'I was worried about him.'

'Why would you be worried about him?'

'I do not know how they have survived, but they have managed. No, not even that. They've remained loyal, and not once have I thanked them enough for their sacrifices.' Rojet sighed. 'Isn't it fair I worry about them? You took our brother to a fantastically Western café, where to him the people dress half-naked.' He didn't let the discomfort of the moment pass. 'Consider how awkward that was.'

Though, more importantly, I should have realized that this meant that Rojet had been watching us walk to Trianon. But he had a frustrating way of taking someone else's wrong and turning it into his own right. Enough for me to profess an apology. 'I'm sorry.'

'I was only explaining my worry,' he replied. 'I didn't blame you for it.'

'Sounded like that to me.'

'You hear what you think is said. Then you wonder why I want you to have time off.'

Maybe that was true. So why was I talking to him? 'I'm sorry.' Again.

'I already told you—'

But I cut him off by walking towards the frozen foods section, conveniently close to the exit. I found myself delayed by the dairy section, lost before various brands of milk. The best was Labanita, which came in little bubbly bottles, mostly white except for blue spots. As Rojet caught up with me, I held it up to him, maybe to see if we could engage each other with things more mundane. 'Is this any good?' But then I felt stupid. How would anyone from Khan al-Khalili know what Labanita tasted like?

'It's not bad,' he offered. 'It'll probably give you diarrhoea the first time, but you'll become used to it and then you'll even recommend it. With caution, of course.' At my astonishment, Rojet started to laugh, just over the hum of the refrigerators. 'You want to know how I know what Labanita tastes like.'

'You want me to listen to you, but you don't want me to know who I'm listening to.'

'You listened before.'

'I'll listen better this time.'

He folded his arms across his chest, and turned away from the dairy products. 'After completing my education, I worked in Cairo for a few years.' He looked at me as if I might start dozing off. Didn't he know he had a beautiful voice? And then he started to speak in English. Maybe to prove something. 'Eventually, I went back to school, to study those things that I always wanted to but never had the opportunity to. I threw myself into Arabic, and also Kurdish—'

'Why would you need to learn Kurdish?' I interrupted.

'My parents neglected to teach me my culture and heritage. They even sent me to an American college. So you could say I went back to school to make myself Kurdish.' While Rojet was staring into the past, perhaps wondering why his parents had forgotten their solemn duty, I slipped two almost-alcoholic grape drinks into my shopping basket. 'Only later did I meet Abd al-Bari, to benefit from his learning. May God have mercy on him.' To which I couldn't have said a thing. We were talking about salvation in a supermarket aisle. On my left were stacks of soda, piled up to catch the attention of the last-minute shopper. That is, me. What were midget pizzas without Pepsi? I took two one-litre bottles, and asked Rojet if he wouldn't mind holding another two. There wasn't any room left in my small basket.

But instead Rojet held up one of the Pepsis as if it was a fish he'd just caught. 'You come to this place and you wonder if it belongs in Cairo, do you not?'

I motioned towards the check-out counter. 'It always seems odd.'

Gihad was at the check-out counter, a young Egyptian who should've been a Pakistani: with his bouffant black hair, he didn't make a convincing Egyptian. Every time he said salam, I had to stifle the urge to converse in Urdu. I bent over to set my basket down, pulling my wallet out at the same time, only to look up and see Rojet paying for my groceries. He didn't even give me the chance to say thank you.

'You should bag your groceries,' he said.

With half the bags in my hand and the other half in his, we made our way out.

'Okay, Rojet.' What was I supposed to call him? Shaykh?

Ustad? Then I shrugged, but it hurt. Most of the drinks, I realized, were in my bags. Unfortunately, I'd picked the bags myself. 'I don't want to keep you. I'll just be going back to my apartment—'

'I'll walk with you,' he said. I was about to protest, but: 'Are you going to carry everything by yourself?'

Well. 'I could take a cab.'

'You could just say that you don't want me to come along.'

Oops. 'I'd just be wasting your time, wouldn't I?' But he shook his head in an emphatic negative, turning to walk the shorter, dimmer route.

Rojet was coming over.

whoever you are, welcome

Rojet asked, 'Will your room-mate be in?' The street ended
and Shari al-Ghayth began, prompting him to pause in
appreciation of his location. I would have, too, had three
mightily overburdened plastic bags not been straining my
reddened hands. Rojet looked up and down both ends of the
street, but especially towards the barbershop, bright even at
night. Thank God it was closed.

'Haris was asleep when I left.' I started to take a step
forward. 'He hasn't been feeling too well.'

'I wouldn't want to disturb him,' Rojet said. Even though
something told me he just didn't want to meet Haris. Up the
steps and into my building's unlit lobby, the doorman
preoccupied with a person I'd never seen before. A friend,
perhaps. I wondered if his friend could understand him.

'Shall I leave the groceries here?' Rojet asked.

'How am I going to carry everything up?' I said, even as
I dropped my bags.

Rojet replied with a question that served also as a
suggestion: 'Ask your doorman to help you?'

'Well, we could both carry them up.'

'Haris may be awakened, even if we don't enter your
apartment.' Then he practically ordered me: 'You should ask
your doorman to help you.'

But why wouldn't my doorman wake Haris up? Still, I

could take a hint. The man didn't want to come up for a visit. He'd been good enough to carry my bags this far and I wasn't about to be a jerk about it. 'I can't really ask my doorman,' I admitted. 'I don't understand anything he says.'

'I thought you were here to study Arabic?'

'I'm still studying.'

I reached for a cigarette while Rojet did what I could not do. Glancing behind me, I saw the doorman touch an honoured hand to his chest. Did he judge Rojet a great scholar? Well, that was fair enough. He certainly had the bearing of one. Probably the education, too, though I hadn't bothered to ask.

My cigarette touched my lips when Rojet returned. 'He'll be happy to take care of it.'

But I was falling on to the marble steps, finding it wonderful to release the pressure that had been building on my legs. Rojet sat down as well, almost directly beside me, though he had trouble making himself comfortable. For some time, his eyes were on both ends of the street, and for the rest of the time, straight ahead, considering what little could be made out.

Finally, he asked, 'Would you sit here, for some time, and listen to me?'

Might we have a real exchange, and not a command, a flourish, or an argument?

But I didn't say that aloud.

'Do you know what the worst thing is?' Rojet asked. But, of course, it was not a question he expected me to answer. 'Hesitation is the worst thing in the world,' he said. 'Had I known the effects of my lethargy, I would have lived life differently. Though perhaps that is only regret, the type that keeps us awake the length of the night.' Or makes us feel as if there is nothing but the night. 'By the time the Order had been formed, the time for it had passed.'

I sensed him turning downcast, so I tried to introduce some cheer: 'The road to hell is paved with good intentions.'

'What are you trying to say?'

Nothing much. 'The road to heaven is paved with bad intentions.' I tried to smile, too, just like he'd smiled at me. 'I think you've got nothing to worry about.'

Except that he did.

Tears gathered at the base of his eyes, a wall of water pushing upwards, till he was looking at me through a sea. I had never been good at dealing with other people's problems, let alone this one. I thought about putting an arm around him, doing something to express some kind of compassion, but that wouldn't have been right. I was young and he was old, I was to learn and he was to teach. I managed to spurt out some clumsy questions, which he answered as well as he could, telling me of the future he'd sacrificed and the painful costs of doing so. After that, could I possibly believe he was lying?

Only some decades in the future, the Order of Light would be much more than a few men clogging a run-down masjid. The Aryan Expanse stretched under Old Cairo, its only promontory a spire that soared over the Citadel: the Tower of Light. The many Cairenes who lived over the Expanse were ignorant of its existence, for most of its existence, while the many Cairenes in the shadow of the Tower thought of it only as a mighty minaret. Until the Sacred Compensation arrived, with the promise of the Great Overturning, when the Order unleashed its armies.

Weapons never seen in the Muslim world were deployed by battalions of the Ummah's stoutest defenders, the Lights of the Sun, the Moon and the Stars. But the enemy was still too strong, and the bold assault on occupied Jerusalem foundered. Then the forces of the Muslim States—or, at least, what remained of them—formed a joint command, to fight alongside the once-scorned Immortals. The Order's stout commanders resisted beyond what mere numbers could suggest, with strategies and tactics that allowed for desperate retaliations. But to what end?

Rojet's younger son, Arayn, was dispatched to Karachi just as the city was pummelled. With the defences decimated and the metropolis fast overrun, Arayn fled north to Kabul, which was raided thereafter by an Indian force as well. The last Rojet heard, Arayn had disappeared in or near Mazar-e Sharif, trying to go north but stymied by the Chinese occupation of Central Asia. Had the nineteen year old tried to creep north to meet up with the dwindling mountain resistance, the most formidable fighters known to remain?

The following year, Rojet's elder son volunteered to take command of a small Muslim company in Tanzania. It was similarly defeated. Christian militias overran Dar es Salaam, capturing Orhan. The last night before Rojet's prayer was granted, his twenty-three-year-old son was declared a prisoner of war, a message that arrived complete with a demand for unconditional surrender. It was over. But it also never happened. The next morning, when the Pole of Poles awoke, he was lying in a masjid, where the Tower of Light had once soared.

the return of salah al-din

One of the barber's young apprentices raced in front of us, dribbling a soccer ball as he went. But he kicked too hard and the ball rebounded off a white sedan just ahead, returning in his direction and knocking him flat on his back. His friends, previously invisible, emerged from the shadows, laughing with childish and furious delight. The boy laughed too, and stared at me with that laugh still on his face.

'Why did I know that was going to happen?' Rojet said, hoping to smile. He waited till the children had passed, and just as quickly, his smile slipped off. 'I was told, long ago, that I would find a man who would refuse mortality. When I came back here, to this time—to your time—I understood. I had to begin things before they were begun for us. Your appearance in our masjid was a confirmation of that.'

There would be no reason, no sense, in making up a story so fantastic. So I hated myself for lying to this man, who mistakenly thought my immature desperation could justify the sacrifice of his sons. So I stopped lying.

'I was chasing a girl, Rojet.'

Rojet had gone out with Azad, but on his way back, he had encountered something unexpected. Me, running. Few people knew about those alleys in Cairo, he said, and probably none who knew ran through them in the middle of the night. And how did he know I didn't belong? Because I ran like a Westerner, with thudding steps. He knew, too, that Zuhra had diverged from her course during my chase, and that very soon, I was running after nothing.

With that revelation, Rojet had no more reasons to hold back, to hide what he really wanted to know. 'Though you have been honest with me, I expect more. I need to know if I am wrong in so honouring your presence.'

Liars go to hell and martyrs to heaven. Can a martyr be a liar? Or, even worse, can a liar be a martyr? But if I told Rojet the truth, I'd do to him what had been done to me. Rojet would be changed, from a decent and grieving man, into a pathetic man like me. That a weakling like me could harm a saint like him.

'Please,' he said, his hand on my shoulder, bringing not touch but something beyond it.

'I'm afraid of telling myself who I am, Rojet.' Maybe it was the trust that was born of our conversation, or maybe it was something else, but my mind seemed to melt into liquids, flowing out of a mouth that had become a spout. 'I don't let myself sleep at night, but I can't stay awake during the day. I want to do a thousand things, but I can't finish the first because I worry incessantly about the last. I can only offer you answers like these. I don't know if that'll help you, but—'

'When you tell me what you are, you tell me what you are not.'

His eyes begged me on, sensing that this was the beginning of the flood. 'I was born sick and near death, but to this day I forget to thank God for each breath. I'm deep and shallow, insecure and arrogant, shy but loud, a loser but proud, simple and decadent, poetic and then prosaic, priceless and pragmatic, making most complex the obvious. I want to drown but I sin for the surface, I'm an optimist like a pessimist, a romantic and a sceptic, a cynic and a tonic, a mystic who's in love with common sense. I'm aged beyond my youth, an advertiser of truth, an amoral aberration, a boy and a nation, an angry child, domesticated and thus wild, a federalist fundamentalist, an individualist Islamist—in denial all the while. I'm down and depressed, the result of the West upon my peoples progressed, the East unseated, like the Turks defeated. I was victorious at Badr but fast asleep for fajr, anaesthetic like an android, strong like a Salafi on steroids. I'm a man who in heaven would long for hell—'

But this didn't satisfy Rojet, because it didn't really answer his question. 'Perhaps it would be better if you told me what you dream of.'

'What I dream of?'

'What do you want?' he clarified.

'Everything in the world comes in opposing pairs, and I can't be happy but with both of them. If there was a way to do away with that, then I would be the happiest man.'

'But the first life is always a barrier to the next,' Rojet said. In other words, I have to end my life to end the divide. But he didn't say that. 'You make it sound so hard, when really it's very easy.'

Easy? But it was. Just as before, words tumbled off my tongue, an avalanche of so much fluff, altered water with celerity and harmony previously unimaginable. 'How can a man like me, who is so many different things, dream of just one thing? I'm rude and crude, rash but brash, rough and tough, a complete coward and a foolhardy fanatic. I'm unable to remember today and unwilling to let go of yesterday, seeking meaning in all things, knowing I'm meant to seek something. I judge people for having the audacity to judge me, though I skip prayers with exclusive regularity. I read the Qur'an and I can't stop weeping, I lower my gaze but I can't stop peeping. I listen to music and then I forbid dance, I love rhythm but I suffer silence, all because I'm a Sunni Ayatollah, a recovering alcoholic with a stomach so sick it's pathetic. I'm a million people, Rojet, and all of them have hoarded too much of me. I but bound from one extreme to a dream, from rebellion to open conformity, thus one side of my mind might accept reality and the other, well, he'll blast me.

'So I turn wholeheartedly to faith, and my darkness cries, "Have you dared betray the cause?" And there I always pause. I'm so compulsive it's repulsive. I'm deceptive but receptive, genetic unlike health, inherited like wealth, motivated and reactive, innovative and active. I always open up and disrupt, speak up and interrupt. I'm angry at my religion, engaged by extremism, saddened by the secular, livid over liberalism, conservative in thought but loose with all I've sought, rigid in modesty but open with theology. I'm migrating to Makkah, corrupted like Madinah, foundering like a pointless hijrah, shrouded in black like the Kabah, bruised and wiser for Uhud, longing for a hud-hud, closing my ears to the hidayah while binding my feet back to the bidayah. I'm a Sufi stumbled into ideology. If I was Atatürk I'd vanish before I was forty but no less; if I was his mother I'd kill myself and then ask for his forgiveness...'

One would not expect the listener of such admissions to burst into gut-wrenching guffaws. But just sitting with him should have taught me that anything was possible. It took him a few minutes to calm his cackling, and even then, his eyes were tired from having laughed too hard.

'Did you hear what you just said?' he asked.

Well, there was a lot to recall. 'About Atatürk?'

'No, no!' He was heaving from exertion. 'Everything you said!'

'Everything?'

'The way those words came off your tongue. Didn't it make you feel free?' But it was not freedom I felt; it was, instead, astonishment. For a moment, I saw in Rojet's eyes what I saw in the eyes of his followers—a calm awe. And then it vanished. 'I tell you, with words like that, you might be able to change the world. Or yourself. The latter is harder, but the latter is also better.'

And then I heard someone yell my name. I looked left and down the street, spotting Muhammad—my barber—gesturing in my direction.

'Salam alaykum, Muhammad.' But I shouldn't have said that: I could've initiated a conversation with several other people walking by. Fortunately, only the barber replied.

'Wa alaykum salam.' He began babbling in his jargon. I began trying to put the words together, making them meaningful expressions. Met your friend. Name weird. (In Arabic, the noun and then the adjective after it.) Asked your address. Told him you.

Me? 'Thank you,' I managed.

'He was running also.' Muhammad grinned. 'All of you like to run.'

I turned towards Rojet, introducing him while rotating my body: 'This is the man that gave Azad directions—'

Except Rojet wasn't behind me.

In my excitement to present my impressive Sufi master/companion, I'd forgotten about said Sufi master/companion. Odd that my interest in someone could be so selfish. I imagined that to be a wonderful topic for a Friday sermon.

The problem, however, was that the best person for delivering that sermon had disappeared. I glanced into the lobby, down the street and even across it, but he was nowhere in sight. Did the barber wonder who I'd been talking to? Did he think I had an imaginary friend? Perhaps one I went running with.

the century when
everything went wrong

The doorman was a good soul I'd never bothered to acknowledge: our groceries were waiting outside our door, placed all in a row. At the least, I should've said thank you before coming up, but I didn't. That was me—always too late. I pushed open the door and then went back outside to drag the groceries in. My room-mate was on the love seat, reading one of the many philosophy books he'd brought with him. For a second, I was possessed of the urge to read something stimulating, but only till Haris—having smelled that unmistakable aroma—asked, 'Did you buy pizza?'

I raised an arm to confirm his suspicions. His face broke into a big smile, so that it seemed he'd been dunked in a vat of radioactive something. He glowed like Lemon-Lime Gatorade. 'Rolls and pastries, too.' I lifted another bag. 'There's apple juice, soda, and even fake alcohol.' I displayed two bottles that looked like wine, proud that I'd gotten two such bottles past the otherwise eagle-eyed Rojet.

'Fake alcohol?'

'You know. It looks like wine, tastes like wine, but isn't really wine.'

We ate to our hearts' content, not speaking a word between us till we'd washed down the little bits of pizza, vegetable toppings and crust wedged in-between our teeth with the kick of bubbly Egyptian not-wine. Who would have thought that eating some store-bought food with Haris could be so satisfying? But sometimes the small pleasures amount to satisfaction beyond anything the greater ones can promise.

In this spirit, I asked him, 'How are you feeling now?'

'I think the rest did me a lot of good.' He burped. 'But maybe I shouldn't go worrying about you anymore.'

'Well, the barber forgave me.' With my index finger, I pointed to my head. 'He even washed my hair for me. For free.'

Haris found this especially entertaining. So I told him, 'Muhammad—that's his name—yanked my arm, quite nearly pulling it off in his haste to race me back to his shop. I asked him what he wanted but he only pointed at my hair. But when Muhammad forced my head down into the sink, I understood what he was so hassled about: my nasty, yucky hair. It'd been some time since I'd showered. His apprentices gave me a fantastically satisfying shampoo, spraying my head all over with water, and I never wanted it to end.'

'I'm not up for class tomorrow,' I confessed. If we didn't go, it meant a four-day weekend. Of course it also meant skipping a class we'd paid a good deal of money for.

'You want to do something else instead?'

'I was thinking maybe we could go somewhere tomorrow.'

'Let's do tourist stuff,' he suggested. Hinting I should get our *Rough Guide*—which I did, ploughing through its pages for a tourist site not yet featured in our many rolls of film.

My eye caught the highlight box for the Citadel of Salah al-Din that contained within it the monumental masjid of Muhammad Ali. Named for the nineteenth century, ostensibly Ottoman but originally Albanian governor who was nearly responsible for the overthrow of the government in Istanbul, the masjid was famed for its eclectic blend of European styles and traditional Ottoman Islamic forms. Eclectic, I would find out, also means hideous.

'How about the masjid of Muhammad Ali?' I asked.

'That's kind of far. Is there anything else out there?'

'Yeah, there's a lot.' I scanned the page again. 'The masjid is inside the Citadel of Salah al-Din, so there's a bunch of museums and old masjids. We could probably spend the whole day there.'

And so we agreed.

Haris announced that the big meal had gotten him drowsy again, and went off to the bedroom, leaving me in my lemonade chair. I was thinking of going off to the bedroom as well. But I'd only woken up a few hours before and I wasn't tired. Unfortunately, I had nothing else to do, other than going into the bedroom to lie down.

A headache came on, but I wasn't quite sure if it was physical or metaphysical. Both were bad. But only one fell to Tylenol. So there I lay staring at black walls, black air, black ceiling and other blackness, each minute that went by negating the evening, the taste of the meal and the satisfaction of having shared it without argument. This was my mind, my greatest enemy, which if allowed too much time could collapse any defence. Were my hands pistols, I would've aimed the barrels of my fingers at my heart, collapsing the pipelines that fed oil to my brain, that devil of an organ that only exploited its fuel. Oil has a rather uniform tendency to make itself the source of great problems.

Born the sick child of wealthy parents, I always doubted what was mine. My talents, skills, dreams, poetry and prose built on a foundation found: the fruits of a forbidden tree, upper middle-class almost-white suburban Eden. Those who came to this religion of their own volition were gripped by an insurmountable faith. Each progress was made by their careful determination. But those like me, born into Islam and taught the perfect past that belonged to their blood, had a legacy for which they suffered enormously. Life was not a journey to Him, as it should have been, but insecurity, the kind of feelings failures feel, sure as we are of only one thing: We can't live like those that handed the faith down to us, entrusting its survival to us. I would rather spend half my life moving the mountains.

We Muslim children of Muslims are the dwarf children of giants, frightened by the obfuscating reach of shadows that stretch from yesterday well into tomorrow. Islam was gifted to us and we drove ourselves mad, to extremities of fanaticism and violence, to prove that we were worthy of the gift unsolicited and undeserved. Crushed like an ill-prepared Atlas, we were nothing, sprung from something we suspected was everything. I doubted anyone in Cairo had thoughts much different from these, which fell harder and harder, ceasing only when the umbrella of sleep finally cast its numbing shade over my mind. Thank God for darkness—blindness, deafness and dumbness come to pass only a period of time, and that nothingness is my sacred refuge.

nineteen years ago

No man can know how he will arrive in the world, and no man can know by what instrument, at which time and in what place he will depart from it, save those given knowledge by God. So Wanand could not have known that the last days of his life would be marked by the sort of shortcomings he'd struggled years to overcome. Events had conspired to bring him to such an impasse, when the only way to obey was by disobeying.

Nineteen years before his return, Wanand wed a woman named Shanazi. For years they struggled to have a child; when Zuhra was born five years later, she came at the expense of her mother's life. But Wanand could not know what it meant to be Zuhra, to understand that one's own life came at the expense of another's. No, not another. Her mother. Who after nine months of protecting her, at a time when the world had grown dark, had been rewarded with death. Zuhra's life had been ruined by someone she had no control over: herself.

Then, the next year, Wanand became enamoured of a different love. In the masjid close to his home, he heard a sermon given by a promising young preacher called Rojet Dahati. After Rojet's talk, Wanand hurled question after question at Rojet. None of them struck, but were all hurled back at Wanand.

This soon became the norm. Rojet and Wanand would spend hours, and then days, talking, studying, and soon enough, Rojet was intimating his plans for the Order of Light, to gather the most promising Kurds and lead them to the salvation they had so long waited for. Wanand was sufficiently taken with Rojet, both as a pious Ustad and a trusted friend, to become the first Murid. He swore that—as an Immortal—for that was what members of the Order would be called—he would keep the Order cloaked. But looking back from the last day of his life, Wanand understood this oath to have been the biggest mistake of his life.

The punishment for revealing the Order was expulsion, but nonetheless Wanand transgressed. He revealed to Zuhra that her father had joined the select because he knew that as a Kurd she would understand the importance of such a revelation. But letting her in on the Order was not only a violation of Wanand's oath, but also signalled great danger. Her own troubled history precluded the possibility of her approaching The Path with a clear mind. But when Rojet learned of Wanand's transgression, he didn't punish him. Rather, he kept his distance from his formerly close friend, a distance that assisted Wanand in his second and last transgression.

During the first few weeks of their return, Wanand believed he'd been dispatched to Agouza to expose his daughter to the past and its modernity, to make her father's departure easier to bear. Maybe even to indicate to her that there was still hope that when her father was gone she could still persevere.

Because Rojet had asked of his Murid one more thing: Zuhra was not to be taken with Wanand, not even to Wanand's point of departure. Having known how impossible this was to fulfil, why would Rojet put on his first follower a burden too great to bear? While her father, and all those who knew of the world she knew, would depart, Zuhra was to stay behind to make things right. What would she do? What choices did she have? Would she return to Cairo's Kurdistan and find her mother, who was younger than her? Would she find her father, who would be only a year older than her?

As Wanand prepared to depart, his Ustad told him what he had held back from him. 'My brother in Islam...' Such sweet softness. 'Stand on the Citadel of Cairo, where our great father Salah al-Din once stood. All who need to find you will find you there.'

Wanand wrapped his arms around his Ustad. The tears fell unchecked and he let them fall, moistening his shirt and fastening it to his skin.

But Rojet did not cry. 'If God is with you, there is no reason for tears.'

But many things are done without reason.

'I know.' Wanand replied. 'I am weeping for my friend. I am weeping because we have failed him.'

'You do not fail me, my friend.' Rojet clutched Wanand tighter. 'Only do not fail God and you will have no reason to weep.'

But Wanand's lips escaped his control. 'I can't believe...'

'All things must end, Wanand. Else, how could anything better begin?' Rojet held Wanand's head between his hands and kissed his forehead. 'I am so jealous of the path you are taking and the place you are going. You will be a martyr, Wanand. Do not ask forgiveness of only yourself, but please seek forgiveness for me. Choose me, on that Day when there shall be no shade but His. I have loved you as a teacher, a brother, and a friend, and this love does not perish, though the world in which it lived will.' This only made Wanand's tears quicken. 'You are the first of us to reach out for God. Is there not, in this, cause for joy?'

'I can't imagine leaving...' It was Satan whispering. And Wanand listened to him. His legs became lead, too heavy to move. But as his Ustad had been there for him countless times before, he was there for him again, breaking bonds unbreakable.

'Do you love me?' Rojet looked into his eyes. 'Or do you love God?'

for the advancement of egypt

My room-mate walked into the bedroom with a towel around his waist. Not the first thing I wanted to see when I woke up.

'What time is it?' I asked.

'Eleven.'

I threw off the blankets in haste, sitting up and looking for my slippers. Haris was also searching, but for clothes to wear, his black hair still dripping water onto the dusty tiles of the bedroom floor.

'You're up late again,' he pointed out, walking a bundle of clothes into the bathroom. Though he was down the hall, invisible to me, he continued. 'I just got up a little while ago, too, but I've taken a shower.' Of course you have. 'We should leave soon.'

'Yeah,' I sighed. That meant yet another hurried shower. My body demanded a very long and thorough one. 'I was hoping I'd wake up earlier.'

Brushing my teeth felt wonderful: with each stroke, the satisfying removal of that ancient musk that had been filling my mouth since Tuesday. My face received several scrubbings, each casting off either a layer of dirt or skin, though I couldn't tell which was which. I allowed myself the luxury of a ten-minute shower because I'd missed a day in-between—in fact, two—but fifteen minutes would have been pushing it. I concluded my cleansing by spraying deodorant all over my body, lest I find myself trapped away from hygiene and stinking again.

At least I made the lobby smell good.

As we strolled through, the doorman was walking up the stairs, towards us. He looked at me, thought deeply and then turned towards Haris, mumbling something urgent.

'He thought we missed our cab.' Haris pointed to the street, where a cab had been waiting. But it was no longer there. 'I guess he was suspicious, so he asked the driver why he was parked outside our building.'

'Well?'

'He was going to pick up someone and take them to the Citadel.'

'But that's where we're going!'

'Very good.' Haris triumphant. 'Anyway, he thought it was our cab. But it was actually waiting for someone else.'

The way Haris was smiling, I knew there was something coming.

'Your girlfriend, yaar.' Haris burst out laughing and ran down the steps.

We spent most of the long ride staring out the windows, judging Cairo's uneven development. It bothered me. But it was just a way to avoid thinking about what was really bothering me. Was Haris pulling my leg?

He prevented me from asking. 'You know—' he began.

'Wait,' I interrupted. 'Did you take the keys?'

He felt his side pocket and said that he had.

'Just checking, because I forgot mine.' All I had was my blue passport. Then I remembered. 'What were you saying?'

'I was just thinking that this is the worst time to go out.' Haris made me look out the window again. 'It's the middle of the day and we're going out to the desert. We must be retarded.'

As was a certain architect.

The masjid of Muhammad Ali sat on the Citadel's highest point, towering over distant Cairo. The most we could make out was a mushy skyline. As for the guidebook's depiction, it was only partially correct. While the masjid was definitely rare in its combination of Ottoman Turkish and West European nineteenth century, it was also unsightly, overdone in the most unpleasant ways. A sad indictment of a suddenly withered creativity.

Haris grimaced. 'This is the ugliest masjid I've ever seen.'

We caught the Qur'an circle right after noon prayers, though I had no interest in taking part. Besides, how was this circle going to compare with the last one I'd sat in? Innocent Haris, on the other hand, couldn't wait to recite his heart out. Probably because his reading was melodious wonderfulness, while mine was a little Arabia broken apart by too much Americana. So while Haris sat down, I headed for the museum, promising to meet him at the main entrance in an hour. Between me and my destination, there was a park in need of green. I hadn't even gotten halfway across when I saw them sitting there.

Parked under the only tree, facing Makkah. Wanand caught my gaze and shifted to the side, his way of inviting. Barely lifting one dragging foot after the other, I moved to meet him. There were no policemen about, only a few tourists hiding from the heat. Why was I looking for strangers? Wanand sat me beside himself, so that he formed an Islamic wall between his daughter and me. I think Zuhra wanted to ask a question (namely, why was I present?), but she just turned her head indifferently away, towards the boring masjid.

'Are you ready?' Wanand asked.

Since I thought the question was for Zuhra, I remained silent. Until he asked again.

Ready for what? 'I was just visiting this masjid and going to see the museum. I didn't know that you would be waiting—'

Wanand cut me off with palpable frustration. 'It is my time! Bas!'

Time to go. His time to go. Bang. Boom. Or whatever noise it was that a person leaving his life made. I felt it at the top of my throat, burning acid torturing the back of my tongue, while Zuhra mimicked a pleasant portrait. When her father rose, she rose, and I was the third to rise, watching them set off to some quiet side of the Citadel where there were no guards or tourists.

'Where are you going?' I asked.

Wanand only said, 'Away.'

haris

I hoped against hope. Maybe he'd gotten caught up in the museum. But considering that the museum was small enough for me to have checked twice, that wasn't likely. Did he see Zuhra somewhere and decide to go off with her? Maybe he decided to spend the afternoon with her. But I didn't think happy thoughts. His absence didn't feel like an afternoon opportunity, several hours of chit-chat about this and that. Something else was going on. I looked outside the Citadel once more, but he wasn't among the tourists.

My consternation caught the attention of a smartly dressed policeman who intercepted me on my second circuit. 'Is there a problem?'

'I'm looking for someone...' And I answered his next question, 'My Pakistani friend...' Then my voice faded, partly out of worry, partly because I felt certain the policeman hadn't seen him. Why did my room-mate always do these things to me?

'Salam alaykum,' the policeman announced. 'My name is Mahmud.'

'Wa alaykum salam. I am Haris.' Then Mahmud introduced his approaching friend, Marwan, another policeman. They could have been cousins. Marwan shook his head as Mahmud explained my predicament. Meanwhile, I tried hard not to confuse the two of them.

Marwan smiled, 'We might be able to help.'

'How?'

'I think I saw your friend,' he said. I asked him where, and he pointed to the entrance of the Citadel. 'But he left from here an hour ago, maybe more.'

'He left?'

Marwan nodded. 'He went in a taxi. He was picked up just from here.' He paused to indicate the Citadel's entrance again. Maybe Marwan should have been a tour guide. 'I wouldn't have spotted him except that he looked very frightened. Or maybe he was late for something, because he was certainly in a rush to leave.'

'Was he with a girl?' I asked.

'No, he was alone.'

Definitely sounded like my room-mate.

Though I could not have been sure, it might just have been my room-mate, liable as he was to do something stupid. So I thanked Marwan and Mahmud and started to leave. Marwan stopped me, though, clutching my forearm as if he wanted me to leave with whiplash.

'Where are you going?'

'Back to my apartment,' I said. 'He's most likely to go back there.'

Marwan told me to wait, and though I was frustrated, I was not going to argue with an Egyptian police officer. In Egypt.

When he returned, both he and Mahmud were smiling. 'It will save time,' Marwan announced, 'if you come with us in our car.'

'You don't have to do that...'

'You come from Pakistan, and you pray in our masjid.'

His eyes hinted at the Egyptian flag fluttering by the entrance. 'These countries are not real. They have been imposed on us. So do not argue but let us go together.' He clasped my hands inside his own and held them there.

Not the best time to tell him we'd actually missed prayers. And that I was Indian.

the river of martyred muslims

My head fell against the window, staring out at the lives of still-living Egyptians: it was a film in slow motion, accompanied by the whine of a Japanese engine; the former scene fake, the latter sound alien, like all of our existence, either artificial or imported. None of those people outside the vehicle, nor even the driver of the cab taking me home, would have to forget the sight of Wanand's head, inflated and then deflated. I rolled the window down, letting in a breeze, hoping the smell of modernity would mask the reek of vomit still on me. Making sure the driver wasn't looking, I wiped the drying blood off my arms and onto his black, possibly plastic seats.

The three of us had been in the Citadel, forming something like a triangle—though this one had a centre. Wanand produced a small, silver pistol from underneath his robe, letting it catch the sun once but only that once. I may have gasped. Maybe when he raised the gun to his head. I wanted him to hold back, think things through, allow the gravity of the moment to weigh him down rather than let his life end in a gunshot blur. But there was nothing in-between the revelation of his pistol and its settling against his skull, except for a loving glance towards Zuhra and a murmured prayer, all of this done with an automatic progress. I told myself not to watch, but the velocity denied me escape.

Wanand's finger pulled the trigger away from his head. A brief pause, followed by a lonely click, the only sound in the whole world, fast spoiled by the boom of a bullet diving deep into his brain. His face grew and shrank in the same second, sending me backwards to the ground as bits of his cranium came raining down around. In contrast, Zuhra was absolutely still, making me feel oddly disrespectful for covering my hands and arms in a hot vomit. I must have stumbled again, on to the ground. Turned and looked. I must have tried to get away, gagging and coughing. Having never seen a man die before. Nor a woman: I saw her only to see her go, the gun to her head and then she was on the ground. She was too young. She should have stayed.

Allah Hafiz, Zuhra.

I should've closed my damned eyes.

And now my eyes couldn't close. A crush of traffic on the Corniche had trapped me only a short distance from the apartment, which might have been a good thing. The more I thought, the more I was sure: I couldn't face Haris. Not after this. I would have to tell him why I'd left him behind, and then he'd know. He always knew. He knew what I was thinking and when I was lying, because he had that sense. Outside, sparse benches, ornate street lights and a well-maintained sidewalk and then a sudden, sharp drop down to the Nile below, barely swimming. But still moving, unlike us.

My driver turned around, agitating the rolls of fat on his face. 'We never have so much traffic.'

But I knew better. He'd gone this way to drive up my fare. And I had too much on my mind to suffer a cheat. So I dropped a few crumpled bills on the seat in front of me. Before another word escaped his mouth I was gone, weaving in-between landlocked lanes of taxicabs, making my way towards the Nile. What I needed was calm, but I had no chance to enjoy the waters undisturbed. Cairenes careened down the sidewalks, talking at an inordinate volume. They were blind. Not just because of their unfortunate taste, their unmatched clothes and gaudy fashions, but because they didn't see what had happened to them. Each of them deserved a scream in the ear, but they wouldn't be fazed by my pitch. Maybe a slap in the face, but they were all talk. They would've walked away. Maybe a bullet to the head. But I didn't have a gun.

I didn't doubt that there was once a land called Egypt. I just wondered where it had gone. Alien apartment buildings, rationalized to a hideous, standardized perfection, all but eclipsed every minaret in the city, except for a few stragglers whose time would doubtless come. Whatever else was left was covered by highways, hiding from sight those sands that were once part and parcel of the people, their every path to their past paradise bulldozed. The times, they were changed. And what did we do? We missed them, even missing most chances to miss them, so that we found ourselves where I was now, asking myself in archaic tongues what use there was in going on.

But if this was destiny, was it worth questioning? After all, it wouldn't make any sense for the Nile to have asked God why she flowed North. Rivers aren't as presumptuous as Muslims: the Nile did what she did, her waters sliding down that riverbed carved ages ago, her exit into that western lake—into which she disappears—intended from a time forgotten. Out here, so close to her end, she was choked on pollution and little more than fuel spat out of an atheist dam still promising potential and prosperity. Once a beautiful blue, a thundering snake with a skin made of the morning sky, she was now a regurgitated green, filled with the refuse of the diseases collected over her history. It would've been far better had she given up in the Sudan. But she went too far and tried too hard, and before me, from near the 6th of October bridge, I could see why the Muslim world needed a reprieve. Bearers of the drive to survive but also the heavy legacy of past glory, it was insufferable to accept that we'd just vanish into another civilization. Had we travelled four thousand miles only to spill into someone else's sea?

Like Karachi, Kuala Lumpur, Istanbul and Beirut—and the list goes on and on—Cairo strikes the observer as a city that doesn't know where she should belong. And her children, the Cairenes who grew in number by the minute, do not know, either. Perhaps they'll accept that they were made to drown. Like good Muslims, they'll choke to death with God's Name on their lips. But it could happen that some of them might announce that drowning is a good fate, and proceed to give up with all the enthusiasm a human being in such a situation can muster. Do I go too far? I see the kids and how far they've gone, and they're well past Alexandria and into the Mediterranean, waves lapping at the shores of the French Riviera, licking Europe like desperate dogs, so happy to see their masters that they slobber all over them. Once in a while, they get a pat on the head.

Cairo's wealthy children dress Western, but it's not the dress that hurts. It's the look in their eyes. Their ability to breathe comes from their appearance. They know it, too. I'm sure these Cairenes would love to have someone pull them out of the Nile, to fly into the open sky above. But they can't fly. It's too late for them now. The water holds them above the surface. Providence gives them the gift of breath. And the current tugs at their feet, pulling them closer to the North. There is little they can do, but sigh and take pleasure in the view.

'Maak filus?' It was a beggar, seeking cash. Waving him off, I spotted Keyf Khoshi alone on a street corner. I ran as fast as possible but Keyf didn't turn in my direction. I would've thought the contrast of a tall brown man, blustering through black-and-yellow vehicles pasted like squashed wasps by the pavement, would've gotten his attention. But his mind was elsewhere. And his hand was on a gun. Somewhere behind me, that beggar was asking someone else for cash. Probably one of those couples holding hands, looking over their shoulders to see if their parents might be trapped in the nearby traffic jam. Meanwhile, my driver was kicking himself for taking the longest route.

Keyf was leaving. I got into the last lane when his head imploded, celebrated by a Pepsi billboard snapping off its moorings. That, but more so the gunshot a split second before, had pedestrians running madly, none of them sure which direction safety lay in. Cab drivers spilled out of everywhere, leaving keys in the ignition and doors wide open. It made me feel uncontrollable pride, the kind that comes when we think ourselves the source of something significant. But reminders of my mortality returned as caffeine-free Pepsi came crashing down, sending me backwards onto the hood of a cab. The heat of the engine singed my back and I spun off, falling to the pavement and wrapping my head in my quaking arms.

haris

We stepped into a smart police wagon, speedy-looking Eurotrash painted legitimating white and reassuring blue. Marwan driving, Mahmud next to him, and me in the back. Our doors slammed shut in unison, a harmony that elicited a brief smile from me. Then the siren roared, Marwan punched on the accelerator, and we tore through the roads past desert and into urban sprawl, swerving around cars that were more than happy to get out of our way. Trying to keep myself occupied with saner thoughts, I began to check for little things. Wallet. Check. Keys. Keys!

'He doesn't have his keys!' I said.

'He's going to be stuck then?' Marwan was almost as stunned as I was. 'Is there anyone you can call to help him?'

There could only be one. 'My friend...'

Marwan reached into his pocket and pulled out a cell phone. I called and waited two rings. When Rehell picked up, I said, 'Rehell, it's me, Haris...'

'Salam mate, Izzayak?'

Forget that. I replied in English, something suddenly encouraging me not to involve the policemen in our conversation, no matter how friendly they might have seemed. They still represented a government I didn't trust. So I told Rehell that I was with policemen, but that there was no cause for worry: they were lending me a hand, as well as a phone, driving me over to his place so that we could put our heads together and figure things out. Namely, where the hell had my room-mate taken that cab? And what made him leave without telling me?

With the help of those flashing lights, we made excellent time. But when we arrived, Rehell wasn't waiting outside his building, which I thought odd. Marwan and Mahmud agreed to stay in the car, while I ran up four flights of stairs. Rehell was just outside his door, engaged in a hushed exchange with Mabayn.

'Salam, Haris.' Rehell didn't smile. 'This is Mabayn, your Pakistani room-mate.'

Uh. 'What?'

Rehell grabbed both my shoulders and shook me. 'We've already decided, Mabayn is going to go downstairs with you and tell the cops that he's your room-mate. Okay?'

'How do you know they're going to believe that?'

Mabayn cut in. 'The policemen need to leave, Haris.'

I wanted to ask why. But they were men possessed.

'They need to go, Haris. Now.' Rehell pushed me back towards the stairs. 'They won't know the difference. Just tell them he came here by himself.'

'Tell them what?'

'Go! Make up a bloody reason on your way down.'

Mabayn and I went out together, but Mahmud, leaning impatiently out the window, spoke first. 'This is your room-mate?'

Perfect. There were urgent messages coming over their radio and neither Marwan nor Mahmud seemed very interested in me—they looked like they were in a lot of trouble. I began to explain what was going on, that Mabayn was sick and had come here because he didn't have the keys and he didn't want to be sick alone, but they didn't care.

Once they were gone, I asked Mabayn to explain what was going on.

'Come back upstairs, Haris.'

Then he went ahead without me. In fact, he ran ahead, forgetting I was behind him. Back in their apartment, Mabayn was parked dead centre in front of the television, in prime viewing position. Even though he had no competition. Al-Jazeera was warning the Arab world. The body of an older man, believed to be about fifty years old, and that of an adolescent girl, had been found at the Citadel. The result of self-inflicted gunshot wounds. To my horror, they showed the corpses, and I recognized them immediately: Zuhra, with her father, Wanand, crumpled beside her.

'You guys were just there, weren't you?' Mabayn asked.

I felt Rehell's arm on my shoulder, but before I could react, breaking news chimed in: reports of a possible bombing at a major intersection in Doqqi, right off the Corniche. Which was just south of our apartment. The exact facts remained uncertain, as the reporters were still on their way, probably abandoning the Citadel even as we listened. Perhaps Marwan and Mahmud were being lambasted for abandoning their charge at such a moment, or maybe they were being ordered to Doqqi. Whatever might be the case, Cairo's police were going to close the major roads and arteries, set up road blocks, enforce curfews, raid mosques and stop cars. In a matter of hours, Egypt would turn upside down.

the pride of the kurds

Kibr spent the last afternoon of his life thinking that everything was working according to the Order's plans. Wanand had given his life at the Citadel; that Zuhra had gone too, that could hardly be blamed on Rojet, who had firmly instructed Wanand not to bring his daughter along. Keyf Khoshi had departed at a crucial intersection of Rojet's choosing; the panic that ensued had forced the security services to close nearby roads to traffic, bisecting Cairo into its northern and southern halves.

In the wake of the Order's actions, the poor would find themselves enraged. Always sidelined by the government, they would be infuriated at once more being on the receiving end of the government's heavy-handedness. The modern, meanwhile, would be terrified. Were these actions signs of Egypt's instability? Would they lose their money and their property to revolution or anarchy? To say nothing of the tourist industry, which would be dealt a severe, if not crippling, blow. Frightened, the government would pursue every lead with vigour. In their searches, they would uncover unexpected suspects, madmen waiting to carry out horrors that had forced the Order of Light's formation. But the Immortals themselves would be gone long before the government was able to identify them.

Rojet returned to the masjid to meet Kibr and Azad, to share their last hours together. He had just come in from a midday march through the cluster of nameless streets, buried beyond the masjid of Sayyidna Husayn, that constituted Cairo's Kurdistan. Since his return to Cairo, it was the only time that Rojet had been out in the bright sunlight, and he understood quite well the consequences of this action. Peering through their windows, both the elders and the youth of the Kurdish community wondered who this man was, this man who so brazenly marched past their houses. And though they were invisible to him, they snapped at attention, in silent appreciation of a man whose Islamic dignity was not only preserved—as so many Muslims look these days, men and women on a fierce defensive and nothing more—but radiated. None walked out to greet him, follow him, or even question him.

But he'd made his point.

For some hours afterwards, Rojet talked with Azad and Kibr, ending their discussions by reviewing with them how and where they were to depart, and at what time. And then, with the full greetings of peace, Rojet walked out the door, revealing for an instant a sky slowly approaching sunset. Pretty like pink and plum purple, gargling orange and salmon, hazardous red and maroon, all those colours—but no blue.

Kibr, too, said his salam to the nervous Azad, thinking that abandoning him in the masjid would be the best strategy. How else could Azad be made to go?

Azad watched Kibr leave, without a gun, instead with a rosary in his hand. Of the Immortals, living and dead, Kibr was their greatest champion. Where the Pride of the Kurds was going, nothing material was needed.

kill me, habibi!

If the sequence Rojet had told me was correct, then it was Kibr's turn next.

I was wandering, looking for Rojet, or more precisely his masjid. Yet after a great deal of searching, it became quite obvious I wasn't going to find my way. My feet groaned, complaining about the number of miles they'd walked. It took me a few more minutes to recall that Zaheed lived in the area, too. His address was in my head, stuck as many things we'd rather forget remain with us the rest of our lives. I had no desire to see him, except that these were my other options: nothing. Perhaps I could rest my feet in his apartment, drink some cold water, sit back and think about three suicides.

Zaheed lived in an ugly four-storey building bullying a shorter one beside it. I recalled his apartment number and trudged up the stairs, kicking shards of wood out of my path the whole way up. Once I was on his floor, I had to choose between two doors, one dirty and the other dirtier. I chose the cleaner one, knocking three times before the door opened. Zaheed paused a second before rushing into me, hugging my disgusting body.

'Hello? Salam alaykum!'

What the hell was he doing, answering a phone? 'I need to talk to you,' I said.

'Of course, of course, yaar...Come in!'

Dragging me into his kitchen, Zaheed set me down in his nicest chair and said he'd be back in a minute. When he returned, I lied. 'I got stuck out here without cash.' Well, I hadn't really checked if I had any. But I *was* stuck. 'Would you mind if I spent the night here?' Why the hell did I ask that?

'No problem, no problem, yaar. Do you need some cash?'

'Not really,' I admitted.

Did that make sense? I didn't think so. But Zaheed was way too enthusiastic to notice. 'Do you want to call Haris and tell him you're here for the night?'

Actually, I didn't. 'Yeah, I should, shouldn't I?'

So I smiled (it seemed the appropriate thing to do), approaching the phone much as I'd approached Zaheed's apartment, both acts mind-boggling tests of what the will can force upon the body. Until the mind reminds the body that it is not necessary to actually dial a number, that one may, instead, merely pretend. So I dialled nothing and, not surprisingly, no one picked up. I turned to Zaheed: 'I've got the answering machine.' I spoke into the receiver. 'Hey, it's me...I got stuck without cash...I'm at Zaheed's place. Everything else is cool. I'll be back tomorrow.'

I placed the phone down, very pleased with myself, until I noted Zaheed's crumpling expression. 'I know you're tired tonight,' he started, 'but my friend and I were going to go see the light show at the Pyramids. If you're not up to it, and I understand if you're not, you can stay here. There's food in the fridge and a bed you can use.'

The Pyramids. My mind moved quickly. Wanand went with Zuhra to the Citadel. Keyf took himself at a major intersection. There was a chance, however slim, that one of them might head for the Pyramids. Probably Kibr, the third—he was the cunning one—and I could think of no location more significant. Of course, I could keep going, looking for their masjid, or I could stay behind, in an empty apartment. Alone, in Old Cairo, by myself? In a building like this?

'It's a bit far to the Pyramids, isn't it?' I felt the only way I could survive the night would be by stealing some of Zaheed's energy.

'My friend has a car. There's also going to be a rave there tonight. We can stop by if you want.'

I slapped the air. Zaheed nodded, not sure if I'd declined the last offer out of respect for him, religious inclinations or sheer exhaustion. His lack of comprehension bothered him.

The two of us waited outside his building for another Pakistani, who by his boisterous manner was probably Punjabi. But I didn't try to remember his name when he introduced himself to me, turned off immediately by his wimpy Japanese car, bursting with excessive bass.

I suffered a back-seat trip, tormented by blaring Egyptian dance music. Somehow, Zaheed and his silly friend managed to keep talking over the repetitive racket. Habibi! Yalla! Habibi! We wound through a small village, parking on a dirt embankment behind a high, wiry fence. Even from there, we could see the Pyramids—unbelievably enormous. Beyond the giant monuments, invisible to the eyes but not to the ears, that rave was in full, un-Islamic swing. Wasn't that disrespectful to the dead?

The light show was the typical spectacle, though much better in production than I would've expected. A proud announcer narrated condensed ancient Egyptian history, accompanied by laser diagrams displayed against the sides of the Pyramids. I found the programme entirely distasteful: a glorification of pagan greed and obstinacy, that same tyranny that had tried to crush our brothers in faith, the Israelites. That Zaheed and his friend were engrossed by the presentation was unbearable. Fellow Pakistani Punjabis, brothers by blood and lustful language, reduced to this. When a civilization begins to die, it commits all sorts of paradoxical acts. For one thing, it becomes obsessed with already dead civilizations. Not willing to take any more recounting, nor anyone's admiration of it, I feigned a need to use the bathroom, rushing out of the tourist area and moving in the direction a helpful employee pointed me—only to bump into a hurrying Kibr.

'What are you doing here?' I asked.

Kibr pointed past the Pyramids. 'I'm going to the rave.'

questions cause questions

Kibr laughed at my stunned expression. 'You seem surprised?'

'That's one way to put it.' I examined his feet. His sandals were plain and black. 'When Keyf, when he—you know—there was an explosion. Was that—?'

Kibr interrupted, not just verbally, but also physically, stepping into me. 'We know what our souls are capable of and what they're not capable of. We keep that in mind before considering a location.'

'How can you tell?'

'Maybe years of discipline, prayer and reflection can teach you things you don't yet know.'

'I'm just asking—'

Kibr grabbed me before I could finish my sentence. 'I need to talk to you.' He walked me to a low stone wall, upon which we sat. Or, rather, he sat and forced me to do the same. 'I have to tell you something important about Egyptians.' He stopped, until I urged him to continue. It was more like he wasn't sure how to.

Egypt would face trials in the coming weeks, months and years, some of which would be of immediate duration and others that would resemble eternal epidemics. What was not to be forgotten, though, was that without weakening, there could be no strengthening. I countered that the Egyptians, like other Muslims, were right to worry that there might be no counteracting improvement, that it was all downhill from here. And for a second, Kibr looked like he was losing control of his own conversation. But that flickered and faded.

'The Egyptian response is either to defect wholeheartedly, or to build a castle and suffer the siege behind its walls. These fortifications even have names: socialism, nationalism and fundamentalism, all of them with a commanding view and a much better chance for defence than the simple huts the people were used to. The problem is that people begin to enjoy their castle too much. They begin to confuse their inside with their outside—their skin becomes thick like granite, the castle walls going up while they come down.'

'So you're saying Egyptians are stuck in castles?'

'Fairy tales, really,' Kibr grinned. His fellow Kurds liked telling fantastic tales. Was that why he found it funny? 'But to get from here to tomorrow, we have to migrate, and this means exposing ourselves to many threats, the full danger of which only God knows. We will find our salvation in this search. To give one's life is not the goal.'

He'd added on that last sentence as an afterthought. 'But don't you have to?'

'Do I? Yes.' Then he paused. 'But it's not necessary.'

My confusion gave way to suspicion: was Kibr jealous of Rojet's interest in me? But while this might have been a tempting thought, I sensed no ulterior motives. 'Why would you choose to do something you don't have to do?' I asked.

'If we only did what we had to, I wouldn't be talking to you.' He sighed. Loudly. 'I will follow Rojet. Or, more correctly, he will follow me.' He paused here, to let me think about that. Except I didn't know how to. 'Many people make themselves what they want to be, so that everyone around them imagines them to be something other than what they are.'

Wait. 'Are you saying Rojet is a fraud?'

Kibr shook his head, but that said neither yes nor no. 'Rojet is looking. Do you know what I mean?' Why couldn't he just spit it out? 'Something happened, which we, as Muslims, should have been prepared for. It made things very bad for us. But Rojet, looking all this time for someone who could turn the tides, has forgotten that all rising tides must eventually recede. As bad as it was, as bad as it's going to be, that's not forever.'

'You think he's deceiving himself?'

'He's deceiving you,' Kibr answered.

'Why would he do that?'

'Is there anything but deception?'

'Why are you answering my question with a question?'

'Why are you?'

I wanted to punch Kibr in the face. That certainly wouldn't be a question.

'If you choose to leave the castle by foot rather than trying flight and coming crashing down on the grounds around, you will do what needs to be done. But he's too scared to tell you this.'

I swallowed. 'Why would you follow a coward?'

'Imagine you knew that you were supposed to believe, believe so strongly that you could hold on to faith when it seemed there was no hope in the world, but that you couldn't bring yourself to believe that way. Then imagine you found someone, like you, who found a way to believe. It would be a great day for those who are afraid of the world. But it would be nothing for those afraid of God.'

'Your master is not afraid of God?'

'I didn't say that.' Though he almost did. 'Islam started

in a pagan society. If in that darkness a light could emerge, then things aren't hopeless. But Rojet doesn't see this. Under the weight of all that happened to us, he began to doubt, and ever since then that doubt has consumed him. He wanted to do what Abd al-Bari would have done, but we are not Abd al-Bari, are we?' Kibr put his right hand on my knee. 'We did not live in his times. And you will not live in our times. The path is for each of us alone.'

'So why are you going to give your life?'

Though I'd asked a question, Kibr managed to answer with a question once again: 'Is that the solution, to give my life?' He withdrew his hand. 'Listen carefully.' That light show was nearing 2000 BC. 'We are the descendants of Salah al-Din's most trusted men. He picked them, by hand, and sent them to live for generations in Cairo's shadows. Can you imagine? All those generations that passed unnoticed. I'm sure not even your travel guide could have told you of this city's Kurdistan. Because nobody knows except us. And you.'

'It's weird that you're Kurdish.' What a moronic thing to say. Thank God Kibr didn't let that ferment.

'Salah al-Din knew the greatest threat to this Ummah was, and would remain, the Franks. He also knew that resisting them could destroy us. And what do you see in this modern Muslim world?' I saw lasers bouncing off Pharaonic tombs and white tourists nodding in agreement: They'd seen this before, on the Discovery Channel. 'The Order of Light is almost entirely departed. Soon there will be no more Immortals. What will become of the world after we've left it?'

'I don't know.' But in fact I did. 'A suicide at a rave...at the Pyramids.' Goddamn. The consequences. 'You're going to turn Egypt upside down!'

'Egypt already is upside down.' Kibr slapped my back playfully. 'We're just turning her right side up.' Then he stood up and resumed his way to the rave.

That was it?

I called after him. And, thank God, he turned and waited as I walked towards him, thinking of the one thousand questions I could ask, having this opportunity to delay.

'Why did you tell me all these things?'

With his index finger, Kibr jabbed my chest, right over the heart. 'Sometimes, we wait too long and we miss our opportunity to act, and then we can't forgive ourselves for acting too late, and we sink into misery and despair, which are the best ways to leave Islam. But in truth, waiting too long is only a mistake, and we all make mistakes. Don't we?' His finger came off my chest and pointed to the heavens above. 'If a mistake is really such a horrible thing, then all human beings are horrible things.'

'But look at me!' No, don't. 'I've become such a horrible thing.'

'When we're gone, only you will remember us as we were.' Kibr, sympathetic? 'You should know by now that I cannot save you. Why would I even want to save you?'

I nodded. 'The path is for each of us alone.'

'You'd make a good student. Except—'

'Except?'

'Soon, there will be no teachers left.'

'But the world will always need teachers.' I didn't believe I had the courage to do so, but I put my hand on his shoulder. 'Stay and teach, Kibr. Stay and help.'

'No.' He eased my hand off his shoulder. 'You stay.'

It certainly was a sight to see. From behind the Pyramids, an explosion made the piercing light of lasers vanish before bursts of catapulting fire, cascading into the sky, throwing violent orange shadows on to the darkened Pyramids. Tourists tripped and fell into the sand, trying to bury themselves beneath it, tossing white fold-out chairs wherever they went. The police, anxious to protect the frightened dollars around them, rushed forward, desperate to do something. But didn't know what. I laughed out loud when the power went out and nothing could be seen but what the slowly diminishing flames allowed.

But I didn't stay.

whom to blame when the time for blaming comes

I found myself on an empty lane leading two ways, both absent of signs. I could have stopped and waited for Zaheed and his friend, who would have been more likely to know the way out, but the idea of stopping and waiting for either of them was repugnant. Instead I walked off the main street, and one block behind, so that I could see the primary thoroughfare but not actually be on it, continuing until there was no chance the pyramid explosion was visible. And so I was free. My stomach burned from the day's retching, my intestines felt like lead and my toes screamed at me, as was becoming their habit. Two hundred pounds out of a nearby ATM, with twenty swiftly blown on a cab; I had a cab driver who had no idea what he was driving away from.

Unfortunately, Keyf had made sure there was no easy path back to Mohandessin. After the bridge, we found ourselves in a late-night traffic jam, the result of a hastily erected checkpoint. One incident was bad enough, and Kibr was sure to double the wait. Handing a nervous cabbie his cash, I was out and in Doqqi, looking for an alternate way to get home. Nobody, God-willing, had seen me with any of the departed Kurds, so none of them would suspect me. I crossed the street, thanking God the street lights were dim, and found myself alongside some shrubbery. Rumblings in my belly said

food first and thoughts later. I was about to consider walking
north, to find myself a meal, but I was prevented by the
pitter-patter of footsteps, tiptoeing past me.

I knew him by his skullcap.

Was he going to take his life on the side of the road? In pity,
I whispered his name—and he froze, stuck to the ground.
'It's only me.'

He heard that and melted. 'Salam alaykum.' I shook his
hand, but on the release, he let his arm flail to the side.
'They're all gone now and I'm supposed to be gone before
Rojet—'

The mention of his name and I missed him again. 'Is Rojet
gone?'

'No, he hasn't gone yet but everyone else is gone
and—'

I was one of them now. Didn't he know? 'Is Rojet leaving
soon?'

'He's on Gamiat al-Duwal and I was supposed to meet
him there but I don't know if I can go.'

In his eyes, there was none of that fabulous conviction,
those eyes like roaring furnaces, common to all Azad's brother
Immortals. Were I to give my life, I suspected, I'd be gone
well before he could even put his finger on the trigger. I
wanted so much to give Azad the conviction he should've
had.

'Are you ready?' I asked. Blinking.

'To cross the street?'

What?

How had Azad gotten into the Order? I didn't know everything
Rojet knew, but certainly I'd have known enough to throw

this man away at first glance. On my lead, Azad made it to the edge of the street. Was Azad really going to 1) cross, 2) look for a way north with me, 3) find his departure point, 4) pull that gun out of his pocket and 5) fire it into his head? I didn't think I could fire it for him, either. Still worse. Imagine if Azad accidentally shot himself in his foot. Or, God forbid, in my foot. I saw myself hopping on one foot, the other gripped by my hand turning red, looking for a policeman, a cab ride, anything, screaming for help and wondering what explanation I could give.

For now, there was blissful relief, as the intensity of the traffic prevented us from crossing. In a moment, though, a clearing would emerge, and then all would be lost. I'd be forced to bring him to Mohandessin. What if we got in a cab and the gun went off inside? Then I would really—but a horn blared and I was back to reality. A nervous Azad, only a foot in front of me, teetered over the curb. To my right, in the middle lane, a white Mercedes truck was barrelling down the road, blaring its horn a second time, as if to confirm its existence to itself. And to me.

'In the name of God,' I whispered, loud enough only for Azad to hear.

Before his mouth could open, both my hands, and all the energy they could gather, grabbed Azad by the shoulders and thrust him outwards. Thankfully, only his left foot landed on the street. The rest of him tumbled and fell, his right arm softening the impact for the full weight of his body. Two taxis swerved in opposite directions, brakes screeching, tyres rolling off the ground from the speed of their unexpected turns. Adrenaline lifted Azad back on his feet in under a second. Unconsciously, his left hand cupped his right elbow, nursing the bruise. When I laughed at this futility, his eyes locked on to mine. Another, third blast of the horn shook Azad—the truck was too close to brake. I've lined the barrel up to your temple. I've squeezed the trigger. All you have to do is take the bullet. He repeated his faith in God, his hand gave up on his elbow, and the truck ploughed into him, sputtering blood that erupted skyward and then descended, dropping on the pavement like fat raindrops. How suddenly I bolted, charging up the street, behind me swerving cars and smashing sounds, not daring to look back, only amazed at how fast I was becoming someone else. When I finally stopped, exhausted, at least half a mile away, I looked down at my guilty hands.

Did you do that?

the history of the defeated

I took advantage of a cab driver's patriotic hospitality. I was a tourist, staying at the al-Nabila Hotel, and I really needed to get back home. He heard: Scared. He heard: Helpless. He heard: Wealthy. Fifteen minutes later, minus forty dollars, I was just a street ahead of the Metro, still open. The West never slept. Fortunately, some of the traffic did, letting me dash straight away to the other end.

The McDonald's employees were in a rush to close. Giant advertisements of burgers and fries tried to lure me in, to take last-minute advantage, but I picked Trianon. Some patterns couldn't be broken. Other patterns, too. My eye caught a wonderful blonde-haired Egyptian girl in a bright red shirt with horizontal maroon stripes. Her faded blue jeans were the best fit in all the wrong ways, really guilty not for tightness—though they were that tight—but rather, because of the wholesome and fertile fullness of her body, which struggled not to burst out of that fabric. I wanted to have a horse and be Manas, Shiban or Bayazid. I'd snatch her on to my ride and race off. But she walked past me and into the arms of a muscular Egyptian teenager. I looked around me, and the few girls still out on the street were held close by proud men, clinging to the one victory they had.

Defeated, I sat at the outside edge of Trianon Café.

Within a minute, that same waitress was serving me, the attractive one, with the confidence to confirm it. She took my order for a cappuccino, but when she smiled, I instantly disliked her and her employment. None of the restaurants here hired hijabis: those veils might've made us think of God and not money, asking us to ponder the poor and thus order less. Putting one arm against the table, I dropped my face on to it; my hair scratched the skin near my elbow and my head looked sideways into the rest of Trianon. I felt like I could've stared into the café forever.

Any promise we had ended in 1918, when our Ottoman Caliphate finally inhaled its last breath. The end of the First World War was a dismal time, not just for the Ottomans, but for their allies, the Germans and the Austro-Hungarians. By the terms of the Treaty of Trianon, vanquished Hungary was forced to give up two-thirds her territory—some of which Hungary had held for over a thousand years—and one-half her population. Then, after the Second World War, the Hungarians lost more territory, this time to the Ukraine and Czechoslovakia. Hungarians became one of the most widely dispersed minorities in Europe. I wondered if the café's owners had any idea of the significance of the name 'Trianon' in the histories of the defeated.

Did Kibr want me to go to Cairo's Kurdistan? Did he want me to tell the other Kurds how the Immortals departed? Would they believe someone who wasn't even a Kurd, someone who met these supposed Immortals just a few days before? But at the same time, I couldn't forget his warnings, nor Azad's from before. The world was changing, and it was going to be for the worse. So many Egyptians trying to be Westerners, as if one could possess God's message and then act as if it meant nothing at all. Even though that was how I acted, it should've meant everything to everyone else, who should've burned this city and built a new Cairo over it, complete with faithful dreams and new beds to have those dreams in. Otherwise, they would be consumed by that which they pursued. That which never accepted their sacrifices. But could civilizations be planned in advance?

Rojet's visits seemed to be. He pulled the chair across from me so carefully that it didn't squeak. I noticed, with a concurrent tug of envy, that he was much better groomed than me, dressed for the first time in Western clothes. His beard, too, was trimmed to a fashionable stubble.

'Salam alaykum.'

'Wa alaykum salam,' I replied, my head barely off the table.

'How are you?'

I pointed to my cappuccino.

'That's not an answer,' he observed.

I picked my head up. 'No, it isn't.' But I showed no hostility. Somewhere, Uighur were starving, Iraqis were dying, Palestinians were vanishing, and Americans were fighting for freedom. Or was it fighting freedom? 'I'm tired, Rojet. My mind, my body, my everything. I'm just so sick of this place.'

'So why even come here?'

I moaned. Not *this* place. 'The coffee's good.'

'So you like what they have to offer'—Rojet winked— 'but you don't like how they offer it? Or why they offer it, if I may be so bold.'

I was expecting him to erupt with another speech, a reflection on the necessity of giving up and giving in. And had he begun, I would've listened, learned and probably accepted. I was all ears. There was simply no energy anywhere else in my body.

there are no in-betweens

Mabayn covered the top of the bottle with his finger and turned the bottle upside down. He dabbed a drop of cologne on his left armpit. Then again, on the right. He looked in the mirror and smiled at what he saw. He was going to surprise Sarah; they hadn't seen each other, or even talked, for an interminably long two days. He was carrying with him his messenger bag, having carefully folded a rose inside it and a poem too, some horribly forced rhymes he'd penned the evening before. With luck, tonight might be that special night. Sarah's room-mate was in Bahrain, visiting family—the idea that people would want to visit Bahrain especially amused Mabayn—and she was all alone, in her dormitory.

Getting out of the house was the easiest part. Though it wasn't time for any of the five mandatory prayers, Mabayn's parents were praying nonetheless. One day, they'd find out about her. In-between a supererogatory act. But that was later and this was now, straddling the tapering line between Thursday and Friday. Busy in devotion, they couldn't have heard him leaving through the side door, sticking the car in neutral to roll it quietly out of its parking spot, turning the engine on only when he was on the main street. The radio informed him about some disturbances, but the report was vague, mentioning only a change in traffic. The short way to Zamalek was cut, so Mabayn would have to go south to Doqqi and then back around the other side.

Mabayn was so nervous he was sweating. Then he worried his deodorant would fail, which only made him sweat more. In desperation, he let the windows down a little, enough to cool him but not ruin his meticulously combed hair. After passing the riverside hospital, traffic eased up, only two cabs ahead of him and a truck a bit behind. So Mabayn relaxed and dropped one hand to the stereo, catching Amr Diab's latest hit. God knew how much he loved her. A horn blared, but he couldn't hear it. Too much bass. Then another, but he still didn't hear. When he finally looked up, more out of habit than concern, he saw those two taxis on opposite ends of the road. His heart leapt, and with it, his hand, which for some reason jumped off the steering wheel.

The truck, which had passed him when he wasn't looking, was braking. But it didn't brake hard enough. A human body catapulted into the air and then the truck jerked left, smashing into Mabayn's car. He screamed hell, slamming on his own horn again and again, but he wasn't heard. Amr Diab was calling on Allah. In horror, Mabayn saw that the driver's eyes had rolled backwards. If they were looking at anything now, it was their master's brain, trying to figure out how he'd just sent a pedestrian that high into the air. Mabayn pummelled the accelerator, trying to break free of the press, hoping to catch a ramp on to the bridge. He'd have a nice story to tell his girlfriend, never mind the explanation he'd give his parents regarding a seriously ruined vehicle. But just as Mabayn angled for the on-ramp, the truck wavered and spun, catching the back of his car and crushing it against the retaining wall.

The first police on the scene didn't notice Mabayn's accident. They'd been sent to pick up the pieces of a man now spread over three and a half lanes. But the truck driver, on regaining consciousness, had gone back to the sight and sound of sirens and informed the police about what had happened. Were it not for his killer, Mabayn's car might have been ignored for much longer. But what was left of Mabayn's car had fast erupted into flames, originating in the truck's overheated engine and quickly catching the mangled remains of Mabayn's sedan, charring everything. Almost everything. They found a photograph of a very pretty girl, and a police officer was chosen to investigate the connection between Mabayn and this woman. Unfortunately, the task fell to a young officer named Hasan—so wet behind the ears that he could've tilted his head at the scene of the accident and put out the fire. He was also to deal with Mabayn's parents, as other, more experienced policemen were being posted to the scenes of actual attacks.

Hasan's task started terribly: first he had to console a truck driver who couldn't be consoled. Not only had he struck and bludgeoned one man, he'd killed a second the instant after. A very uncomfortable Hasan forced the man to the nearby hospital, leaving him to the care of its medical staff. That done, Hasan got back into his police car and drove to Mabayn's residence, which was nearby. He didn't have the time to think through how he would ask what he was supposed to ask.

Hasan rang the doorbell, praying he wouldn't vomit when it was answered. A large man, with a beard covering his neck and a Qur'an in his hand, filled the entrance. As if the night couldn't get any worse, a veiled woman appeared. Though she was only one more person, her presence made Hasan's duty much more difficult. It was as if he was informing a million parents of a million deaths.

'Does your family own a car with this licence plate number?' Hasan astutely gave them the number (instead of the mangled plate).

'It is my son's car,' Mabayn's father replied. Then, it sunk in that Hasan was a police officer. 'Has something happened, sir?'

'There was...' Was it good to delay? Or better to let it out all at once? 'There was an accident.' Though he'd mumbled, Mabayn's mother heard well enough, soon sobbing in fright. 'There was an accident in Doqqi,' Hasan continued.

'I wasn't aware my son had left the house...'

Hasan was taken aback. 'It is very late, sir.' But then he reminded himself: This was not the time for chiding the parents. They'd do that to themselves later, and probably for the rest of their lives. 'It was very late to be driving...'

'My son...'

Hasan shook his head and didn't answer.

'Where is his body?' Though tears poured out the corners of his eyes, Mabayn's father's speech was quite clear. But Hasan noticed that his fingers were clutching the Qur'an so hard that they had turned white.

The young officer moved away from the door. 'At your convenience, sir, we would like to ask you some questions. Please call me—'

He was reaching for a pen, but Mabayn's father interrupted: 'You may ask them now.'

What Hasan did next, he had to. But not a day has gone by that he hasn't regretted doing what needed to be done. From out of his pocket, Hasan produced the photograph the police had recovered from Mabayn's car. He turned it around to show Mabayn's father and asked, 'Do you know who this girl is?'

Did his son kill her in the accident? Was she in the other car? Was she in Mabayn's car? What difference did that make? All the difference in both worlds. This one, and worse than that, the next one. 'I've never seen her…'

'Her name is Sarah El-…' But Hasan had forgotten the last name. Neither did it seem that important, since Mabayn's father didn't know who she was, anyway. Why Hasan carried on, he still doesn't know. 'This photograph was in the glove box of your son's car.' We couldn't save your son but we saved it instead. 'You've heard of the suicide bombers?'

Mabayn's father stepped back. 'Not Mabayn!'

'No, no,' Hasan shook his head. He had merely hoped this would lessen a father's pain. How stupid was he? 'The driver, whose truck…well, before it happened…he hit someone walking on the road…and then we think the truck driver fainted…' Mabayn's father began to weep, and Hasan apologized. 'I am sorry, sir. We will return at a better time.'

But Mabayn's father held Hasan's arm. There wouldn't be a better time. 'I would like to know. What does this girl have to do with the recent attacks?'

Hasan had become a police officer so that he could support his family and keep good people safe. Never had he pictured himself in a situation like this. He wondered if Mabayn's father hated him. 'Sarah was studying at the American University, but only for the summer. If you recall the suicide attacks near the Pyramids a few days ago…' Hasan paused to gather himself. 'She died in the attack. The only casualty, actually.' Hasan reached forward and gave Mabayn's father a hug. 'To God we belong and to Him we are returning.'

other people's eyes

'I want to tell you something,' I said. 'Please don't be angry with me.'

'I would not be angry with you.' Rojet smiled. He was not angry. Did that mean I could continue?

I said it. 'I don't want you to leave.'

'Why not?' At least he was still smiling.

'Okay, this is why you can't be angry.' Was I really going to say it? But no more time for holding back. 'When I was walking here, I'm sure you were behind me or something, but I don't think you saw what I saw, because you weren't looking that way. There was this beautiful Egyptian girl. I mean stunning. You could stare after her walking away till your legs gave out and you fell onto the ground so hard it knocked you out, but even then, you'd have dreams about her till you came back to your senses. And then you'd only want to know where she'd gone. But—surprise!—she had a man. All of them do.'

Rojet laughed, though there was no anger in his laughter—so he'd kept his word. 'Every man wants a woman. But there are, beyond superficial persuasions, deeper reasons,' he said.

'All I've known, from my youth, are sickness and disease. Other kids, they had those special years when they thought they were invincible. I never had that luxury, Rojet. I wish I had, so badly.'

'Why do you wish so badly for that life?'

'Superficial things let me know I'm real.' I looked down, like that would let me look at myself. What was I trying to say? 'I don't feel this world, Rojet, like everyone else does. Or at least like they appear to. You said it: We live in an age that glorifies the body, and all I've known from mine is failure. I'm a broken idol. Can you imagine everyone around you is a god but you can't be one, because of mistakes you had no part in, shortcomings you never asked for. They're perfect and beautiful, and I'm ruined and ugly.'

Rojet completed the thought for me. Better than I could have, of course. 'The world tells you that you are an idol, and so, in order to live up to the world—no, no, that is too simple, too immature. Let's put it another way. The world tells you that because you are a human being, you are an idol. So in order to belong, in order to be real, as defined by the apparent omnipotence of the culture that has always been around you, you must be worshipped as all other persons are. Of course, an idol that isn't worshipped is discarded. But there is also a second reason for the way you feel...'

Stunned by his analysis, I mumbled, 'What?'

'You believe you are capable of more. So you believe you should receive more.'

I looked at my cappuccino, not sure how I might react to that. 'But I'm still alone.'

He said nothing for two minutes, another two minutes for which I was alone. 'God, too, is Alone.' The spell of his words! 'You want more attention, but none of these girls, none of these empty lifestyles, can give you the attention you want, because you—like the Immortals, like myself, like a few others in the world—understand the depths of attention that human beings need.' I had forgotten everything but him before me, and the things he said to me. 'We are not self-sufficient, the protests of the deficient aside.'

Rojet reached for the spoon by his fingers and slid it to the middle of the table, as effortlessly as he took me and moved me. He was an uncommon comic-book hero, read about in books or wrongly portrayed in movies. The person that most people never have the chance to meet, only imagine: draw/film/write about/study. But it was his unforgettable voice that most drew me to him.

'I can't survive like this, can I?'

'We're only mortal.'

I didn't expect to smile, but I did. If he was not angry, then I should not be either. 'Why is it we always end up talking about death?' I asked.

'At least we're not extremists,' he said. 'They kill other people. We only kill ourselves.'

have your birthday at mcdonald's

When the waitress came with the bill, Rojet asked, 'Where are you going now?'

'Nowhere,' I answered. 'I don't have the keys to my apartment.'

'Well, is Haris home?'

I nodded as he stood. 'He's home, but I don't want to wake him.' Realizing just then that Haris definitely wasn't asleep. He was probably frantically searching Cairo for me.

Rojet walked out and aimed for McDonald's, letting me trail him. He looked every few steps to his left, drawing attention to the vanished traffic, probably the effect of the roadblocks, the security concerns, the panic, the late hour. But I missed Trianon.

'I'm tired, Rojet. Can't we go back to your masjid? I could rest there.'

He returned at a brisk pace to my side, surprising me with his aggressiveness. Not only that, he faced me directly. 'You would use my masjid as a bedroom? You never care for us, though we care for you. You only look down on us, though we never look down on you.'

A second ago, he'd been happy with me. 'I don't look down on you, Rojet,' I said.

He looked down one end of the block and followed the

buildings to the other end, as if he were preparing an architectural sketch. Slumping against the wall, I was dithering between seated and sprawled. All that held me up were the few calories and plenty caffeine provided by a cappuccino.

'The police are looking in all the right places.' He was ecstatic. 'Anyway, how could they look for us? We're already gone. We never existed.'

I motioned him downwards, making him face me. 'Why are you leaving?'

He met me, carefully. 'We don't belong in this world.'

But instead of arguing again, I thought of another question. 'If you came from Cairo's Kurdistan, are you still alive? You have to be, right?'

Then he sat all the way down, resting on his ankles, as Muslims do in prayer. 'What's today?'

'It's Thursday, I think.'

He squeezed my hand. 'I was born tomorrow.' He squeezed harder, rounding it off with an enormous grin. 'Do you want to go see me?'

'No.' No? 'I mean yes.' Trianon was far away now, and everything else was empty. 'I can't believe you're going to do this.'

'I have to go.'

'It's wrong, Rojet.' I put my hand on his knee. 'You can stay and do something for Islam, for Egyptians, for us. I mean, if things have changed, and you know how they could have been—'

'Years longer than you have lived, I have been thinking.' He slid my hand off his knee with some hastiness. 'Don't tell me what's wrong.'

'Taking your life is wrong.'

That's when he exploded.

He launched forth with words I cannot remember, accusations I'd rather forget, but some of it still sticks. My appeals to my efforts, my recollection of Azad's demise, none of that stayed his assault. He condemned me for my presumptuousness, and in such a casual tone. 'Forget even arrogant,' Rojet bore into me. 'Maybe Azad wasn't the bravest of men, but he stood his ground while that truck raced right for him. You, on the other hand, you would have run straight into the truck, proclaiming yourself a visionary who had miraculously seen the light—and, oh, how bright it was!'

I'd tried to make him stay, out of care—out of love?—for him. 'I don't want to hear this, Rojet.'

'Are you afraid to?'

I raised my voice. 'Yeah, that's exactly it, Rojet. Does that satisfy you?'

He said, 'Somewhat.' Making me want to scream. Didn't he understand the purpose of rhetorical questions? You don't answer them, Rojet. 'Why, then, are you so keen to accuse us?' he continued. 'Do you think we are afraid of something?'

'Maybe we're not supposed to react. Maybe we're supposed to act first.'

'You blame us because you hate yourself, but you are too afraid to believe what you really believe.' His voice became tense. Terse. Upset. Impatient. 'You hate your life, not because you haven't got what you want but because you know this life cannot offer you what you most want. There are other levels of existence, yet they are only for those brave enough to ascend to them. This has not only crossed your mind, but pitched a tent within it.'

'Then what am I supposed to do?' Enough of the rhetoric. 'Am I a Muslim or a Westerner? Am I traditional or modern? Islam is the answer, everyone says. It's plastered on half the masjids in this damn city. But that's just a lame slogan.'

'People who expect posters to change their lives have deeper issues.'

I almost smiled. That would make a great slogan. Damn him, then, for distracting me. Damn him, too, for making me damn him. 'I don't believe the posters are actually going to change my life.'

'Exactly!' He hit upon the word as one might strike upon a drum. 'Yet, while you know no person is uplifted by slogans or posters, chants and rallies, you expect them to do so nonetheless. It is as if you believe in gravity, yet curse the world when you return down to it after every leap.'

One way of putting things. But there were many other ultimately hollow ways. 'Whatever you say, there's still the fact that people put those words on those posters—and for some reason, Rojet. They say they have the answer. But every answer I've heard doesn't tell me how to change what I am.' A pause, and something clicked. Not a trigger but a joint. 'Maybe a piece of paper can't become a tree and I'm stupid for thinking it could. Or even that it should.'

Rojet stood up, like he was looking for a tree. 'If a piece of paper wants to be a tree again, it should stop worrying about seeds, soil, roots and, most of all, trees. It should let itself be written on, and endure patiently, even when it is crumpled up and deposited in the garbage, and even while that garbage is thrown into a bigger pile of garbage, where it sits and stinks and rots. When a piece of paper decomposes, it returns to the earth, becoming part of the soil from which new trees shall one day grow. We Muslims do not rise and then submit. Rather, we submit and then we rise.'

'You can say that, but what does that even mean?'

'The desert Arabs had Islam, but they did not have faith.

That means you have to obey before you understand why. It's a choice, but make enough choices in this regard—and this regard alone, unlike all the other things in your life and anyone's life—and you will know what lies behind those choices. It's what the Children of Israel told Moses, peace be upon him. That they would do, and then they would comprehend.'

But that didn't want to make me throw my fists in the air. Or even be proud of myself. Or even care about myself. 'I'm supposed to come to Islam because I've failed at everything else?' No. 'All my life, I've only been told that I'm not white enough, not strong enough, not good enough, not handsome enough, not brown enough. And after all that, I'm supposed to accept that less is more? That we just give in and eventually, if God wants, He lets us figure it out? That's not a choice, Rojet. That's being forced against the wall and told you have freedom.'

Rojet leaned into me. The better to judge me. 'Not secular and not a believer, but somehow the two together. And where has this taken you?'

The north end of Gamiat al-Duwal, probably by now a shade past midnight, locked out of my apartment, not having eaten properly in days. Were Rojet to leave, I'd have to add 'alone' to my unspoken answer. 'It's gotten me nowhere,' I said.

'If that was your destination, you've done well.'

'I don't appreciate the sarcasm.' That is, if it was sarcasm.

'God has dealt you defeat after defeat, that these might humble you, but what do you do? You are the Ummah. You modify, but for a while. You pray, but for a few days. The minute the threat recedes, you revolt.' He receded from me. 'You stank of yourself that day you walked into our masjid.

How could I not follow you, with your scent strong enough to track from anywhere in Cairo? I did not choose you because I saw potential or promise. I chose you because your ego had to be cut down.'

'Other people are worse, Rojet.' I said it while turning my head away.

'Is that your excuse?' His voice was reddening, the words out of his mouth molten calligraphy. 'God has done everything for you. But what have you ever done for Him? Always defending yourself, always offending others. Always protecting yourself, always attacking others. You are a piece of paper who has made himself into a tree, a trunk of hate, denial, indifference, thinking nothing of humility, modesty and perspective.'

Perhaps it was his rage. Or, more appropriately, me realizing he was right. 'I'm a hypocrite...'

'Is that what you think? You hope for life, when you've known from childhood that life is a mirage. You were granted wisdom where others had to climb out of ignorance. So why do you still reach for what is false?'

'Because I want fantasy.'

'You have to wake up from fantasy.' Rojet crossed his arms. 'Life is from death, death is from freedom, freedom is from faith, faith is from submission, submission is from humility, and humility is from honesty—the honesty of seeing what we have tried for, what we have denied, what we have accepted and what we have refused. Now, you see yourself. So do something with this sight. Cut yourself open and put it in your blood so that it might sap your falsehood from within.'

Rojet's speech stopped there, and he put his hand over his head, revealing that he was carrying something like a satchel.

Were I eagle-eyed, I might have noticed it earlier. It was open too, releasing the smell of fried foods, a Qur'an wrapped tightly in cloth, a large wooden block and a full bottle of water. When he pulled out that block, I saw that it was a Qur'an stand.

'There are no egos without the Ego. Unless He is first, there can be nothing after. There, really, was your mistake: You tried to be Descartes.' Rojet laughed. 'You tried to prove yourself and then your Lord. It doesn't work that way.'

'I misunderstood Islam,' I admitted.

Abrasion charred his voice. 'You began with your self and not with God. This is not simple misunderstanding. You are too smart for that. You are, rather, guilty of *shirk*, the only unforgivable sin: of associating with God. That, you must know, is the one sin that cannot be forgiven.' I swallowed and too loud. I'd considered myself a bad Muslim, but never so bad as to be guilty of *shirk*. His voice slid towards soothing. Soft. Sleepy. 'But seeing and speaking—these two are not the same as believing. Our masjids have become homes for the living, far from the tombs and graveyards of the believers that they should be. Deny these mechanisms and ideologies; leave for yourself your mortality. You will toil till you see yourself as you truly are, so that your children's children might one day stand under a humbling sun. And do you know why? Because this destruction will bring creation. Our elimination elicits illumination. The gods are dying, the ego is fallen, the West is overthrown, the traitors betrayed, capitalism disarrayed and paganism has, at last, again commenced perishing. The times of old are around the corner. If only I could meet them, as you are destined to.'

In the middle of the night, in the middle of an empty street, victory sounded all right. I tried to raise my pitch to a steady tone, and I nearly succeeded. 'I'm ready now.'

'You are not,' Rojet countered. 'You most definitely are not.'

'I will be.'

'You cannot give yourself until you know yourself.'

'I know myself.'

'You do? Good.' Rojet looked too pleased. 'Who are you?'

'I'm nothing.' I added, 'And now that I believe this, I must give myself up. I must show that I really believe it.'

'But isn't it a sin to take your life?' Rojet remembered our first argument so well that he mimicked me.

'If I'm nothing, then I'm annihilating nothing. So where's the sin?'

Rojet stopped to pull at the end of his sleeve, revealing his watch. 'I have done many things in life, but all of them are nothing, except what God may reward me for. Be my witness, then, that I have handed you the axe-handle and pointed out the idol.'

Then he gave me a strange responsibility: I was told to hold that bag of food. McDonald's, it turned out. I asked, 'Is it yours?'

'Just hold on to it.'

'Are you going to eat with me?'

'I think you've asked too many questions.'

haris

I'd run down the stairs to see if the doorman knew anything, but he was asleep. I figured if he did, he'd have shared it with me. Besides, had my room-mate come back, why would he remain in the lobby? So I spent the evening mostly in the apartment, with the upsetting news Rehell shared with me. He called, and came over a couple of times. He had friends at his place who'd let us know if my room-mate showed up while he was away.

I was worried by the way my room-mate had been behaving. Having spent two years at New York University with him, I'd seen him from the outside and within. During our stay in Egypt, he'd opened up to me on a few occasions, sharing frustrations, exasperations and humiliations. So when Rehell summarized the last conversation he'd had with him, I began to panic. Fears I once dismissed or discounted, I now felt very stupid for passing over. Could he have anything to do with the attacks? A massive blast had struck a rave party at the Pyramids. Only one person had died, a Syrian girl, if I remembered right. Power was cut from much of southern and eastern Cairo. Word spread to international news networks, and Egypt, having taken Israel's place as the Western vacation haven, was looking at serious trouble. So when the phone rang, I ran towards it with both hands extended.

'Salam, Haris.' It was only Rehell, so I sighed. 'You

thought it was him,' he said. 'I'm sorry, mate.'

But before I could answer, someone else's voice interrupted. 'Rehell, get off the phone and get over here!' One of Rehell's random friends, whose names I could never remember.

I heard Rehell pushing the receiver away from his mouth. Then animated conversation, but I couldn't make out the words. Finally, Rehell returned.

'Oh my God!' he was screaming. 'Get here, Haris. Get here now!'

I slammed the phone down, checked for my keys in my pocket, shoved my feet into shoes and sprinted out the door again, motivated by the urgency in Rehell's voice. The police post at the end of our street was empty, but I heard sirens in the distance, too far to tell if they were coming this way, or just repeating repeated warnings. Please, God.

Up four flights of narrow stairs, a dull mix of grey cement that oozed a desperate blueness. At the end of a similarly constricted hallway, Rehell's place. The first of my knocks pushed open Rehell's unlocked door. Rehell and two of his European friends were huddled around the television set, that al-Jazeera logo in the corner. Mabayn wasn't sitting in his usual, uncontested spot, right in front of the screen. Strange. Stranger still: they were staring into a blank screen. Cameramen were trying, but police roadblocks—and a frightened government—were preventing al-Jazeera from receiving access.

The reporter narrated in stuttering bewilderment, as if Qatar was in Cairo. There were credible reports that someone had bombed the Gamiat al-Duwal McDonald's. Not just the two-storey restaurant, but everything around it for two big blocks in both directions had been completely gutted by the explosion.

those who believe,
and do good

Rojet marched in front of the McDonald's, choosing the restaurant as his launching pad, choosing me as his audience. So I asked no more questions. I threw no more barbs his way. I did not pull at his hand or clutch his shoulder. Nor did I give him a parting hug. The best thing I could do was fish a cigarette out from my pants pocket, next to my passport, and put it in my mouth. Rojet produced his water bottle and then his Qur'an, setting it down on the stand before him. He twisted the bottle cap off and poured its contents over his hands, splashing his face, his arms (up to, and including, the elbows), through his thick black hair and then over his feet. A strong smell of something familiar caught my nostrils, but its nature escaped me. Not that it mattered, once he started reading. The tossing of Abraham into the fire, the verses attacking the night sky. It was impossible to fight the tears. My left hand held on to his useless food, the other had nothing to do.

I turned around, found a match in my other pocket and struck it against the back of the matchbook awkwardly balanced on my raised leg. Not quite steady, and always all thumbs, I dropped the lit match on to the ground. A bubble burst behind me, knocking my unused cigarette out of my mouth. Time slowed and then accelerated, throwing me on my face.

I could taste blood on my lips, dribbling down my chin. But his voice never faltered. The Arabic was stunning, the delivery mesmerizing through the screaming fire. Each second that passed, the flames lifted higher into the sky, growing whiter around him, till many such seconds had gone by and his body was nothing but a distant shadow. Rojet leaned forward and touched his forehead to the marble floor, bowing through the flames—a sight my eyes could not be pulled away from.

The windows along the second floor of the McDonald's trembled and then tore apart, a crack surfacing on one end and spreading, left and right, in innumerable branches. I dropped on to my strong leg to run, but it was too late: I was sent a good ten feet back, pinned against the ground. Once I was up again, I scuttled backwards, to a place safe to dare stare at the McDonald's building. The restaurant was consumed by flames the size of ten men, fire following the block in every direction, the whole stretch of shops and restaurants burned away by a fireworks celebration of negation.

Prior to this moment, had anyone asked, I would've said that Rojet was as all humans were. He was possessed of his own life, if even fated by God to intersect mine over a series of days, the end of his existence and the muddled middle of mine. But no longer. Had God created Rojet to teach me how not to stay but rather how to leave, and had he been made only for that? Cairo was no longer confusing, condemning, or crowding. Rather, Cairo was as it would have been. Egypt was not an alien country, nor even an Arab country, but seemed to vanish in the light of this lighthouse fire.

I looked behind me, expecting Rojet to have gained a crowd, standing in appreciation, but instead there were only sounds of distant police cars, starting up from where they'd stopped—near the site of Azad's departure? Though that must have been more than an hour ago. It must be, by now, blessed Friday. Why didn't the minarets erupt into praise, filling these boroughs with ovation? I thought I heard distant windows opening, the sounds of Egyptians in their apartment buildings staring out at this wonderfully intense sight, but of course it would only frighten them. Another burst and I stumbled again, stubbing my toe on a bottle cap: Coca-Cola. The loopy letters laughing. Even our garbage was Western.

Was I going to go back to see Haris? Was I going to answer his questions? Were the police going to interrogate us? Enough questions, enough doubts, enough hesitations; I overflowed with the excuses, which were all that Muslims had and all that were ever implemented. I did not intend to let anyone ask me anything more, nor know any more of what had happened here. As the teacher went, so too would the student. Else when everything quietened down again (to burst forth another day), I might return to New York—if the police didn't detain me forever—bringing nothing back from this summer but traumatic memories. The clash of civilizations was over. We clashed and they won, because they began to believe more and we less, losing our conviction, our motivation, and then, once these two were gone, our lives. If ever anyone could have described the most devastating defeat, it would have to be this. We gave them a good run and we'd almost ruled the world, but only almost, and since when has almost been good enough? A century ago, the Ottomans were the sick men of Europe. A century later, we are the sick men of the world.

The world had been emptied of five good men and one

young woman. And what was I? If only someone else could have stayed in my place, to tell Kibr that I did not intend to. Taking one step ahead, followed by a second, more painful one, the result of a bottle cap's bite. Laughing, thinking about throwing myself into a righteous kiln while bitterly resenting a childish wound. A braver step closer. To where I could stick my hand out and feel too much. But I fast understood that I couldn't do this step by step. The only way was to take a leap of faith, to concentrate, bend slightly at the knees and catapult ahead. I'd have to start far enough away not to be scared, but close enough to come down deep in the inferno. Prayers for myself and my parents, for my sins to be forgiven and my sacrifice to be accepted, prayers for the Immortals, for Rehell and for Haris.

But at the end of it all, it was not my own effort that threw me towards those thirsty, merciful flames.

bukra

tomorrow

Bulleya,
Who knows who I am?
I'm not Moses nor Pharaoh.

Bulleya,
We're not going to die:
In the grave, it's someone else

—Bulleh Shah

the kurds of the end of days

What would have happened could not. Not any longer. In Afghanistan, the Base activated itself prematurely, its hand forced by the unexpected events in Egypt, of which it had no foreknowledge. Their spectacular strikes, designed to escalate the contradictions within Muslim governments, which would force the rise of the Islamic peoples, would have to be summarized. Some of the Base's combatants were withdrawn, their energies redirected, so that the primary operation would still be able to succeed, if not the other assaults, intended to coincide with the four mighty blows against the Great Satan. Thus the war would begin on a lesser scale. Yet the Base's activities were not going to be enough to destroy the Islamic peoples, as they had previously.

Muslim governments were uniformly shocked by the attacks in Egypt, and would be similarly stunned by their sudden cessation. Never very fond of their own people, these regimes were ready and eager to begin their crackdowns. They resumed intrusive searches and illegal seizures, breaking up any organizations with hints of Taliban connections, unearthing other militants, but more than anything, accomplishing the increasing oppression and alienation of the people. That America supported these endeavours would mean trouble for her. Though that would mean little in the short term: there was no chance for Afghanistan. Still less for

Iraq. But the anger that consumed the world, in another, ended universe, was not to come. Only America had been attacked. The Order's sacrifices had spared Europe and East Asia, and thus secured some public sentiment. When Iraq fell, and the lies were inevitably revealed, the Muslim Nation was enraged. But none of this compared to what stirred within the alleys of Cairo's Kurdistan, expectant generations finally becoming conscious. Not because of the Promised One's arrival, but because of events that forced reaction.

The Kurdish elders had noted an unknown elder walking proudly through their streets; later, alone amongst themselves, they discussed his presence. Who was he and why had he gone to that abandoned masjid? The next day, they sent a group to search it. They found notes, left in tattered notebooks, which opened a world to them, because these notes were not only in English and Arabic, but in Kurdish, too, languages referencing events that had taken place and that would (but would not) take place: warnings, fears, dreams. Things that could not be waved away. Thus the elders gathered and questioned the community, though it turned out that none had heard of these Kurds, the self-proclaimed Order of Light, nor had any had any contact with them. Still, all present agreed: these must have been the same Kurds who had so recently panicked Cairo. So the elders wondered: Was their community about to be discovered, or would they be able to remain hidden, as they always had been?

'With or without the Promised One,' Yusuf ibn Imad al-Din, one of the most pious and respected elders, warned, 'now is the time for us to act. These events affect our Egyptian brothers and sisters, even if they do not impact us directly.'

Another disagreed. 'We must remain quiet and wait, as we have been told to wait.'

'The time for quiet is gone,' a young Wanand countered. 'How can there be quiet when the world is hearing this noise?'

Yusuf understood. 'This is a sign from God. Two of their bodies were found where our father, Salah al-Din, stood surveying the city that was his.'

'It remains our city,' an elderly woman agreed, 'so we must protect it.'

And so they debated, long into the night and also the next night, and conversation continued in their homes; discussions on developments, hearsay, history and rumours in a potent combination. Yusuf ibn Imad al-Din and Wanand ibn Warith were in favour of creating some sort of organization, which would firstly guarantee the security of Cairo's Kurdistan. And secondly?

'This government has gone too far,' one of the elders said.

Another elder, Jalal al-Din, jumped in: 'This government is our enemy, not the Franks. If there were no such regimes, there would be no problems with the Crusaders. They would be afraid to harm us.'

'Our governments are a reflection of the people.'

'Then the people are corrupt!'

Wanand rose, and his unyielding voice boomed: 'Then the people need to be changed—but what is the chance that, in such an environment, any such change will be allowed?' Others murmured their agreement. 'We must bind ourselves and defend ourselves. If our task is to help the people, then we must be able to defend them from those who would do them harm.'

'You want us to fight the state?'

A boy stood up, and with his words, lifted the fog of

indecision. 'We know that the government will fight us. Either we go to them, or we wait for them to come to us, just as they come for others sinless, whose only fault is to wear a beard, to demand justice, or to be offended at the corruption and iniquity of society.'

'We must fight.' Wanand beamed. 'Kibr is right.'

abandoning arabic

My face smashed into the marble floor, which wasn't as hot as it should have been. I felt something small rolling through my mouth, making me think I'd been shot. Through the back of my head? And I'd caught the bullet between my teeth? Rather, it was a tooth, come loose from the force of the impact. My head was throbbing, almost burning. It was a foot from the flames, and someone's arms were on my legs, wrenching me backwards while violently trying to lift me up.

He turned me, held my shoulders and squeezed them. 'We have to go!' He shook me again, so hard I almost swallowed my tooth. I held it under my tongue. Maybe I'd need it later. 'Hello? Let's go!'

'Haris?'

'Yes!' He pulled me, but my left foot gave way and I fell on him. Another popping sound, but this from the firestorm behind me. Haris screamed again, 'Let's go!'

I staggered to my feet, wobbled and pointed to the flames. 'He's gone, Haris.'

'The police are coming.' Again he tugged, but I wanted to give him a hug. So I did and he clenched me back, using the opportunity to pull me off the curb. Sneaky bastard. 'Can't you hear the sirens? They're coming. We need to get out of here.'

He tried to whisper while he ran, but his panting prevented

him. I ran too, picking up my pace to match his, though there was a terrible thump in my ankles, my feet preferring the left over the right. Something had to be broken. We charged off the main street, past a gas station, and the only thing I could make out, between the rhythms of our feet and the weight of our tired lungs were emergency sounds. Haris and I were factories, with shared energy supplying us with the intensity necessary to get us where we were going: The police checkpoint at the end of Shari al-Ghayth.

Before we got too close, Haris yanked me aside, urging me to catch my breath, which I did only because he told me to. He could have been ordering me in Urdu, I couldn't tell. I only understood enough to go along, not thinking where going would get me.

'I was going to jump,' I said.

Panicked, Haris sealed my lips with his finger. It was weird. 'Shut the hell up.' We shifted. The police had noticed us, so we started walking towards them. Casually. Gasping. Sweating. Me dragging a lame ankle, grimacing with each step. Would they notice I had a temperature—of sorts?

Then they drew their guns.

I abandoned my Arabic.

'I'm an American!' I might not have had my keys, but I did have my passport. Yanking it out of a tight pocket, hoping I'd produce it before Haris produced his Indian identity and got me shot a dozen metres from a barbershop. That wouldn't have gotten us anywhere. 'See?' It's blue. It paid for your uniforms. Bastards. 'American!' So let me go. To wherever the Indian's taking me.

The interrogator lowered his gun, but the two policemen behind him didn't.

'We went to McDonald's.' I bent over, faking exhaustion. Faking? 'Then we went to Trianon Café'—would they have any idea what that was?—'to get coffee. But there was an explosion—'

'We ran all the way here,' Haris added. He grimaced. To look scared. More scared than he was.

'Did you buy coffee?'

There was a reason these guys were Third World. 'We didn't get coffee,' I explained. I shook my head, to look less confident. 'We couldn't. There was a big explosion.'

The policemen jotted down our names and our address, worried because we lived across from Mister Important Minister. They lost all interest soon thereafter, mostly because of the food.

'Can we see the food?'

My hand twitched and I realized I was still clutching the bag of McDonald's food. Alhamdulillah. Alhamdulillah. Alhamdulillah. The interrogator looked at the bag, curiously. It did look pretty beaten up. Like someone had fallen on it a few times.

'This is your food?'

Haris said yes.

'For the two of you?'

Haris hesitated. And I prayed. 'Yeah. For both of us.'

as apple pie

We were escorted back on to our street, watched until we got past the barbershop, and then we were free. We reached the steps, my slippers slapped cement and I was in the lobby and heaving. Soft yellow from the street lights threw happy hints of butterscotch, splashing against angles of the wall in a mindless manner. It almost made me want to smile. As did the sight of the doorman, curled in a foetal position. He looked so helpless. So alone.

Then Haris's question came down on me like gallons of water: 'You were going to jump?'

He was standing at the bottom of the steps, in the exact middle, with such a look that he thought himself a Hosni Mubarak who'd conquered Palestine, but incapable of believing himself responsible for such an act. He came back to his senses slowly, trying to string a better question together for me.

It came in quanta. 'What in—the hell—were you doing?'

I opened my mouth but I only coughed. An ugly, rasping sound, pathetic in its echo. My helplessness melted his consternation, so that he became the room-mate I remembered.

'Are you okay?' Instead, I sat down on the steps. Haris didn't react. He only shifted his feet. 'You were going to jump, yaar, weren't you?'

'I want to stay.' And then I motioned for him to sit down beside me.

'You want to stay?'

'Yeah.' I felt a disgusting weight in my gut. I needed to use the bathroom.

'In Egypt?' He laughed and put one foot on the first step, his hands on his hips. 'Well, never mind that. Do you want to spend what's left of the night on the steps?'

We stepped into the elevator as it arrived. Pushing for the fourth floor, I stepped to the centre, Haris adjusting to give me some space. Then the mouth of the bag opened, allowing the smell of French fries to waft out. When the elevator bounced at four, Haris went forward first and shoved the door open, which for some reason wasn't locked. I could have gone home all along. But then, I would have missed everything.

I sighed, so loud and long that it could've been a sentence, complete with a subject and an object. 'I need to eat something.' I found myself staring into the McDonald's bag. Shouldn't I have done that before the policeman did? 'There's two combo meals in here. With fries. But you can probably smell those.' I laughed and then I noticed it. 'There's an apple pie, too. But only one...'

This made Haris break into a humongous smile. 'How'd you know I like apple pies?' Then his smile withered and he became upset. 'Do you realize what you've put me through?'

'Don't say anything,' I shrugged. 'That's easier for you and me.'

'I hate you.'

'No, you don't.'

And I was right. The apple pie only sealed the deal.

I put my arm around him and we tried walking in, momentarily getting stuck in the doorway and teasing one another about it a minute later. Then I fell on to the love seat, announcing how much I had missed the place.

Haris dawdled by the dining table, unaware that I had prepared our schedule. The two of us would devour fast-cooling food, pray—some hours remained before dawn—and then collapse. But before that rest, though after eating, Haris was owed an explanation. He had, after all, finally done what he was all this time supposed to do: run after me.

I tore open the bag. 'Do you want the apple pie now?' I asked.

'Yeah.' He strode towards me. 'Please.'

'I thought you'd like it,' I said. 'I figured, after putting you through all that, it was the least I could do.'

The Almighty Says in His Book

I will divert from My signs all those unjustly proud:
If they see any sign, they will not believe in it;
and if they see the way of uprightness, they do not
take it for a way;
and if they see the way of error, they take it for a
way.

—The Qur'an,
The Ramparts (7), Sign 146

Author's note: The following time lines contain information regarding the progress of the Order of Light. Since they reveal events relevant to the progress of the novel, they are best read after completing the novel.

the world that could have been

1967 Yusuf ibn Imad al-Din is born.

1980 Mabayn is born to a family living in the Indian subcontinent. A few years later, his family moves to Egypt.
Rojet Dahati is born.

1981 Haris is born.

1985 Wanand ibn Warith is born.

1986 Kibr al-Akrad is born to Yusuf ibn Imad al-Din.

1988 Shanazi is born.

1998 Keyf Khoshi is born.

2001 A force called al-Qaida launches a series of spectacular attacks on American, European and East Asian targets, killing tens of thousands and sending the global economy into a tailspin. The resultant depression stretches through the decade, causing a series of ever-escalating conflicts.
Osama Bin Laden, alleged mastermind of the attacks, is never found.

2002 The birth of Keyf Khoshi's only brother.
He dies defending Cairo, around the year 2029.

2008 Rojet Dahati marries. His wife's name and fate remain unknown. They are known to have at least two children, both sons.

2010 Rojet's first son, Orhan Dahati, is born.

2013 Rojet's second son, Arayn Dahati, is born.

2014 Wanand marries Shanazi.

2019 Zuhra is born to Wanand and Shanazi.

2020 The Order of Light is formed.
Sometime thereafter, the wars intensify. (Little is known of the nature of these conflicts, except what the members of the Order had revealed during their brief return to Cairo in 2001.)

2030 Cairo is attacked and mostly obliterated by a nuclear strike. It is suggested that other major Arab and Muslim capitals are similarly pummelled, leaving the Middle East a depopulated wasteland.

2032 Karachi falls to Indian forces, which then go on to raid Kabul. Rojet's son Arayn disappears, though it is suspected he had attempted to link up with Muslim resistance forces in the Ferghana Valley. (The rest of Central Asia is under Chinese occupation.)
The Aryan Expanse is destroyed along with much of the Tower of Light, in the last assault upon what little survived of Cairo.

2033 Rojet's son Orhan takes charge of a Muslim company based in East Africa, which is quickly overwhelmed by unknown resistance forces. Taken prisoner, his release is made conditional on the complete surrender of the Order of Light. (This demand likely indicates that the Order of Light was a primary component of the surviving Muslim resistance forces, and that their surrender would be pivotal to ending the wars, and Islam.)

the world that was

2001   (May) Rehell and his European friends arrive in Cairo, living in the neighbourhood of Agouza. Shortly thereafter, Rehell meets Mabayn.

(June) Haris and his room-mate arrive in Cairo, to begin classes at the International Language Institute, in Sahafayeen.

(July) Police break apart a protest during the Mawlid of Sayyidna Husayn, inside the masjid of Sayyidna Husayn. The conspirators are found to have ties with foreign networks that will assist police investigations greatly during the 9/11 attacks.

Over two days, suicide attacks rock Cairo, though only two bystanders are killed. Though the damage is by and large restricted to property, Egypt's economy experiences a severe recession.

(September) New York City and Washington DC are attacked. Most Americans hold the al-Qaida movement responsible, though this is greeted with disbelief throughout the Muslim world. In response to increasing unilateralism, the European Union distances itself from the United States.

(October) Invasion of Afghanistan in response to al-Qaida attacks. The poorly equipped Taliban militia is swiftly toppled.

2003   The United States defies world opinion, invading and occupying Iraq.

Saddam Hussein is captured in late 2003, possibly through the invaluable assistance of unknown Kurdish intelligence agencies.

2004   The United States and its few remaining allies are forced to admit the lack of any real grounds for the war against Iraq. Supposed weapons of mass destruction are never found, while scandals over abused prisoners cause widespread outrage.

acknowledgements

In His Name.

God bless Comrade Suhayla Gafarova, for babysitting this book from its birth. It and I wouldn't have been realized without her persistent love, wit and wisdom. For that, I am obliged beyond words: you are first on my list because you are first in my life because you are first in my heart.

Benjamin Adams is always listening. Maybe that's because I'm his ride, but I like to think it's also because of the bigness of his big heart. Ali Hashmi: investment banker, existential therapist, all-around hero. Hasan Kazmi, who has this gift among countless others: he can turn any frown upside down. Agha Khaled Hosseini, a moving, astounding and inspiring writer and a still more wonderful person, and not just for taking the time out of his well-deserved success to answer my queries. Khurram Gore and Heba Nassef, each in their own way. Asad Husain, for appreciating the novelty of a novel and then offering the ear to hear it evolve. Rabia Kamal, for helping me learn how to learn. Zeeshan Memon didn't have to read through the dismal early drafts, but nevertheless did.

How can I thank big brother, not only watching, but examining, reading, editing, advising, helping, hand-holding, smiling, sharing, guiding and in every way teaching? (Thank you, Umar Bhai.) Khalil Sayed, for technical assistance. (Let's just leave it at that.) Ameer Shaikh: I don't know what to say to someone whose closeness to me goes beyond the best descriptions of friendship. Except, of course, 'No! You're not!' Rahilla Zafar, for helping revive the city of the living dead. I admire Adnan Zulfiqar in sundry ways: for his brilliance, his sincerity and his support; among Muslims, he is all too rare; he is the Muslim I wish I was and pray I can one day become. My friend Daanish Masood, there with me in apartment number whatever on that dismally overheated street in that delightfully bemusing Cairo, eight weeks spent trying to figure things out—including ourselves. It wouldn't and couldn't have been a summer without you.

No matter how many hours I spent hunched over a computer, often at the weirdest and worst hours of the night—my lower back will vouch for me—this project couldn't have come to fruition without Penguin India, and especially Diya Kar Hazra. When my manuscript landed on her desk, she set about trying to make something out of it—however far this book has come since, it is her skill alone.

My Apa Khala read primitive drafts in record time; Faizan Ghori really knows his Qur'an; Hugo Munda was inspirations galore; Nabeel Hazratji spread the word when it needed spreading; Professor Mehdi Khorrami is the most fantastic Farsi teacher this side of Ahvaz; Mr Thomas Malone, my twelfth grade English professor: I cannot help but hope this meets with his approval (it is, after all, probably too late for extra credit); the late Mr Gerald Perreault, for first kindling in me a serious interest in societies and histories; the smiling, obliging, amazing staff at Somers Public Library, by far the world's greatest; Steve Pugnacious; Sufi Zikr Guy™ and, undoubtedly, my love, respect and prayers to and for my parents, for everything they have given me over the years.

Finally, my grandfather, who would find his traces on every page of this book.

God grant him the highest station of Paradise.